Penguin Books
Rooms of their Own

PHOTOGRAPH: RUTH MADDISON © 1986

Jennifer Ellison was born in Melbourne in 1957. Since leaving school, she has travelled, worked for a Melbourne publisher, studied English and Drama at Melbourne State College, written arts reviews for various publications, run a Melbourne radio programme on books and writing, and held full-time positions with the Victorian Ministry for the Arts. She researched, recorded and edited the interviews for this book over a twelve-month period.

Rooms of their Own is her first book.

ROOMS OF THEIR OWN

JENNIFER ELLISON

PENGUIN BOOKS

a white kite
production

First published by Penguin Books Australia, 1986
Penguin Books Australia Ltd,
487 Maroondah Highway, P.O. Box 257
Ringwood, Victoria, 3134, Australia
Penguin Books Ltd,
Harmondsworth, Middlesex, England
Penguin Books,
40 West 23rd Street, New York, N.Y. 10010, U.S.A.
Penguin Books Canada Limited,
2801 John Street, Markham, Ontario, Canada
Penguin Books (N.Z.) Ltd,
182-190 Wairau Road, Auckland 10, New Zealand

Copyright © Jennifer Ellison, 1986
Interview with Blanche d'Alpuget:
copyright © Jennifer Ellison & Blanche d'Alpuget, 1986

Typeset in Galliard by Dovatype, Melbourne
Made and printed in Australia
by Dominion Press–Hedges & Bell
Designed by White Kite Productions

All Rights Reserved. Except under the conditions described in the
Copyright Act 1968 and subsequent amendments, no part of this publication
may be reproduced, stored in a retrieval system or transmitted in any
form or by any means, electronic, mechanical, photocopying, recording
or otherwise, without the prior permission of the copyright owner.
Except in the United States of America, this book is sold subject to
the condition that it shall not, by way of trade or otherwise, be lent,
resold, hired out, or otherwise circulated without the publisher's
prior consent in any form of binding or cover other than that in which
it is published and without a similar condition including this condition
being imposed on the subsequent purchaser.

CIP

Ellison, Jennifer, 1957–
  Rooms of their own.

  ISBN 0 14 009218 8.

  1. Women authors, Australian — 20th century. 2.
  Australian fiction — Women authors. I. Title.

A823'.309'9287

For Dorothy Ellison (1926–1983)

ACKNOWLEDGEMENTS

Thanks are due to the writers in this collection, for writing their books and for so generously giving their time and support to this project, and to whom I remain indebted; to my friend, editor and packager, Sally Moss, without whom this book would not have become a reality, and who held my hand from beginning to end; to Trevor Sinclair, for so many reasons, but especially for his constant encouragement, patience and belief; and to my mum and dad, for being there.

Photographs on pages 152, 172 and 212 by Brendan Hennessy.
Photograph on page 50 courtesy of John Fairfax & Sons Limited.
Photograph on page 70, by Anne Zahalka, and photograph on page 132 courtesy of McPhee Gribble Publishers.
Photograph on page 110 by Tony Nota for *Follow me* magazine.

CONTENTS

INTRODUCTION	1
BLANCHE D'ALPUGET	8
JESSICA ANDERSON	28
THEA ASTLEY	50
JEAN BEDFORD	70
SARA DOWSE	90
BEVERLEY FARMER	110
HELEN GARNER	132
KATE GRENVILLE	152
ELIZABETH JOLLEY	172
GABRIELLE LORD	192
OLGA MASTERS	212
GEORGIA SAVAGE	230

INTRODUCTION

> 'A woman must have money and a room of her own if she is to write fiction.'
>
> Virginia Woolf, *A Room of One's Own*, 1929

In the 1980s women writers enjoy a prominent place in Australian literature, and their writing embodies a diverse range of styles and approaches. But under what conditions do these authors write, and why has the number of women writers increased so dramatically? To what degree does the feminist movement account for this rise? This book was motivated by a curiosity about the answers to these and other questions.

The writers interviewed see themselves as writers first and foremost. It was pointed out that to be described as a woman writer can still be seen as being damned with faint praise. The historical implication is that the woman writer and her work are of less importance than the male writer and his work. And women writers are not by definition feminist writers, as is now often assumed. The interviews therefore voice some concern about the use of gender as an ordering principle at all.

Most of the writers interviewed here applaud the feminist movement but do not attribute their success as writers to that movement. They speak from a conviction that, whatever their success, it has been achieved through talent and persistence. But being female casts them in a social role which inevitably affects their lives, and, consequently, their work.

A number of writers in this collection grew up believing that what men did was central and what women did was peripheral. The legacy of that period persists in one form or another. Thea Astley says in the interview, 'I always felt that [men] wouldn't read books written by women, because it would be like listening to a woman talk for three hours, which would be intolerable. When I started to write ... I'd have opinions about things, but I knew they didn't rate, and I didn't know what voice to write as.' 'I still have trouble even now with the thought that I'm not as worthy as a man ... I mean as a writer,' Helen Garner says.'An act of will isn't enough to break out of female conditioning.' Jean Bedford observes, 'Men still have a stronger sense of themselves as people.'

Kate Grenville points out that she persisted with her writing because she believed there were other women like her (women, that is, who were neither extreme feminists nor content any longer with traditional conceptions of women in literature) and believed there was an audience for her work — an audience markedly different from the one Thea Astley had in mind.

Work by these writers sells. Is this because, suddenly, women are writing 'the best stuff'? Or is it that there is now a demand for books which reflect female experience? Certainly, more women than ever before have money to spend on books of their choice.

Considering the success of these writers, it would be reasonable to assume that attitudes to writing by women have changed. However, Thea Astley cites an example of a male student who refused to read Henry Handel Richardson's *The Fortunes of Richard Mahony* on discovering that Henry was a woman. She adds, 'I can't imagine a man in a plane being seen dead reading *The Home Girls* ... And that's not a criticism of Olga Masters'. 'If you're writing about the real world, real people, [the divisions between the sexes] will come up,' Olga Masters explains, 'because that's the way it is and the way it was.'

These interviews continue the debate about whether the sex of a writer is relevant to his or her ability to write of the opposite sex's experience. Elizabeth Jolley maintains there is no difference between a perceptive male writer and a perceptive female writer. Others feel less confident with their male characters than with their female characters. Perhaps the significant elements here are that female characters are now a legitimate focus for novels and stories, and that the social and cultural changes for which the feminist movement was largely responsible have allowed women to enter traditionally male domains. Women can write of experience previously denied them. Sara Dowse's *West Block*, for example, could not have been written in the 1950s.

In 1958, when Thea Astley was first published, there were few women among the critics, publishers, academics and others who shape our culture. The McPhee Gribble publishing house, run by women, has published a third of the writers in this collection. Helen Garner believes *Monkey Grip* either would not have been published at all, or would have been published in a very different form, had she been dealing with male publishers.

Concomitant with the changing role of women has been a profound change in attitudes to Australian culture, including literature; and this, too, has been reflected in publishing trends. Beverley Farmer quotes Roland Barthes: 'Literature is what is taught', and points out that Australian literature wasn't taught twenty years ago.

Australians have a new-found nationalism and want to read books about their country. For all its benefits, though, there is a danger that this nationalism may descend into narcissism, as Gabrielle Lord points out. 'I'd like to write a musical called *Come on Ned, Come on*, in which Ned Kelly rides Phar Lap across Anzac Beach and beats the Americans. Now I reckon that'd be an absolute winner, with Ned wearing a nice tennis outfit or something.'

Gabrielle Lord also points to the importance of writers for the society and culture from which they spring: 'I'm starting to feel now that writers are custodians of the culture, that they're vocal and that they can shock and they can check.'

What value does this society place on its 'custodians of culture'? Jean Bedford pithily observes that the artist's position is akin to the 'nuns or whores' syndrome to which women historically have been subject: 'You get the worst of both worlds. People think there's something mystical going on if you can create a piece of art, but at the same time they think that because it's special it's not part of society so they don't have to pay for you to do it.' Many of the authors in this book are aggravated by such a paradox.

Money was a key part of Virginia Woolf's 'opinion on one

minor point' regarding women and fiction. Most of the women interviewed here are too busy trying to make some money to be sitting around forming the Australian equivalent of the Bloomsbury set. Only a handful write full time and they haven't earned that luxury from royalty cheques. 'You name my books and I'll tell you the household goodies [they bought],' says Thea Astley. And if having time is a luxury, time is the *only* luxury some of these writers have. Most have no luxuries at all, and have had to come to grips with the precarious financial status endemic to writers.

Writers have to be resourceful and creative in more ways than one in order to survive. Selling the film rights to *Fortress* enabled Gabrielle Lord to resign from the Public Service. Blanche d'Alpuget shrewdly set about writing a best-selling non-fiction work to buy time to write fiction. Others live from job to job, on an occasional grant, from teaching, freelance journalism, and so on. 'One's urge is to sit in a room and push the pen,' Helen Garner says. 'I like to be obliged to get out in the world — well I don't *like* it, but I need to.'

The writers in this collection have had to adapt their working methods to suit whatever time is available to them. Correspondingly, their writing habits are idiosyncratic. Georgia Savage writes in bed for two or three hours every morning. Jean Bedford likes a clean desk with a vase of flowers when she sits down to work. Olga Masters gets up at four in the morning and writes every single day. Blanche d'Alpuget sleeps, eats and breathes a project until it is done. Both she and Beverley Farmer need a 'still centre' in order to write. Elizabeth Jolley and Helen Garner take notes all the time, even if not working on a specific project. Blanche d'Alpuget says, 'Everybody I know says, "You should take notes", so I take notes and then I can never find them afterwards.' 'I think a lot about a story,' Beverley Farmer says, 'and jot down notes and work my way towards it, almost looking in the other direction.'

Whatever their habits, none of these writers would deny that writing is a hard and exacting job. These writers have to create the time to work and must use that time effectively. Thea Astley, who wrote ten novels while in full-time paid employment, says 'it's yakka, pit-digging.' For Helen Garner, the difference between the artist and the non-artist is that 'the artist is the one who does it. Almost everyone thinks they can write a novel.'

Generally the writers interviewed see themselves as loners, and the reality of their working conditions reinforces whatever sense of separateness they may have. Loneliness is an occupational hazard for writers. They don't have colleagues to toss around ideas with, and most of the writers in this book say that a trusted companion or mentor would be enormously helpful to their work. 'It must be wonderful to ... have a lovely wife to hang on your every word,' Gabrielle Lord quips.

Some of these writers do enjoy close relationships with editors, publishers or agents. Even so, it appears that the process of writing remains a solitary one. Surprisingly few of the writers interviewed for this book had met each other, and although there is an informal, encouraging and supportive network between some of them, most were bemused by the idea of being part of a literary milieu.

The interviews record a variety of perspectives on becoming 'a writer'. The early work of many of these authors was repeatedly rejected and, although they received little or no encouragement, they had the tenacity to continue to write and rewrite, believing they would eventually be published. And they were. But even when Gabrielle Lord had two books published and people asked, 'What do you do?' she still said she was a clerk in the Public Service. In Helen Garner's experience, few men writers hesitate to call themselves writers. For Helen Garner, Gabrielle Lord and others in this collection, claiming the title of Writer involved a gradual building of their own confidence in their work and in themselves.

Being published is not a guarantee of success or acknowledgement. Instead, it is often the beginning of a new round of assaults. Writers are sometimes (mis)judged as people on the basis of their writing and are rarely given an opportunity to debunk or confirm theories publicly woven about them, let alone the theories formed privately by readers. On the other hand, affirmation — in the form of public acclaim or private correspondence — is for most of these writers a validation of their work and a real measure of success.

However, success of any kind is not without its costs. Beverley Farmer believes the people close to the writers are the ones who suffer, not the writers themselves. At any one stage of the writing process, a writer may be distracted, absorbed or obsessed, or a combination of these. Blanche d'Alpuget says, 'When I'm writing fiction I am emotionally and psychologically absent from other relationships.' The issue of social roles again comes in to play when she adds, 'I don't think there exists any man, or many men, who will put up with that kind of thing from a woman ... [Women] stay in relationships, often to the detriment of their writing'.

In some of the interviews in this book it is argued that any time-consuming and demanding job can create conflict and tension in personal relationships. For the record, however, six of the women in this collection were living alone when interviewed.

Why do writers write at all? It's certainly not for riches, nor is it for fame: 'I'm not going to be so famous that when I walk into a room everyone will know who I am,' Helen Garner says. Blanche d'Alpuget considered the fame she found through the Hawke biography detrimental to writing fiction. And writing is not always a happy lot. The accumulated weight of criticism of Thea Astley's work has led her seriously to entertain thoughts of stopping altogether. Jessica Anderson gets 'tired of all that paper'. She is also irritated that the writer is the only negotiable element in the publishing chain, 'so naturally he's screwed.' The personal investments and costs associated with being a writer are substantial and the financial gains modest.

Writers defy both capitalist and socialist molds of useful production. They don't generate wealth and, as Jessica Anderson says, they cannot 'be commanded to do what is for the general good. There's a great deal of anarchy in art.' Writers are in the invidious position of being 'necessary evils'. They do examine and check the society in which they live, if only by reflecting it. Perhaps governments cannot afford to acknowledge the value in that, but readers always will. And perhaps this is the most significant reward for writers.

Simone de Beauvoir said, 'I write to be loved.' Helen Garner, for one, has come to appreciate the truth of that statement. Kate Grenville says, 'there is actually a power in the written word ... The fact that something I wrote was able to reach somebody ... I found astonishing, and slightly spooky, and wonderful'. These writers are surprised and delighted by the power of the word, but it is rarely, if ever, uppermost in their minds when they sit down to write. Most of them say they write stories to entertain and amuse, and that they write largely for their own satisfaction. 'Literature *does* instruct,' says Jessica Anderson, 'but it is not the job of the writer to *directly* instruct.'

And yet, interestingly enough, Jean Bedford says she was criticised by feminists for not offering constructive role-models for women in *Country Girl Again*, and Helen Garner says some people thought she was 'recanting' in *The Children's Bach* because in that story a woman returns to her husband, presumably to live happily ever after.

Jessica Anderson says she feels privileged to be a writer because to be able to do anything well is a privilege — a sentiment shared by many of the writers in this collection. Others take Beverley Farmer's view: 'I've done what I wanted to do.'

Through their fiction, these writers have each established a voice. They have determined whether it be sonorous or shrill, melodious or dissonant. By contrast, the voices in these interviews are spontaneous and responsive, lively and anecdotal, as the writers tell stories of their lives and work. Perhaps it is ironic that, as a collection, the interviews read like an extraordinarily good piece of fiction: there are countless resonances, they speak volumes on a wide range of issues and they illuminate the human condition, especially the human condition of writers. Yet, like a photograph, each interview captures a certain truth and reality about the individual. Collectively, these interviews constitute a snapshot record of a critical point in the social and cultural development of Australia, particularly its literature.

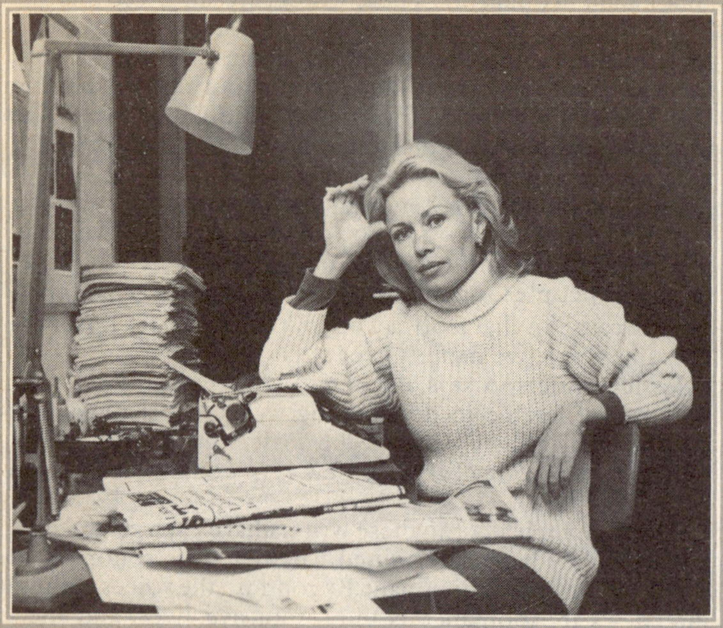

BLANCHE D'ALPUGET

'When I'm writing fiction I am emotionally and psychologically absent from other relationships. I don't think there exists any man, or many men, who will put up with that kind of thing from a woman.'

What prompted you to write your first book, the biography of Sir Richard Kirby?

I'd been living in Indonesia and I'd known Kirby for a long while. It was through our shared interest in Indonesia that I became interested in Kirby and doing his life. I knew I could get a biography published and once that had happened it would be easier for me to move on to fiction. I really always wanted to write fiction and the biography was a vehicle. Similarly with the Hawke biography — I just had to make some money. I mean, that wasn't the only reason, but I had that practical reason. Nobody can expect to make money out of writing fiction, so I wanted to write a book which I thought would finance me for a couple of novels, which it has.

When did you first start to write fiction?

Very late. Thirty, almost in the grave! I didn't ever see myself as a writer. I really wanted to be a scientist. It was only after the birth of my son, when I was twenty-nine and he was about five or six months old, and I was living in Malaysia, that I tried writing a short story. Then, just before I turned thirty, I came back to Australia and wrote a couple more short stories. I had the feeling that I had had a lot of very vivid experiences through spending five years in South-East Asia and another couple of years in England and France, and I wanted to write about some of these things. So I just wrote off three short stories — rewrote the first one and did two more — and I sent them off to my stepmother, who was a publisher's editor, and she said to me, 'You're a born writer'. That was on the Australia Day weekend of 1974. I decided on the spot that's what I would be, at least for a while. At the end of the weekend, on the Tuesday, I sat down and started to write a novel. It took from February to September that year to complete, and of course it was quite awful. I'd given about ten minutes' thought to the plot before sitting down and starting to write. So 1974 was really when I started to teach myself how to write.

You must have worked fairly intensively throughout that period to get it finished so quickly?

Monkeys in the Dark is a short book, and I was only able to work four hours a day, because my son was quite small. I had him minded for those hours so that I could write. I didn't have any idea what I was doing. I was getting some extended thing on paper, which I'd never done before. Ever since then I've always kept to very tight schedules when I've been writing. I don't find the discipline difficult at all. People always ask, 'How do you get the discipline?' What they don't realise is that your motivation is so great that it's the interruptions which are the problem, not sitting at the typewriter.

Did you start work on the Kirby biography after you'd finished Monkeys in the Dark?

No, I didn't. I then sat down and I wrote a bit of another novel, which was no good at all, and I threw it all out. Then the Kirby thing came up. But in the meantime I'd had a piece of absolutely critical encouragement, and also the birth of my son seemed to release some creativity. I think actually giving birth to a son is an interesting thing for women, particularly if they've got a very strong male aspect, as I have. For me, it was extremely psychologically satisfying, as if there was the male, incarnate. And I think that actually did release a creative process. But the crucial piece of encouragement was that I won prizes for the two short stories from the Victorian Fellowship of Australian Writers, beating some good writers. I'd also won a commendation for the manuscript of the novel. A few days later I had dinner with Kirby and the idea of doing his biography came up.

How did Monkeys in the Dark *come to be published in its final form?*

As soon as I finished the Kirby biography I went back to Indonesia for the first time in five or six years, for a month. I refreshed myself and then came back to Australia and rewrote it, in six weeks. I'd been living with the book for so long that the unconscious had actually done the work in the meantime, and so the rewriting was very quick. Then I only had to polish it. But I must say that one of my great flaws as a writer is writing too fast, and I wish I could discipline myself to write more slowly. I'm given to impatience anyway. I want to get the thing out of my system and once I have, I lose interest in it.

Do you find it difficult to rewrite then?

Yes, yes. And I'm never able to re-read a book once it's got past galley form. I mean, once you get the galleys you think you'll vomit if you look at the bloody thing again. I'm sure Beverley Farmer really spends time, she really crafts, and that is my idea of a very good writer. But I have a combination of impatience and energy, and sloppiness, which drives me mad about myself.

What sort of developments did you feel you had made, as a writer, by the time you'd completed your second novel, Turtle Beach?

Well, more confidence, obviously, which gives you more authority. I'd learned a lot more about structuring a book. It is a well-structured novel — I think that's one of its good points.

Does structure particularly interest you?

I could never explain to anybody, including myself, how to structure a book, but it's something for which you develop a feel by doing it. Also, through doing the Kirby book, because I was dealing with a lot of potentially dull material — wage cases and economics — I'd learned about narrative pace, which was good. By the end of *Turtle Beach* I felt that I knew a lot more about shaping a book, and I knew how to make it go fast and slow. I thought I was better on dialogue, and

I was getting better on character, but my precision of language was my very weak area, and I still consider it weak. I admire Beverley Farmer tremendously, and Helen Garner, for their precision, and Helen for, as she says, leaving things out. I'm given to flinging in everything, including whistles and bells. I've done that in *Winter in Jerusalem* — the novel I've just finished. Actually, it's a badly structured book. I think it's good overall, but it's got the lot: truffles and cognac and a cherry on the top.

Do you do any formal research before you start to write a novel?

Yes, I did for all three. I had to do a lot less for *Monkeys in the Dark* than I did for *Turtle Beach* because I didn't know anything about the boat people. I had to go and investigate all of that, read up about it, go to those camps, interview people. For my latest novel, *Winter in Jerusalem*, I had to do a horrendous amount of research. I thought at various stages I was certainly biting off more than I could chew because I don't speak Hebrew, and I'm not Jewish. All the main characters are Jews. It's easy enough to turn yourself into somebody from a different culture, but you do have to know a certain amount about it. To write about Israel, I had to learn an awful lot about current and past Israeli and Jewish history, and the Jews didn't exactly spring out of the ground in 1066.

Did your idea for this novel arise out of the Hawke biography?

Yes, I had to go to Israel to do the research for Hawke, and I had no interest in the place one way or the other before that. I went there in '81 and I was struck by the country — its towering antagonisms, among other passions. It was in many respects a reckless decision, because it was obviously a different matter to set books in South-East Asia — one in Indonesia and one in Malaysia. I spoke Indonesian and Malay, and I'd lived in both places for a long time, and was at home there. By the time I left Jakarta I knew it as well as I knew Sydney, for example.

Did you ever feel like abandoning Winter in Jerusalem?

Oh, about 7000 times. I had awful difficulty writing it. I had writer's block, a year ago, which had never happened to me before, and it was a chastening experience. I couldn't write at all. Towards the end it was so bad I couldn't even write notes to the milkman. It lasted about a year overall. A lot of that time I went on writing, but it was drivel. In its very critical form, when I couldn't write at all, the block lasted about three months.

Do you have any theories about why that happened?

I think it happened because my life was taking a drastic change of direction, and I was going through a big psychological shake-up. I'd reached a huge psychological barrier. It was a process of just getting over that barrier and dismantling a lot of things, a lot of patterns, I mean. My marriage fell apart. It was a very long marriage. It had been falling apart for ages, but it takes a long while to say to yourself: this is just not working, and it's not on, and I feel bad about it.

It was the year I turned forty and I didn't like myself. I didn't like my life and I didn't like the people I knew, and I didn't know what to do about it. I hated being famous, which is what I was after the Hawke book. I found it very detrimental to being a writer, because you go around for years writing, being nobody, not needing a defence system because nobody gives a hoot about what you're doing. They talk over your head, you know, and ignore you, and it's great. You can sit there and listen to them without having to say anything. And I'd had years of being a diplomatic wife — I like the double meaning — in which case you're just talked straight through, you're sort of a well-dressed servant. And that increases one's feminist consciousness. But because of the Hawke thing, everybody in the world was wanting to talk to me, and ask me questions.

Were you not conscious that would happen when you started to do the biography?

I knew it would make my name well known, but I didn't give any thought to what effect that was going to have socially, that I would suddenly be unable to go out and meet strangers without being pestered about this thing, and without being seen in a certain light. Once that happens you start building a mask for yourself, and as time goes on you build it more and more strongly, in self-protection. I've got a lot of social skills anyway, so it's very easy for me to slip on a mask, and to keep it up, but the necessity of having to perform, and feeling like you're on show, I find horrid.

Were there any concrete benefits from doing the biography?

Money. It's been very convenient in that respect and in other ways. It brings privileges. People take one seriously. Because of my appearance, for years and years people hadn't taken me seriously. You know, a fluffy little blonde. I am only five foot two and a half, and I am naturally blonde. I was very pretty when I was young and I do have quite a gay sort of personality. I like laughing and being frivolous. All of those things added up — in the stereotype of the fifties and sixties — not to an air-head, because you can't disguise intelligence, but certainly to somebody who wasn't to be taken too seriously. But I learned to play the role too well. The mask got stuck.

Both Turtle Beach *and* Monkeys in the Dark *have a political backdrop. Are you particularly interested in politics?*

I was, because I had a dramatic introduction to politics. I went to Indonesia from Menzies' Australia. I'd been in Europe in the interim, but I went to Indonesia when I was twenty-two and it was in a state of absolute upheaval. It had the third-largest Communist party in the world, after China and Russia, and it was still a very left-wing country. The army was in the process of not just decimating the Left, not just getting rid of one in ten, but wiping it out completely. So it was a combination of seeing a genuine clash between Left and Right. I mean a really bloody clash, in which hundreds of thousands of people were being killed, and tens of thousands arrested without trial and tortured. And also the excitement of seeing very progressive legislation. For example, women had equal pay there. They enjoyed a legal status far higher than the legal status of Australian women.

Was that political awakening linked to a feminist awakening in you?

Yes. What particularly stimulated my sensitivity to the treatment of women was the fact that while there was legislative strength for women in Indonesia, polygamy was still legal. It was a completely male-controlled society, with the women fighting back on a seditious level. Also, I was in an Embassy where the women were just wives, and as such were really pieces of baggage. Their views were ignored because the Foreign Affairs Department was staffed almost exclusively by men, and their spouses were generally a downtrodden lot. If you look at Julie in *Monkeys in the Dark*, she was a typical victim of that system, and I suppose there's a recognition that one was not only a victim of it, but a willing victim, that masochism always goes with sadism in the one person. That's what we forget.

Is there some political intent, or some statement that you're trying to make, in your novels?

Well, that's perhaps for others to judge on the ones already published, but *Winter in Jerusalem* has a war in the background. *Monkeys in the Dark* had an internal war as background and *Turtle Beach*, of course, had the Vietnam War in the background. But in all cases, and much more consciously in this one, it's a story device and a metaphor for the characters' inner states. And war does interest me. It's what we read in the newspapers every day, and see on television every day. The twentieth century is a century of war and politics. Personally, however, I'm not politically oriented. I can't find it in myself to be ideologically committed. For example, it's very wicked to say this, but I will admit, as a member of the Labor party, that the day the Whitlam Government was sacked I was excited. People who are really political were terribly distressed about it and I felt ashamed that I couldn't be, but I couldn't. I have a different reaction to those things: I don't identify with governments. They're not my boys.

How did you come to do the Hawke biography?

It was because of the Kirby book. If I hadn't done that, there's no way I would have got to write the Hawke book. I wouldn't have been interested; nor would Hawke have been. While doing the Kirby book I was outraged by the sheer inefficiency of the arbitration system, and the fact that our economy, and therefore a great many people's peace of mind, depends on the decisions of this thing. So I developed a very genuine interest in that. I'd interviewed Hawke a lot for it and he knew that I knew about it and was seriously interested. The other point, as I wrote in the Kirby book, was that Hawke had wanted to write a PhD thesis about the arbitration system. In doing the Kirby biography I did a part-history of that system. And there was a genuinely shared curiosity: you know, if you've once dreamed of going to Krakatau and then you meet someone who has travelled there, you want to talk to him or her. One other biography was being written at the time, and Hawke wasn't entirely happy about it. We'd known each other for a long time and he liked me, and I liked him. He knew I was a good hand, and that I'd work properly.

What kind of difficulties did you encounter?

I've tried to forget them. Actually the overriding one was the pressure of time. Hawke is somebody who works as if there are twenty-eight hours in the day, and he must be working the whole twenty-eight of them. Just to get him to sit down, and get quiet, and talk for two hours into a microphone, was really difficult. Sometimes in one hour the phone would ring fifteen times, because a strike would start, or would be in progress, and there was no question of his being out of contact with the world, at any time. He always has to be in communication. And it was just nerve-racking, the constant interruptions. So time really was the biggest difficulty.

Did you have a deadline for completion of the manuscript?

Yes. I have attacks of being politically canny. I was absolutely certain, in January 1980 when I started work full time on the book, that Fraser would hold an early election as he had in 1977, and I knew I had to have the book out before the end of 1982. Otherwise, if he did have an early election, and Hayden was still leader, which I thought was what would happen, Hayden could either win it, or he could lose it. Obviously if he won it, that was the end of Hawke. And it would be the end of my sales. So I had in mind that I had to have the book finished by early '82 and I had to have it printed in Australia. It's terrifically smart getting stuff printed in Hong Kong and then there's a strike at the wharves and the bloody thing's held up for three months. Also, I had to have a publisher who could get the thing out fast, which is what Morry Schwartz did. I got it finished in May, and it was out by the end of September, or October, which is very fast for a book that size. And as it turned out, the timing was good. People ever afterwards said, 'Oh isn't Hawke clever!' It's faintly irritating. I had to consider all these bloody things, all the timing. Bob had no idea of the timing, in fact for ages it was unreal to him, and it was only right towards the end of the process, when I started showing him the manuscript to read, that it started to become real. Up until then he'd been interviewed by at least five million people, and it was just something that he did. Part of the day's work.

Would you care to speculate on any differences of interpretation that might have occurred had Hawke's biographer been a man?

There have been two male biographers. Also, one million male political commentators, from every planet in the galaxy, have given their interpretations of Hawke. I had a lot of disadvantages, as a woman, interviewing old trade unionists, simply because I can't join in that ethos. I can't go to the pub and have a few beers. I don't drink beer and I hate pubs. That was a terrible drawback, and also many of the men of the sort of age I was talking to find a young woman threatening, and frightening. However, I had advantages, too, because women are often much better listeners than men, or at least men perceive them to be better listeners. Whether they are or not is another matter. And so they talk more freely.

Are you intending to write Part Two of Hawke's life?

Certainly not at the moment. And it's not something that I could face, or think about, in under ten years. One would have to see if he had an interesting prime ministership.

Given that the publication of Hawke's biography was bound to be a fairly momentous occasion, what were your feelings leading up to publication?

They were the same as leading up to any publication. You're just so sick of the thing, and you've got to get through the day somehow or other, and make the speech — I have a terror of public speaking — it's just a hurdle to be jumped, and if you make the jump without falling on your kisser, it's a huge relief. I'd been nervous all along about how the news media were going to sensationalise it, and indeed — bless them, at least they're consistent — they did. I've still got the Melbourne *Truth's* poster somewhere, which says 'Sex Scandal!' with a photograph of me underneath it, smiling my face off. I was dreading that, not so much on my own account, but on Hawke's and on his family's, and it was just something I knew I would have to live through. Also, there's the terrible author tour, which is one of the aspects of hell on earth exclusive to writers. It's part of the price you pay. Publication is the price you pay for writing.

Are your approaches to writing fiction and non-fiction significantly different?

In both my non-fiction works I've done an overall structure

of the book before I've started to write, just a synopsis of the thing. I do all the research, I get the whole thing in my mind, just by cramming it in my head — I never use cards or any of that stuff — and then I get an overall shape of the book. Finally, I go through and I work at it — where I'm going to start, and how it'll progress. There may be one significant line of dialogue, or a fact, or something that has to be in each chapter, and I'll put that in, and I type all of that up.

For fiction I do the whole book, not chapter by chapter, because I don't know how long the story's going to be until I start writing it, but I get the characters, and the main storyline, and the main ideas, so at least I've got a skeleton for the novel. It's a much lighter skeleton than for a biography, particularly the Hawke biography, which I think is a well-built book. I think it's got good structure. It's internally strong. I was actually thinking of the architecture of a Congregationalist church I'd seen in South Australia when I was writing it: well-proportioned stone, four-square. The novel is more like a fish skeleton.

Are there any authors whose writing you particularly admire?

Yes. In Australia I particularly admire Helen Garner, although I wish with her tremendous talent that she'd take bigger subjects. That, naturally, is a psychological projection on my part, because I take big subjects. Then there are Peter Carey, Jessica Anderson and Robert Drewe. Those four are my favourites.

What about non-Australian writers?

I adore Nadine Gordimer. I think she's a genius, and every now and again I have an attack of trying to write a sentence like hers, and I fall in the mud. I haven't read a lot of her recent novels but I read her short stories, over and over again, like people read the Bible. She has a sensibility and an intelligence that are spellbinding to me.

At what point did you begin to think of yourself as a writer?

Not until I'd had two books published. It was a growing realisation. People kept asking me what I did. And I'd say, I used to be a journalist, and I've written a biography of Sir Richard Kirby, and I've written a novel. Then one day I started to say, I'm a writer. It was shorter.

What are your ambitions as a writer?

To continue. I hope I'll be able to continue writing fiction. That hope's based on two things: A, that I'll find the material within myself; and B, that I'll be able to make a living.

What has been your experience of the Australian publishing industry?

I've been shockingly promiscuous with publishers. You know, a writer and a publisher are meant to settle down together, but I've had about six so far and I'm still not married to one. It's said that incompetence is a special prerequisite for anyone wanting to become a publisher. Some of them grow out of it. And some, like Peter Ryan of Melbourne University Press, succeed in spite of competence. The things you want from a publisher are decent blurb notes, that is, accurate and enticing blurb notes, but much more than that, distribution. Distribution, distribution, distribution. If there's good editing too, you're in heaven.

Have you changed publishers so often in order to pursue these things?

Oh no, they've pursued me, generally. They've come up with a good offer. But I must add, I've had very important guidance from publishers and editors. For example, when I was having my first book published, Peter Ryan taught me a tremendous amount. He held my hand through all sorts of difficulties, often not in a direct way, but he used to write me a humorous letter almost once a week, drawing my attention to things, and saying, 'Have you thought about this and that?' It was a protégé relationship which was very rewarding and gave me confidence. Penguin is a good house, with some good editors. I've also had a wonderful editor for *Winter in Jerusalem* — John Herman in New York. Herman, who is now a boss cocky at Weidenfeld & Nicolson, was the toughest editor I've had, apart from my stepmother. He wrote me notes asking, 'What is the point of this ugly scene?' and 'Is it your intention to bore us with mindless blither?' If he'd not been 10,000 miles away I would have poisoned him.

Do you find there are any personal costs in being a writer?

The greatest one, and it's very specifically related to being female (but I don't want to generalise, I'm just talking about me), is that when I'm writing fiction I am emotionally and psychologically absent from other relationships. I suspect that's so with anybody who's writing fiction. While women can go on being the spouses or live-in partners of male writers because they're used to the role of looking after the great man and the great talent, I don't think there exists any man, or many men, who will put up with that kind of thing from a woman. Suddenly, for, say, nine months (which is what it normally takes me to write a novel), you're just not there, and not interested. In fact you're in love with other people, the people in the book. I've never been as in love over a long period with a real live person as I have been with the men and women in my books. The thing that I've had to come to terms with, and it's painful and frightening, is that I just can't have, and in fact don't want, an on-going relationship. And that gets very scary, because writing itself is such a solitary occupation, and then if you have no family at all, and you can't have any continuity of relationship, you can see yourself becoming isolated and lonely in the times when you don't want to be, the times in between books. And also there's the danger of falling into an artificial life, because it's not normal to be as alone as that. There's a danger of not writing about real people, of getting more and more abstracted.

I've been fearful of that for years. It was ten years ago that I started writing and first experienced this complete absence. It puts tremendous strain on a marriage, and I was really lucky. My husband has been very long-suffering and good about it, but in the end it's too much, and the thing broke down. I was really scared about leaving the marriage and then being totally alone. I think a lot of women are terribly conscious of that. They compromise and they stay in relationships, often to the detriment of their writing, because it is such an abrasive thing to have a relationship with a real human being when so much of your energy is going into the characters within you. It is more complicated when you've got a young child. My son's only twelve at the moment. I'm emotionally absent from him, too, when I'm writing, and one tends to feel guilty about it. We've just recently worked out a way around this: my husband's got a very nice girlfriend, and she wants to have a baby. So we're going to get a big house in which, when I'm not writing, we'll all live together, and then when I am writing I'll just move into my own little place and I'll go and see them in the evening and on weekends. That gives continuity for my son.

Obviously you have intense relationships with your characters while you're writing. What about when the novel's finished — do they live on?

Yes, yes. I have for them the affection one has for old lovers, you know. Yes, they're always there.

What about your working methods? Do you take notes?

No, I'm very disorganised about that, and I just spend a lot of time mucking about. Once I get an idea for a novel then it's a process of feeling it and sniffing it and turning it upside down and looking at it. That takes months and months and involves going off in all sorts of odd directions. It goes all over the place and I start a lot of odd reading, and go up wrong avenues, and can't decide on characters, and change my mind, and that's the cooking process. It is disorganised, but I haven't found any better way to do it. I'm not a good note-taker and I have attacks of guilt over that, because everybody I know says, 'You should take notes', so I take notes and then I can never find them afterwards.

How many hours a day do you work when you're in that intensive period of actually writing the book?

Twenty-four hours a day, thinking and dreaming about it. After a while I can't get to sleep. Then I begin to take Mogadon, and become addicted to it. It's an awful bloody thing, Mogadon withdrawal. I find, once I start to write, that I have to get on to the Mogadons if I'm going to get to sleep and going to be able to write the next day, because as soon as I get into bed I start thinking — what about that adjective, what about the adverb, I must say this, I must say that — and I'm awake till three in the morning. So then I get on the Moggies and they cut down the dreaming, which is bad for fiction. I think the more dreaming, the better. It is really twenty-four hours a day, eight or nine of them at the typewriter. That's why you're absent, because you're actually thinking about that all the time.

Is physical environment important to you?

There's only one thing that's important and that is that there are no interruptions, that the telephone doesn't ring. I have to get very deeply inside myself and I have to get very still. If you have to stop suddenly and talk to somebody, you've got to put on this whole new personality to meet them, and it just pulls you out of that place of stillness.

Are you conscious of an audience when you're writing?

I'm purposefully trying to get less and less conscious of audience. In the novels that I've been writing for Australians about Asia and about Israel, there's a certain amount of explanation one's got to do, because otherwise one is just not saying anything at all, and one owes that as a kind of politeness to the reader. But, ideally, I would like to write just for myself and then the consciousness of the audience becomes an aspect of a desire to craft the thing properly. But, as for wishing to please them and so forth, no, I think that's deleterious.

Are you particularly conscious of your nationality?

I don't know. Well, I see myself as an Australian but I'm an outsider writer. I'm a kind of alien in every situation. I was an alien in those two biographies. They were very male worlds — industrial relations, ALP politics, and the ACTU and so forth are completely male domains. And the three novels are also about a stranger, in those countries. So, to that extent, with the three novels I'm conscious of nationality, but I think it's a different thing. I think it's a general feeling of being an outsider, which is what I feel about myself. I've always felt like an outsider. It may well have something to do with having such a florid name. A name like mine is remarked upon from childhood and people ask 'Is that French?' or 'Were you born in Australia?' I've had that all my life, the constant questioning of where I'm from and what I really should be.

What are your thoughts on book reviews and reviewers?

I think writers make the best reviewers. Unless you've written, you can't read — or that was my experience. I realised after I'd written a book that I'd never properly read a book before. I think it's the same as the difference between somebody who enjoys concerts and somebody who has learned to play a musical instrument and enjoys concerts. We can in fact all read and we think that we do it well, but writing seems to me the other part. You start noticing structure and all sorts of stuff which you don't know about, or can only sense, subconsciously, if you haven't written yourself. I think maybe writers have broader sympathies than academics, to whom reviewing falls so much. Writing, or any practising of the arts, should broaden one's sympathies. A very fine education does that as well, of course, but very fine educations are becoming scarce because there's so much information in the world now.

What do you value in a review of your work?

I have found some reviews very useful in pointing out weaknesses that I wasn't aware of. Always a writer is aware of a huge number of weaknesses in her book which somebody else won't see. Many reviews have pointed out things that I just haven't seen, and it really has been something that I have been able to think about afterwards and say, yes, that's right, and I'll try not to fall into that again. There are some good reviewers in Australia but the majority of them are bad. I don't read too many Australian book review pages any more but I read the *New York Review of Books*. I've been a subscriber to that for about four years and I think their reviews do justice to the books. They are three or four pages long. I mean they are often 6000 words. It's very hard to write about something as complex as a novel, even if it's not a good novel, in 600 words, which is the practice in Australia. One way and another, it's two years out of somebody's life, and 600 entertaining and bright words in a newspaper are not going to do justice to what's in that thing, whether it's put there well or put there badly.

George Orwell said that book reviewing is pouring your immortal soul down the drain a half pint at a time, and that's exactly what it always felt like to me when I used to do reviews. It just doesn't give emotional and psychological satisfaction.

I must say I try not to read the newspapers at all. I think they cause brain damage. I'm serious. Really. We don't know how bad for us the information is that bombards us every day. I work on the view that if something really significant has happened somebody'll tell you about it. Newspapers are distracting. You're told too many trifling things which pass away, and which take up energy and entice the attention away from ... more important things.

Canberra, March 1985

Select bibliography

Mediator, A Biography of Sir Richard Kirby, Melbourne University Press, 1977.
Monkeys in the Dark, Aurora Press, 1980; Penguin, 1982.
Turtle Beach, Penguin, 1981.
Robert J Hawke, Schwartz in conjunction with Lansdowne Press, 1982; Penguin, 1984.

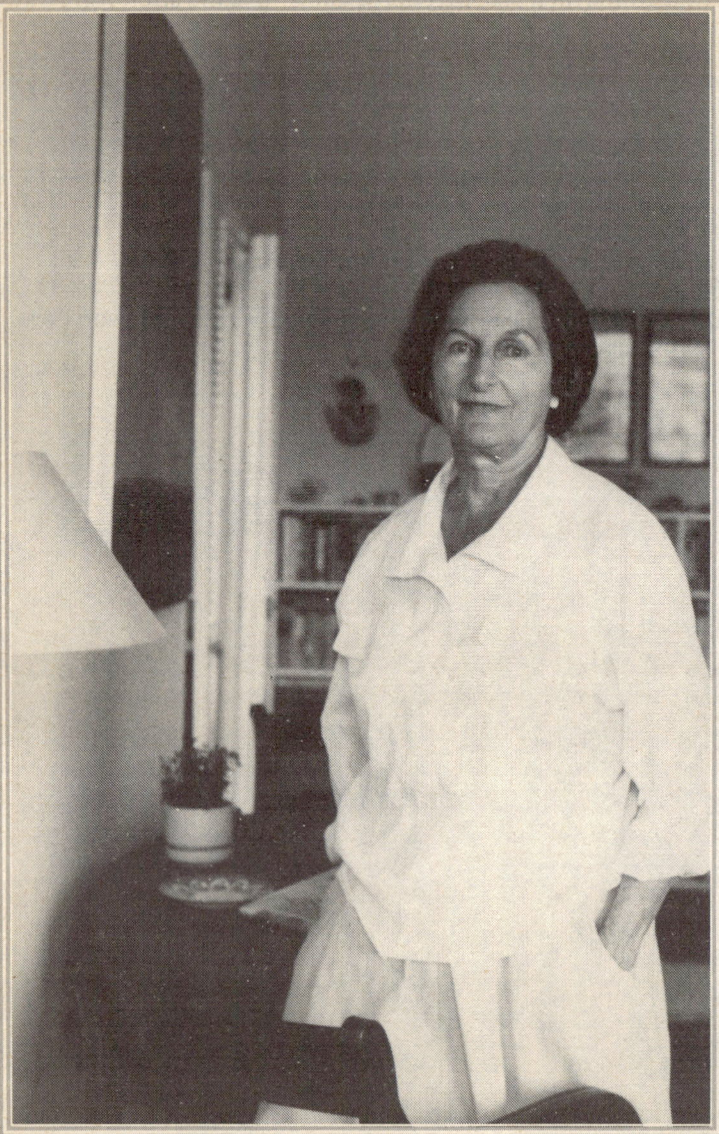

JESSICA ANDERSON

'I don't think a writer's experiences need to be extraordinary. I think the power of reaching them is the critical element, of being able to draw up from the place where all impressions and observations go, the reservoir, the well all of us have in us.'

What writing had you done before your first book, An Ordinary Lunacy, *was published?*

Some stories, all commercial work, and radio plays. The stories were short stories that I wrote purely because I needed the money. I always needed the money. I published under pseudonyms. They were bad stories, but the better they got, the more likely they were to be refused. They got better of their own accord and they started to be turned down all the time.

Where were they published?

Oh, newspapers and magazines, particularly the evening papers. They were 900 or 1000 words each, and all of them had a twist in the tail. It's a formula style of writing — dangerous to do, because it's not easy to forget. The tricks you learn keep getting in your way later. You must un-learn them if you can.

An Ordinary Lunacy *seems a very mature and sophisticated first novel. Was it in your mind for a long time before you sat down to write it? Or how did it come about?*

I started to do a radio play. I'd always meant to stop all this commercial work and do something I liked, but circumstances and my own character, lack of courage perhaps, meant that I left it until I was close to forty. Well, that scared me. I thought I'd better start doing it. I started a play, and after three pages I thought, this is a good idea: I'll write a story. And then I thought I would turn it into a novel, and I started it. It grew much too big. You know the character Possie in it: I allowed her to have a whole life that swamped, or weakened, the main story. After I started I just couldn't stop. It grew and grew until it was absolutely huge. I could see it was bad. And I left it for a year perhaps. Then I peeled off all that story. I remember how I enjoyed it. I just peeled it off, and threw it all out and burnt it. It was a lovely feeling. And I left the stem of the story in. Perhaps I cut it too hard, but I enjoyed it so much, getting the shape out of it, you know. I'd spoilt it, and I was retrieving the shape out of it, and I typed it and sent it off to London and they took it.

Was there a long gap before you started the second one?

No, I started immediately, but it's never been published. I took three years to write it, and I worked on it very hard indeed. I sent it to fourteen publishers, and The Bodley Head agreed to publish it, if Collins here would distribute it. But as soon as I saw the name Collins I knew I was sunk. They refused. They didn't like it at all. It is awfully long. It's still in my cupboard. I can't bear even to look at it.

And do you still feel that your unpublished novel is worthy of publishing?

Yes. It was rejected at a time when sex was new in writing and everything had to be strongly sexual or violent, you know. James Bond had captured the publishing world — no wonder — and mine, as someone remarked, seemed humdrum. The settings of it were humdrum, they told me. I think it was obviously worth publishing or no one would have offered to publish it at all, particularly The Bodley Head.

How did The Last Man's Head *come to be published then?*

After that I returned to radio work. I was absolutely discouraged. It's hard to just keep on when you have flopped, it's hard to get up again, so I returned to adapting. I adapted Henry James for ABC radio — very healing — and Dickens, and slowly I returned to wanting to write again. I just started on *The Last Man's Head* and it went well, much easier than either of the other two. I took about eighteen months to write that, or perhaps two years. I've forgotten.

Did you find that adapting books for radio helped your writing?

Well, you learn a lot. You're adapting marvellous writers, who can construct and who are extraordinarily skilled, and you have to comb it all out and analyse how it was done. You can't help but learn. You'd be rather foolish if you failed to learn. It's excellent training, I believe. For me, anyway.

What was the public's response to The Last Man's Head*?*

Well, I thought it ought to have been released as a plain novel, just an ordinary novel. I did not see that the inclusion of a detective as a main character made it a mystery. But they released it as a suspense novel, and one reviewer said, quite rightly, that the characters were too highly developed for the genre. And it fell between two stools because, I believe, it was published in the wrong way.

Had there been a big response to An Ordinary Lunacy *in Australia?*

It was widely reviewed, but the response — widely reviewed, how I love those words — the response in England and America commercially was better, but not much, you know. It was a good start, that's all.

After The Last Man's Head *you wrote* The Commandant. *What led you to tackle the subject of Australia's beginnings?*

Well, I was interested in Mrs Fraser. I thought I'd do a radio piece on her, and she was in Moreton Bay, as you know, so I went to the Mitchell Library and I read everything in the Moreton Bay file. I came across the letter Logan's lieutenant had written to his superior officer to explain Logan's death, and instantly I put Mrs Fraser away and started to read that instead. I could almost see the whole thing. It was thrilling. It took years of research. I loved writing that. And of course I come from there, and the river, the territory, were so familiar to me.

Those first three novels seem concerned with the prescribed law in conflict with a sort of moral law. Was that something which particularly preoccupied you?

I think it was a preoccupation of the times, and is still, but I think, too, I was very much, and always have been, preoccupied with people who are strangers in their society. That's why the setting of a penal station appealed to me. They were all strangers. Everyone was a stranger.

Why do you think that was a particular preoccupation of those times?

Since the war, there's been a struggle between libertarians and conservatives, hasn't there? Particularly in the sixties. There has been for 200 years, I suppose, ever since the French Revolution, or even earlier actually. You can't think of a time when there hasn't been, can you? It's always there, either underground or overt. At times it is very much to the fore, and ours has been a time like that, I believe.

I think it was on the cover of The Last Man's Head *that you were quoted as saying you feel out of place in Australian literature because you feel your work has a dramatic, rather than a documentary, focus.*

Yes, I do too.

Do you feel, then, that most Australian writing has a documentary focus?

It's changing slightly now, I believe. There's more dramatic writing, now. But I think for quite a long time it had a strong documentary bias.

Perhaps the documentary style really only started to emerge more recently, say, from around the sixties, because before that there was the great tradition of English literature, which was very much based on telling a story.

I feel that I belong to the English and American traditions, but particularly to the English tradition. I started out in the world reading English novels and American novels. I did read Australian novels, but they didn't supply much for me. They were mostly blokey and outback. They don't supply much for a girl or a woman. Women were either mates, or martyrs in the kitchen, or chopping the wood, or killing snakes.

In Aspects of the Novel, *Forster asks three different men what they think a novel should do, and the last one shakes his head solemnly and says something like, 'It should tell a story. Oh, indeed, yes, a story.' Do you agree?*

Yes, I believe that, too, and of course radio work does support that tendency. But it isn't absolutely imperative. There are writers who can just weave a spell and you don't care, you just read them for pleasure. But it's rare. Even when you can't easily find that plot, it is there. Even in novels like *To the Lighthouse*, you care if that child gets to the lighthouse, you want to know if he does.

Do you still feel out of place in Australian literature?

If I do feel out of place I no longer care enough to make the statement. Perhaps I should put it like that.

Did you have any formal education in English literature, or was your reading all self-motivated?

At school I did, but you could hardly count it. I took hardly any notice of it. I read and read and read, from the time I was three onwards. My mother said I could read when I was three. Perhaps it was four, you know what mothers are like.

Were there any writers that made a particular impact on you when you were younger?

I think dozens of them. Everything I read, apart from 'Twinkle, Twinkle, Little Star', perhaps. Dickens must have been a tremendous influence on me. I read him so often when I was a girl. Jane Austen, perhaps. You know, all the old books that were in the house. Henry James I read very thoroughly in my twenties. The Elizabethan poets and prose writers were a tremendous admiration of mine. I don't think I've been influenced by some people I particularly admire. They are out of my range, like Cervantes, you know — *Don Quixote*, I love that book, but I am not influenced by it. It's too different from my concerns. *Moby Dick*, Saul Bellow, *Catch 22*. Patrick White I admire tremendously, but I can admire him without being influenced by him. Christina Stead — I could never write like her, she's so voluminous and so copious, but I admire her greatly and I think she had an effect on me just by writing about Sydney. She gave me courage. She did. But her style never affected mine. I don't know who did. Probably so many people that I can't enumerate them. The English writers, Waugh and Henry Green and Muriel Spark, I like those, too. I love Henry Green's novels, I really love them. I think they're... beautiful novels. If I could choose which novels I'd like to have written I would choose his, all of them. They're lovely, aren't they?

All your previous works had at least three or four main players, whereas Tirra Lirra by the River *is concerned with the interior, singular world of the central character. Did you consciously set yourself that challenge?*

No, no. I never did. But if a challenge occurs during the construction I often take it. For instance, I don't like to move from eye to eye. I like to have one spectator in one section of a story or a novel, the point of view of only one person at a time. I don't like multiple points of view all together in one chapter, and I suppose I thought that the first person form gave me a chance of having to stick to one point of view, without all the devices you use otherwise. But chiefly *Tirra Lirra* was a story. It started as a story of 20,000 words. It didn't work terribly well. I enlarged it, and I showed it to Alan Maclean in England, and he said it was very well done, but it was an awkward length. So I put it away again and went on working. Then I dramatised it for radio, and while I was doing that I thought, well, it's been a long story, a longer story, a radio play, now I'll do the final version of it. So I did, and I sent it to Macmillan in Melbourne, not wanting to send it back to Alan Maclean in London, because he'd seen it already. That's how that came about. Macmillan took it and, as you know, it got a prize. (Prizes are important in this country, in all countries.) It was popular immediately. It is less complex, I think. Or it's easier to read than most of my others. The single voice makes it easier to read, and of course it's in the schools, and so it has done extremely well, and it's done well in paperback in America too. It's had very good reviews in America. They published *The Impersonators* as *The Only Daughter* in hardback, and it's doing splendidly too. They're good, you know, the Americans.

Do you feel that Tirra Lirra *is your best work to date?*

No, I don't really. I don't, but it's the most popular. The public has made its decision and that's it.

Which, then, do you think is your best book?

I like *The Commandant* best, maybe because I enjoyed writing it the most. It was set in the past, so I didn't get that feeling of the ground shifting under my feet, which I'm apt to get when I'm writing about the present. Or do I like it best because hardly anyone else does? Perhaps. But I don't think so. It has no funky spots.

Did winning the Miles Franklin Award have any direct effect on you?

Oh, well, I was pleased, naturally. I adored the money, as I was so broke at the time. And it's encouraging to win a prize. But the success of *Tirra Lirra*, plus the prize it won and the two prizes *The Impersonators* won, made me feel less private and more vulnerable, and I had to get over that in order to go on at all. I had never been interviewed before, or I had never been asked to be interviewed, and suddenly I had all these interviews. It was a challenge I found hard to meet. I almost wished I'd kept writing under a pseudonym as I had begun, and had my lovely privacy still.

Tirra Lirra's heroine, Nora Porteous, seems to be something of a victim. Do you think she was typical of that period, or were you more concerned with Nora as an individual?

I think I was writing about a woman who was born at the turn of the century who, for a start, had those three great events — the First World War, the Depression, and the Second World War — fracturing her life, and also a woman (and this is more important) who was actually a born artist, but was in a place where artists, although they were known to exist, were supposed to exist elsewhere. She was born among that kind of people, and she herself doesn't know that she's an artist. She struggles through, trying to arrive at her art and never succeeding.

So is that what you feel to be the backbone of the novel, the plight of the unrecognised artist?

Not an unrecognised artist, but a person who *is* an artist but doesn't succeed even in being *conscious* of being an artist. She had a kind of buried talent, buried in herself. The sewing, the tapestries, had to be something acceptable to her society. She wasn't a strongly original person. Not many of us are.

Novels written in the first person inevitably seem to suggest a stronger autobiographical basis than others. Is Tirra Lirra *perhaps more autobiographical than your other novels?*

No. But you don't make any character that hasn't something of yourself in it. She was within my range, as all of my characters are.

In all of your novels at least one of the characters is engaged in some aesthetic occupation, and many of them have an aesthetic sensibility and awareness. Do you have any ideas about where that comes from, or why that's there, in your work?

Well, I'm interested in appearances, I suppose, I'm interested in architecture. I'm interested in painting, I'm interested in music and films. I'm interested in all the arts. I suppose, naturally, if I look at anything I assess it. If I look at a building I am assessing it. If I look at a cup I'm looking at it for functionalism and harmony, you know. You do, it's just a natural thing, I suppose. It is in my work, I know.

And it's uncommon.

Yes, fairly.

And it's very beautiful, too. I enjoy all that immensely.

You do enjoy it? I'm glad. I have been accused of being patronising because of it, because I have been critical about a certain slapdash quality in Australian town planning, and ugliness, and I have seen Sydney gradually being almost turned into trash. I think it's improving now. I do feel strongly about these things.

With The Impersonators *you did treat more overtly the awareness of, and indifference to, aesthetics. Had you been building up to that?*

Yes. Well, that is about the England-Australia conflict that exists to some degree in *An Ordinary Lunacy*, too. Though it's more symbolic there. I didn't intend it to be there, either. I mean, you do these things unconsciously — subconsciously — and afterwards you see what you have done. In *The Impersonators* I just started to write about a woman coming back to Australia after a long absence, and I am interested in families — I always have been. They are interesting — you know, the tangle. The aesthetic interest just became part of it. I know so many people, including myself up to a point, although

I'm by no means the worst case, who are always saying, 'Oh, isn't that awful? Isn't that terrible? How dare they build that!' I just like to express it sometimes. I like to have a character like Hermione, who is an extreme of that type, who is so sensitive that she can't stand it. I can stand it easily, but she can't. Sylvia, too, is sensitive to the spoilation. A lot of us are, you know. I am, but not to a degree that it rules my life.

No, but I think people who are extreme in that way are very valuable.

Yes, and we need them, too. Extremes must be stated.

A lot of your female characters are very strong, independent-minded people, but there's never any strident feminism apparent. Does this mean you see the women's movement almost as a non-issue?

Oh no, I don't think it's a non-issue. I think it's an important issue. I think it's a marvellous movement, and it's a movement that has occurred again and again over the centuries, and at last I think it has a chance of succeeding. Biology has defeated it before, always, but with contraception as it is today, it has a chance. Mind you, as all of us know, there are gains and losses, but there have been great gains.

I'm sorry for all the hurtfulness of it: the men who've been hurt, and the women who have been hurt — to say nothing of the children, and the extreme stances that have been taken. But again, extremes have to be stated, and I believe that generally speaking it's been a very good movement. When did you last hear a joke about a woman driver? When I get on buses and see women driving I'm always so pleased. And I see some marvellous things. Men in supermarkets carrying their babies, and they look so good, they look so natural. And it's very nice, isn't it? It's encouraging. It truly makes me believe that we can't go back now. And men often believe that too. But there's a very angry backlash against it. I don't know what will happen. But I hope it goes along.

You don't seem to have any qualms about writing quite intimately about male characters.

No. I don't feel quite so much at ease with them, but I do my best. I mean, I've known a large number of men, and I suppose I know what men are like, you know. I don't feel they're my most successful characters, though.

Do you spend a lot of time redrafting?

Oh yes. I don't fiddle with individual words, although if I think it's a bad word I'll get another. But I try to get a tone of voice and sometimes, if the tone of voice is right, the whole thing is all right, and at other times I get off the rails, and I'll write on and on and I have to throw away all that part and start again. It's very hard to describe. It is trying for a particular tone of voice, and if that's right, what I say is more likely to be right. Not always. It is hard. It's hard for me. When I was a child I wrote most freely and eloquently and simply. I wish I could do it now.

When you say tone of voice, is that something that goes through the whole novel?

Yes, it does go through all of them. All of them have the same tone of voice. It's my tone of voice. It's the writer's presence in the book.

With a work like The Impersonators, *where there are a lot of characters all being managed at one time, do you decide on a basic structure before you begin?*

No, I don't. There'll be a group of characters coming through in the background, with one in particular. And there'll be a theme, but not a plot. I don't make a plot.

So it's the characters who begin the plot?

Yes. I get a big piece of cardboard, and when all my characters are there, which is usually after twenty pages or so, I write their names on this card, or sometimes in an exercise book, but I prefer a big card, and I attach a few biographical details to each. Then I write on until I feel the need of a plan, halfway or two thirds of the way through. So then I make a careful plan on another card. It often turns out to be a sort of visual diagram, so it's no use describing it. After I start writing, according to this plan, I always have to go back and change bits in the early part, and these always turn out to be bits I wasn't satisfied with but let pass. It isn't possible to make a whole plan at the start because, though I have the theme, I don't know the story. There's a rough idea of the story, and often an inkling of the ending. It doesn't do to allow an ending to be too precise, because it may change. In fact, it never does change much. It'll change, but only in details.

Do you write every day?

I try to write from nine to three every day, and usually I do.

Are you always working on a specific project?

I always have something, either a story or a novel or something, in my mind. But occasionally I don't work on it. I have breaks of a month or three months, and I don't do anything. It's rare. I don't like it much when I don't.

Would that be writer's block, then?

No. I don't call it a block. I sometimes feel kind of drained. I feel there's no water in the well. I feel I just need a break. When I have been able, I've gone away during those periods. But I haven't really had the money to travel much, until recently, and now I don't want to travel. I've made a garden, I've gone out, you know, I've entertained myself, I've read, I've enjoyed it, but always in those times there's been something else I felt I ought to be doing and wasn't. It's a curse, I suppose, in a way. I think I would like, after my volume of stories has been published — and then after I've written another, God willing, and you know how unpredictable He is — I would like to retire from writing. I'd like to do something else entirely. I know I won't, but I'd like to.

What would you like to do?

I'd like to make something else, you know. I get tired of all that paper. Though I must say I've had these low points before. It's a kind of biannual event. I don't like the business side of being a writer. Publishing, to me, is a worry. It's a real worry. I hate the negotiation. I think that the writer's position in the publishing world is very unfortunate. They come with their job already done, and they come to a buyer's market, and they're placed in the publishing chain, where all the others, publishers and printers and so on, have to be paid, and most have the protection of unions. The writer is the only negotiable element in the chain, so naturally he's screwed. Almost invariably you have to be highly successful to make any claims on publishers. And that hurts my sense of justice. It aggravates me.

Do you not have an agent?

Well, I have now. I have an agent in America. I believe, I hope, I have an excellent agent now in America. Here I may continue to do my own business. Penguin are good publishers, enthusiastic, and they've taken more chances ... no, I don't think they've taken more chances: they've been well supported, but their enthusiasm is good. They're a good team. Their managing editor, Jackie Yowell, commented on this volume of stories, and I found her comments good. I didn't change them in the direction she suggested, but her comments were pertinent and skilled. She is a skilled person, and enthusiastic and knowledgeable, which not all editors are.

Do you think editors are important in fiction?

Yes, I do. I think they're most important. I don't like the kind of editors that are reputed to exist in America, who will take a book and alter it completely for the market. But often I could have done in my life with a person to whom I could show something, when I was in trouble, and even if they didn't suggest the right thing, to talk about it is often a release — to talk with a knowledgeable and sympathetic person. I think if a writer has an editor of that kind it's a great help, but of course they're almost as rare as good writers.

Do you have much contact with other writers?

No. I know people here and there. I should think I know a number of writers, but I don't know them well. A few I do, but our type of writing is so different that we don't affect each other's writing or talk of each other's work much.

Do you think there have been any personal costs in choosing to be a writer?

Oh yes. But there are personal costs in choosing to be a doctor, or a nurse, or a housewife, or a bus driver.

You don't think the costs of being a writer are particularly great?

I think it must be hard to be married to a writer. They do get very much engrossed in their work. It's understandable that wives and husbands of writers sometimes feel a bit left out of it. People try to understand, but there's this ... shadow that comes across their face when they come home and you're still working. It's understandable, isn't it? But there are many successful marriages among them too. I think it's slightly more of a hazard, I should say, but there aren't any gross difficulties there, I don't believe. If you reverse the position, and look at women who work, with husbands at home who are writers, they are equally susceptible to this feeling of being excluded or put down a little bit, or taking second place. I have heard women say so. So it isn't a masculine thing only. Although I think men are more prone to it, because they're more accustomed to exclusive attention. Perhaps today it's changed, now that men and women so often both work from the start. When I was married, and writing at home (writing was my second job; my first job was the house), I never longed to go out and work in an office or a supermarket. I thought I was terribly lucky to have three hours a day or five hours a day I could sneak in for writing. I never craved to be out in the workplace, as it was being called at the time, never. Of course, when you are home, writing, you're earning too, but your earnings are spasmodic. The earnings that are keeping the house going are your husband's, and so he has the primary position in the house and he feels — most husbands feel, I'm not talking personally — the prime earner has rights over the secondary earner, and perhaps they have a case. Money comes into everything, as a character in one of my books remarked.

Some of your novels focus on the issues of class and money and culture, and whether having money makes people cultured. For example, in The Impersonators *the money theme seems to connect somehow with the theme of being Australian.*

Well, I started off meaning to write a novel where money has a very clear influence all the way through. Actually I often said, 'This is a novel about money.' And my second unpublished novel, too, is called *A Question of Money*, which is a dreadful title, but it was so much about money that I had to include money in the title. Well, it's a natural subject, isn't it, in a society that is so extremely conscious of money, where we don't have a leisured class who just take their money for granted, and where everyone's trying to get it. And you can understand that. It's security, isn't it? I mean, who doesn't try for security? The universities are the closest thing we have to a secure, cultured class, but I don't think scholarship is quite the way to do it, do you? On the other hand, who would want an hereditary aristocracy? It's a problem, isn't it? Not all problems have deliberate solutions; the solutions have to come slowly. I'm not prophetic. I just comment on things as I see them.

In The Impersonators *Sylvia remembers that when English people had asked her about Australia's classless society, she had replied that 'though there were no divisions of the rigour of the English classes, difference of income, sustained through two or more generations, was often visible and audible in the people.'*

Yes, well it's true, isn't it?

It is. And it's also true that anybody can, theoretically anyway, get money and therefore prestige, and thus become cultured.

Let's have a Utopia. The ideal is for us all to have enough money, and to choose what life we like, and then the people who are truly interested in choosing what is called a cultured life would choose it and then we would have a class that was really interested enough, and engrossed enough, in it to choose it, and they would hand it down to their children, and it would go on to *their* children. That way, you would have a cultured class. While the rest of them could be as crass as they pleased. They could be interested in other things, and why not?

Did you ever have any idea that you would become a writer?

Yes. I always did. As a child I said I was going to be an artist or a writer, and I could draw, not very well, and I could always write, and I was always writing, you know, poetry and stories. As time went on it was quite clear that I was going to be a writer. I never doubted this. That was why I oughtn't to have been doing all those bad stories.

I thought at one time I would be an artist, and write. Then I thought I would earn my living as a commercial artist, and write. But when I was a child I attempted to write more often than I attempted anything else. It was my strongest intention, my strongest desire. At one time I would have liked to have been an architect, but it seemed at the time absolutely impossible for a girl to be an architect, particularly in Brisbane, where I lived then. It was not on the cards at all.

Are you happy being a writer?

Yes, I am. I think in a way it's a privilege, because anyone who can do something fairly well is a privileged person, aren't they? And I feel that. I think I've been lucky in being able to be a writer.

When you are writing, are you conscious of the reader who will be reading your work, or is it only yourself that you're seeking to satisfy.

I would love to know. I feel that I have readers in mind, but no particular reader. I certainly am addressing people, but who they are, I don't know. I never think of critics, or any particular kind of person. I'm just talking to someone, I know that. But I don't know who. I suppose I'm just writing for a kind of person who understands and likes that kind of writing. An ideal imaginary audience, whoever they may be.

You don't ever have a fear of running out of material to write novels?

I don't see how anyone can ever run out of material. You run out of the energy and ability to put that material together effectively, but to run out of material is impossible.

Do you have any general views about the function of literature in society?

Well, it defines people's surroundings. Can you imagine England without its literature? It would have far less standing in the world. It defines it, not only to the world, but to the people in the country. I think it is very important. I don't think TV has started to take its place. TV is defining, too, but I don't think it takes the place of literature yet. It may. It kind of hollows out a subject too much, as it were. But to return to literature, its function, there's the question of enjoyment too, you know, and amusement, and entertainment. I think that's important. I don't think the function of literature is to directly instruct, but first to engage, to entertain. Its broader function is to define, but that isn't a function that concerns the writer as she or he writes. It happens anyhow as you examine your particular surroundings, and your particular world. I think all people have a fund of observations and experiences, and a writer is different only because he or she can reach those experiences, as most people could if they tried. But it isn't their concern to reach them. They don't bother to, and if they do, they don't want to put them into words. But I don't think a writer's experiences need to be extraordinary at all. I think the power of reaching them is the critical element.

What exactly do you mean by 'reach'?

It's partly a matter of observation, and partly a matter of reflection, being able to draw up from that place where all impressions and observations go, the reservoir, the well all of us have in us.

You said that literature doesn't necessarily instruct, but then what do you use these experiences, this re-creation of experience, for?

To make stories, to tell stories. Literature *does* instruct, but it isn't the job of the writer to *directly* instruct.

So it's the reader who takes instruction from what the writer says.

Indirectly, perhaps. Certainly I've never had the slightest desire to instruct anyone. Never. But I have had a wish to tell a story, and to entertain, to share, and to ... well, to *make* a thing. The making, the construction, the carpentry, you know. The business of making something is important to me.

Is it that, as Helen Garner mentions, art tries to impose order on experience which is not orderly?

I think order is right. But isn't that only another way of saying it? Out of all those disparate materials you make something — that's imposing order.

A moral order?

I'm very confused about morals. Very confused indeed. Very often I really believe that art must be amoral. And for this purpose I'll call writing an art, because it's true of writing too. I believe that's why totalitarian governments have such trouble with artists, and artists have such trouble with them. Artists cannot, and writers cannot, be commanded to do what is for the general good. There's a great deal of anarchy in art. That's why I'm slightly afraid of government patronage. Our government sponsorship has been most benign and undemanding. It didn't start off quite that way, if you recall? Menzies refused Frank Hardy a grant because he was a communist. It could happen again.

But you wouldn't describe your novels as anarchic, would you?

No, but they're not the kind of novels that would be tolerated by a communist or a fascist society. There's an element of anarchy in them. You know, Lenin made an interesting remark. He was a very intellectual man. He said that whichever path you choose, art or politics, you're bound to meet the other along the way. That's interesting, isn't it? And I believe it's true. There are politics in everything. The Soviet Government approved one type of music, and banned another because it was . . . what did they call it? . . . decadent. Well, words are far more direct than music in their statement. Words are known to be extremely dangerous. They get banned first. People are actually fortunate here, and in Britian, and America. They can say what they please.

Solzenitzin is quite evangelical about literature and its place, and how the art of democratic societies has become corrupted and given up its function and role.

Oh, I think he's wrong. *Because* we are democratic societies, because we already have a measure of freedom, we don't need the zealotry that writers needed — still need — in Russia. If the need arose, I'm sure there would be writers to meet it. There always are. But it's a grim prospect. If we did have to become politically zealous, evangelical, in our work, don't you think we would look back with longing at the times when writing could be simply amusing if it pleased, or entertaining, when it could include playfulness? No, I believe writers — all writers, whatever their range — have one political duty, and that's to guard freedom of speech, and that has to be done all the time. The rest is optional, thank heaven.

Sydney, May 1985

Select bibliography

An Ordinary Lunacy, Macmillan, London, 1963.
The Last Man's Head, Macmillan, London, 1970.
The Commandant, St Martin's Press, New York, 1975; Penguin, 1981.
Tirra Lirra by the River, Macmillan, 1978; Penguin, 1980.
The Impersonators, Macmillan, 1980; Penguin, 1982.

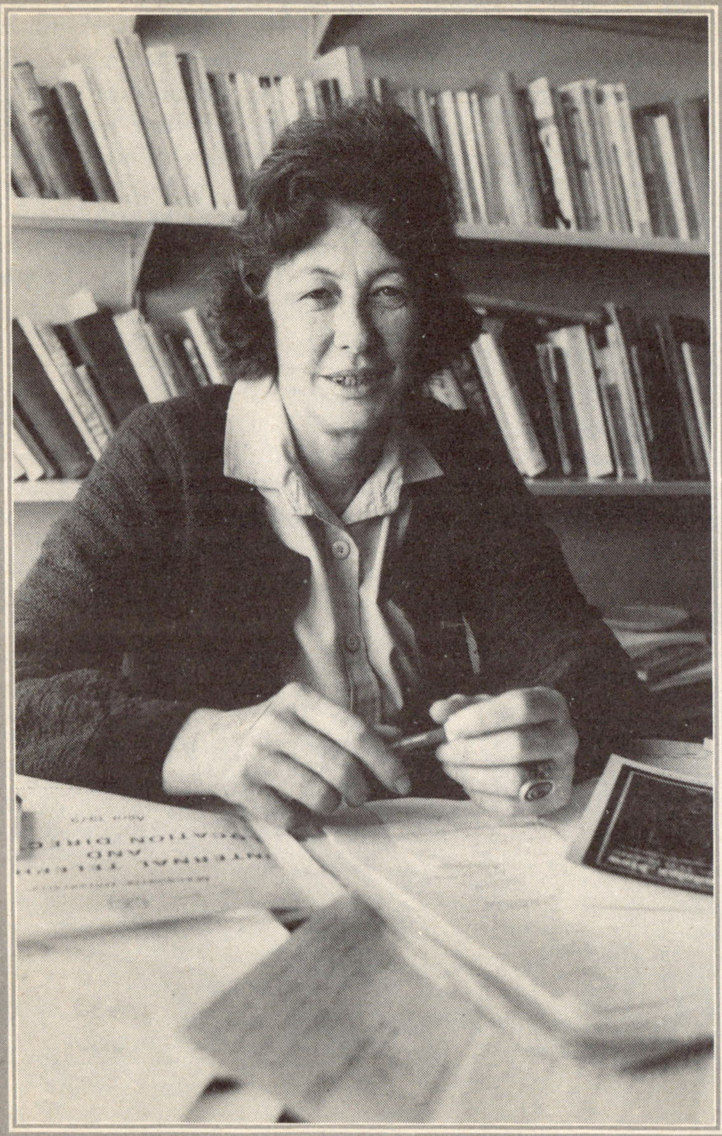

THEA ASTLEY

'When you write a novel you're not writing about anything really except yourself, which is an awful thought, but how do you know what anyone else thinks? You can see a reaction, but your interpretation of it is your own.'

You once said that a novel lasts only six months, unless it's War and Peace. *Do you still think that?*

Yes, I think novels should probably have a date stamped on them, like milk. 'Read by 18 October.' Because the publishing world is so big, and because everybody in the world seems to be hitting a typewriter, I think that a tremendous amount is being published that naturally must fall by the wayside. I can't help wondering whether some of the books that have survived from the nineteenth century have survived purely because there wasn't this enormously fecund publishing industry there is now. And maybe books from that period, assuming that they had modern subject matter, wouldn't find a publisher today. I don't know. I just feel so much is being published.

Do you think there's too *much being published?*

No. I wouldn't say that. I think we live in an age where we're used to disposables. I think people have been geared to regard a lot of the printed word as throw-away. And I think a lot of the stuff *is* disposable. Probably what I write is disposable, probably what a lot of people are writing is.

But isn't it encouraging that A Kindness Cup *is still on the HSC list so many years after it was first published?*

Oh, my dear, I didn't know it was on the list. It seems to be the only book that little royalty cheques keep appearing for, so I suppose I should have guessed, you know, but no one would have told me it was set. I know some of my books are occasionally set at universities . . . But just because *A Kindness Cup* has done the best for me financially doesn't prove it's not disposable, does it?

Well, it proves it's enduring.

I don't know about that. We're in the decade of the minorities.

I suppose there are relatively few books written by Australians about Aborigines. There's *Jimmy Blacksmith*, which I think is an absolutely superb book, and there are books by Colin Johnson.

How long does it take you to write a book?

The last book I wrote, *Beachmasters*, I was thinking about for at least two years, and then I did a lot of reading and research for another year, and I went over to the islands in the Pacific. I guess I put in three years' thinking. The actual writing took me a year, but I lived with the idea for about three years.

Do you feel disappointed that you put in three years on something with a shelf life of, say, six months?

I hope it'll have more, but it probably won't. Actually, the publishers will tell you this themselves, that if a book hasn't sold well in the first couple of months after it's published, that's it. I mean most of the sales come in the first few weeks.

So why do you keep writing?

Now that's a good question. I'm thinking seriously of stopping after the one I'm writing now. It all seems pointless. I've had a lot of criticism levelled at me over the years, all in all. My style irritates people; and I don't do it to irritate. I just can't help my style any more than I can really help the colour of my eyes. When I try to make it simple — I remember I tried to with *A Kindness Cup* — some critic wrote that there was an enormous number of short sentences. I just feel that I can't win any way at all. Even though I might like to write other things, and I'm constantly being stimulated by people and situations, I think possibly I won't.

Do you have a fear of running out of material?

Well, not as long as there are people at bus stops, and in trains, and sitting in cafes at the next table having arguments with each other, no. That can give you a whole novel. You know, it's something you see or hear. And it can be of the most ephemeral nature. And then it's hard, getting 60,000 words to fit round it. But whether one should go on writing about these things is another matter.

Do you have a favourite among your books?

Yes, *The Acolyte*'s the one I like best. I don't even remember the pain of writing that. I enjoyed writing it and wrote it fairly quickly. I wrote it in less than a year, and I only did two drafts. I wrote very slowly. I wrote only about two hundred words a day, and when I came to retype it I hardly made any alterations at all. I was working at Macquarie University at the time, and the corridors were ringing with the sound of symbols, and I wanted to write an anti-symbol novel. I always remember the time someone rushed down the corridor and said, '*Moby Dick* is actually a giant penis'. I got tired of this extrapolation of symbols from novels and I thought, I'll write an anti-symbolic novel and I'll use as many symbols as I can, and send them up. That's why Vesper built a gigantic sling — it was really a giant phallus!

Where did you get the inspiration for that novel? Was it more than a reaction to the symbols fad?

Oh yes, yes, it was. It had been on my mind for a couple of years. I think it was Ken Russell who did a documentary on Delius, the composer, and I'd seen it. In the last few years of his life Delius was blind, and paralysed from tertiary syphilis, and he had an amanuensis from England, a musician, go and live with him and write down his compositions for him. In this documentary the BBC made, which I saw twice, the egotism of Delius — and I think he's a superb musician, but I've read somewhere that towards the end of his life he listened to no one's music but his own — the egotism was appalling, and the way in which he treated his amanuensis, his acolyte, was appalling. I thought I'd like to write a book about a 'great man', but from the doormat's point of view.

Has it been difficult, always having a full-time job apart from writing?

Well, not that difficult, she said, being ungrammatical. No, I think if you want to write you will write, whether you're given grants or not. I remember reading something Graham Greene said once about writing. He said he gets up each day and he does his 500 words till lunchtime, and he stops. And inevitably by the end of the year you have a novel.

Do you spend much time rewriting?

Mm, I do. And I scrap a lot of stuff. And then sometimes after I've scrapped it I'll look back and think, I wish I had kept that. You know, it's awful, really. And I'm only a two-finger typist. I find typing the most tremendous strain, especially up here in the heat.

What sort of changes have you noticed in the Australian literary scene since you were first published?

Well, there are a lot more people writing, a lot more people getting published, but the sort of thing they're writing about I think constitutes the greatest change. I think it's become an urban writing. Even if they're writing about country town, or bush, it's an urban, a more sophisticated approach, an approach that doesn't just accept the laws and values of the bush, a more analytical approach to what's going on in the backblocks. I don't know whether this is due to more widespread education since the war. I mean people seem to be more probing, more analytical, not as willing to accept the Australian myths at face value. And I think this is excellent, and I think a lot of it, too, has been induced by the multicultural society we've got here. I mean if it hadn't been for that, we mightn't have got those marvellous stories of Beverley Farmer's in *Milk*. I do think the migration programme has made a difference to our attitudes, and these attitudes obviously come out in the writing. Also, we have access to American writers, and I think they've been very influential. The New

Journalism of Tom Wolfe has been very influential, in my view.

Vance Palmer said, in 1923, that a man wants of novels vivid character, robust humour, a tough philosophy, and tragedy without a superfluity of tears. And that seems to me to describe your work. Do you think that men and women each want different things from novels?

I think they probably do. Women certainly want different things from the ones men offer them on the relationship level, so I would imagine they might want different things from their intellectual pursuits. I used to think we were all humans, men and women (there wasn't all *that* much difference), and I know a lot of pleasant, sensitive blokes who loathe what happened in Vietnam, who are caring about their kids, and so on. But you do get the feeling that, overall, men demand more violence, or aggression. I honestly don't know about this. I said to someone in an interview once that I grew up believing that women weren't really people, and didn't matter in the scheme of things. You've got to remember my age. Men didn't listen to women when they expressed an opinion. I always felt that they wouldn't read books written by women, because it would be like listening to a woman for three hours, which would be intolerable. And when I started to write I knew I had thoughts going on in my brain, you know, and I'd have little opinions about things, but I knew they didn't rate, and I didn't know what voice to write as. You see, it wasn't popular in my day to talk about menstruation or periods or the angst of having children. That was just a step above Ethel M Dell, or Mills & Boon, and I felt I'd been spiritually neutered by society. I get infuriated when they talk about women as castrators. I remember talking to Brian Matthews about this: I said, but men have done something quite different to women, they've removed their brains, you know, and substituted genital organs where the brain should be, and he said, 'Yes, let's call them vulvators.'

So when I came to write, I thought, well, no one's going

to listen to me, or read me, or be interested anyway, but maybe there'll be a chance of being read if I concentrate on the male characters in my book, or write as I did in *The Acolyte*, using a male character's point of view rather than a female's. And I can't say I felt particularly comfortable doing this, but I suddenly realised, at fifty-plus, when I came to write *An Item from the Late News* and I had a female voice talking throughout the whole book, that I didn't know how women thought. Although I had my own ideas, when I tried to write as a woman speaking, I suddenly realised I didn't remember how I thought when I was fourteen, eighteen, twenty-five, because we were not supposed to think. I used to read books by feminist writers and I was filled with envy, and admiration for the way in which they made women's problems and the woman's voice seem not only intelligent and interesting, but totally credible. That was my first reaction to *Monkey Grip*, as a matter of fact. I thought, God, isn't it marvellous the way Helen Garner can deal with female situations of getting meals (I've always avoided meals, you know) and deal with the mundanities of a woman's day, and make it alive and intelligent and believable, without its looking twee. And I thought, I can't do this. How the hell do they do it?

I read an article about your work which said it's possible that you use males as central characters because many women perceive male characters as not marked by gender, but female characters as distinctly female.

Well, it's true. I think it is true. And consequently of little importance. That's the next step in the syllogism.

But you do feel that's changed?

Not for me, but I feel it's changed for a lot of women writers, and I think they've managed to make women and their pursuits intelligent and alive and interesting, which they always have been. I mean, all right, housework was dreary and drudgery, but now they manage to say it's dreary and it's drudgery, while being amusing about it. They're not whining all the time, you know; they do use it for humour, and also for making a sociological point, whereas I've avoided it like the plague, because it was one of those grey areas of living that men knew went on back there but didn't want to hear about.

Can you tell me a bit about your first novel, Girl with a Monkey — *about writing it and getting it published?*

I wrote that round about 1955, just before I turned thirty. I hadn't written much prose before then. I wrote poetry, because everyone does, and I was really doing an awful lot of autobiographical pieces. I think most first novels are largely autobiographical, and I fictionalised a lot of stuff in it, but fundamentally it followed through my stay in Townsville, when I was a teacher there. I entered it in a literary competition in the *Herald*. It didn't get a prize, but it got an honourable mention. So I thought, what have I got to lose? I sent it in to Angus & Robertson's and, fortunately for me at the time, there was an editor called Beatrice Davis, who has been one of the most effective forces in Australian literature, in moulding and guiding it. Beatrice had worked at Angus & Robertson's, before she left and went to Nelson's, I suppose for about forty years. She was a most encouraging and tremendously brave woman, I think, in taking on poetry and novels which were obviously not going to be big sellers, but she had enough intelligence to see that she was encouraging a different form of writing from the *Bulletin* school. She knew that Angus & Robertson's would always get by with bread-and-butter stuff like Frank Clune and Ion Idriess, and so on. I owe an enormous debt of gratitude to Beatrice Davis, as do very many other writers in Australia. I couldn't believe it when they took the book. They knew it wouldn't be a seller but they were prepared to take a punt on it, I think, hoping that I might do something better.

Did she edit it heavily?

No, no, and she is the most discriminating of editors. She's taught me a lot about punctuation and grammar, too. She's a meticulous editor. I don't think there are many editors like that around now. They leave it mainly to the author. No, if Beatrice ever made a suggestion that I should change something, and she didn't do a lot of that, I knew it would be for my benefit, because an outsider always has a better eye, and you're a fool if you don't listen to the advice of someone who obviously doesn't want to make you look foolish but is trying to help you. I think it shows an insane egotism to ignore the advice of someone who's been in the game all their life, and knows what will wash and what won't.

Since Girl with a Monkey *came out you've had a book published virtually every two years. It's a fairly consistent output. How do you manage it?*

It's only ten. I'm now sixty. That's one every three years.

So you don't consider yourself prolific?

No, I don't. I've had a full-time job, or just about full-time, since our son Edmund was about three. For the last thirteen years I was at Macquarie University, and I think if you do a job conscientiously it's hard to fit in writing time.

How did you manage, physically?

Well, in those days, when I was teaching in high schools all day, I'd write at night. I often went to bed and instead of reading I'd write. But not for long, you know. I wouldn't do more than a page or something like that. But if you do a page every day it's staggering how it mounts up. When I was at university, I wrote *The Acolyte* before I went over to take classes. I'd organise the year so I didn't start till ten or eleven in the morning. I had the house to myself and I'd write from eight o'clock till nine.

In your more recent novels, An Item from the Late News *and* Beachmasters, *you have become more overtly political. The nuclear issue in* An Item from the Late News *is an example.*

Well, that's really what the book was about, but you're the

only person who's ever mentioned it to me, and thank you very much. I mean that. You're the only person who's mentioned it to me. Yes, that's why I wrote it.

Do you think it's important for writers to tackle social/political issues?

Yes, it is. I probably should have done it years ago, but someone like Olga Masters, say, in *The Home Girls*, is very much tackling social issues, while doing a Jane Austen, which is why I admire her work so much. You know, she's dealing with this tiny canvas of living, but she's tackling things that are much wider than that, and that's marvellous.

Do you think writers have a role in helping society to evaluate itself?

Yes, I do. They're always talking about big themes for us. I'm not sure what they are, because, you see, in those stories Olga Masters has touched on one of the big themes of this decade, of women's issues, without for one moment sounding off and sounding like a strident feminist at all. She's merely telling the stories, and their brutality is absolutely entrancing. I mean, you can write wider-issue novels, Rambo-type novels, like *From Here to Eternity* and all these war books that have come out since World War II, and I suppose there are publishers for all the big themes, but also they're subscribing to that Vance Palmer theory of what the male reader wants. I can't imagine a man in a plane being seen dead reading *The Home Girls*, unless he happened to be an academic who's giving a paper on it. And that's not a criticism of Olga Masters; that's a criticism of some constant in our society which no one is ever going to change. I remember once, when I had been lecturing on *The Fortunes of Richard Mahony* at Macquarie, I mentioned that Henry Handel Richardson was a woman. One of the boys in my group came up to me afterwards and said, 'Are you telling me that *The Fortunes of Richard Mahony* was written by a woman?' I said, yes. Now this happened in 1970. He said, 'Well, I shan't read it.' I said, 'That's fine, I shall make it a compulsory question in the examination paper.' And he didn't read it, and he didn't answer the compulsory question, so he failed. But he'd done so badly on the other questions that he would have failed anyway.

You said once, 'My novels are a plea for charity'. Does that still hold true?

Yes. I'm probably not particularly charitable. I'd like to be. One must try to be. I'm talking about the Pauline concept of charity: 'Though I should give all my goods to feed the poor, and deliver my body to be burned, and have not charity ...' Paul meant kindness of spirit — '... it profiteth me nothing' — that was the charity I was talking about. And yet people talk about the acerbic quality of things I say. But very often I'm genuinely filled with sympathy for the things I'm knocking, because they're part of me. I mean, either qualities in myself, or characteristics of my own that I'm criticising. When you write a novel you're not writing about anything really except yourself, which is an awful thought, but how do you know what anyone else thinks? You can't possibly know how they'll react. You can only see a reaction, but your interpretation of it is your own.

In An Item from the Late News *and* A Kindness Cup, *there's a real rage against small-town pettiness.*

No one knows the horror of the small town! I've taught in it, in Queensland. The incident in *An Item from the Late News* about the raping of the dummies in the shop window actually happened in a town I visited. I'm not making it up. Life *is* stranger than fiction. Some of the stories I heard were so awful I didn't use them, actually. Generally speaking, though, country people are great. I like small-town living. Lots of nice things go on in the country. I do honestly believe that hard-working country people are the salt of the earth, and there's something about country haberdashery stores that breaks your bloody heart ... The hats from the season before the season before ... It's sad.

How long have you been living in North Queensland now?

Oh, full time since the beginning of '80, but we've had a place up here since '72, so thirteen years. And now, because it's turning into the Gold Coast, we're leaving. Along with other places, it's lost that 'small town' quality. Cairns was Graham Greene country for years.

Do you feel, living up here, that you're isolated from culture?

Yes, I get a real buzz when I buy the *Weekend Australian* and the *SMH*, but I am also very conscious that I'm 1800 miles away. Very conscious of it. In fact, for a long time I tried not to look at the *Weekend Australian* or the *Sydney Morning Herald* at the weekend, because you do get this enormous sense of being cut off. And I think people in Perth have it too. You talk to Fay Zwicky, it's like another country. I mean there are only two towns that really rate in the cultural world out here, aren't there, and they're Melbourne and Sydney.

I live here because it's physically beautiful and it makes it all the more pleasurable if I go to a conference, like the Canberra Wordfest. But after about forty-eight hours I've had conferences. Enough is enough is enough. In fact, dare I say more like thirty-six? It's just great to see people who are in it, and have a yak and a coffee, but I'm not intellectual. I'm a bit of a loner, I think.

Even so, do you find writing a lonely occupation?

Yes, yes. And I don't know why I'm doing this interview because I don't think writing's something you can talk about. I never bore people by saying, have a look at my manuscript. It's something between you and the publisher. And I don't usually talk about it, because it's boring for other people, except those you know very well, who are in the same game. I never talked about writing at university. I don't think anyone was interested in what I was writing. I talked about the students' writing, because the students were doing a Creative Writing course with me, and I talked about other people's writing, but I didn't talk about my own. I was probably aggrieved that no one wanted to. You think, gee, no one cares.

What about the craft of writing, though? Do you feel you taught yourself that, or picked it up intuitively?

No, I think you teach yourself. You learn from other writers, you learn how they pace their descriptive passages and their dialogue passages. You learn from reading other people's books how it's done technically. And sometimes I've been so filled with envy of a particularly long sentence of, say, someone like Updike, I've analysed it and I've broken it down into its structures: conditional clause, noun clause, you know, object and adverbial clause of time. I've put all these things down and, because I love the rhythm of it, I've tried to construct another sentence using exactly his structure. Now this is a form of grammatical plagiarism, but not a form of verbal plagiarism. It's structural plagiarism, because I don't naturally write sentences like that. Maybe John Updike doesn't naturally write sentences like that either.

Do you set yourself technical challenges with each new novel?

Yes, I do, and I do use grammar quite consciously if I find that I'm repeating the same sort of sentence structure. Sometimes I jot down a list of adverbial introductions: you haven't used a 'whenever' clause, or a comparison clause, or what about using a conditional, how about starting your next sentence with 'if', or starting with a noun clause subject — 'That he was a fool was obvious to everyone.' Just to vary the structure.

Did you have any idea when you were young that you would be a writer?

I always wanted to do some writing. I think probably because Dad was a journalist, and he wrote, and my mother's father was a journalist. Yes, I think I always wanted to do something like that. But I'd much rather have been able to sing lieder.

I have a range of about three notes. God, wouldn't it be marvellous to be able to burst into some Schubert? Or I'd like to be able to play jazz piano like Oscar Peterson, just for half an hour once before I go. And I can't. I haven't got that creativity, and I don't know enough about chords, or theory, or anything. But I think that must be one of the most satisfying forms of creativity there is — extemporising on an instrument.

Do you find writing arduous?

Oh yes, it's yakka, pit-digging. And I think writing novels is far worse than writing poetry. I don't know about writing good poetry, but I mean you've got so long to go, just with all the *the*s and the *and*s, before you see a result. Sixty thousand *the*s before you see the whole thing, whereas at least if you're writing a poem the chances are that it will have formed in a few days.

Why haven't you ever explored the short story form, apart from Hunting the Wild Pineapple*?*

I do occasionally. I'm doing some now. I'm trying. I think it's a much harder form than a novel, and I think probably a play is the most difficult of all. I couldn't write a play. I think you need wonderful techniques to convey mood and character and movement and emotion just through dialogue. I think one of the best story writers in English of the last two decades is John Cheever. I think he's absolutely marvellous, and I'm re-reading Cheever, trying to stimulate myself.

You know, I'm always surprised when people such as Beverley Farmer, say, or Olga Masters, start off on the short story, because of its difficulty. I've always said, the novel's like charity, it cloaks a multitude of faults. You're so exposed in the short story. It's got to be so good, because of its size, for a start. I've just been reading Morris Lurie's *Outrageous Behaviour*. I think he's very good. You have to do so much in so little, and if you can't do it, it shows straight away.

Do you think writers who are being published now might be having an easier time than you did when you were first being published? Do you think there's a more supportive network?

Yes. Yes, I think there probably is, and I think that's a good thing, and I think a lot of it's due possibly to government funding, really. I mean, God, look at the support sportsmen get. Isn't this an incredible country?

But you're fairly patriotic about Australia, aren't you?

Oh, physically I love the place. I love it. Now how is one patriotic? If you mean would I lay down my life for it, the answer's no. Look, it's home, Australia, yes, it's home and I love it, but...

Are you conscious of writing for an Australian audience when you write your books?

I don't know. I think you reach that stage where you're writing for your buddies. What will so-and-so think? That's a dreadful thing, isn't it? Up till now, up till the last, say, five years, unless you were as successful as Tom Kenneally or Patrick White, you weren't writing for any other audience at all anyway. Even if Angus & Robertson's or Nelson's published your books in England, it was a very limited number they sent over. You were forced to write solely for an Australian audience unless you had an overseas publisher. If you used local publishers out of a sense of patriotism you were writing solely for an Australian audience. I think things have improved. I mean I was quite surprised that Viking liked *Beachmasters*. I'm delighted, but I would have thought they'd have gone for something like *The Acolyte*, really.

Do you think there's a distinctively Australian literature, now?

Look, I don't know. They always ask that at conferences and everywhere. Actually I do honestly think if you were given unknown passages by British writers, American writers and Australian writers, you could spot the British very easily. There's a kind of cold-climate moribundity, isn't there? Even if all place names were eliminated, there's a kind of tone. I think Australian writing now would sound more American. I'd like to think that Australian writing is becoming denationalised and has a more international flavour at the moment. If I'd read Beverley Farmer's *Milk* without knowing where she came from, and all place names were changed, I think I would have said it was American. I don't know why I would have said it. Maybe this is what's Australian now, that people are floating loose, as if they're not attached to the shores here, as they were at the turn of the century.

In a lot of your work you have attacks on the Church and Christianity and Catholicism. What's all that about?

Do I attack them?

I think so.

Oh, I was brought up as a Catholic. I'm not a practising Catholic now. I miss it very much, but I do believe in God. I don't like the trendiness of the Church. I think they've sold out to the twentieth century. I could understand the Church better when it didn't bend sideways, when it was inflexible, and you knew where you stood. I liked the Mass in Latin. But I do regard most of the Christian churches — I'm not talking about the Catholic Church alone, I'm talking about the Anglican Church as well — as sorts of great PR organisations, like multinationals, and I think if Christ came back, He wouldn't know which door to go in. He certainly wouldn't recognise what He set out to establish. I think the residue of what Christ taught lingers on with priests who are working in places like Guatemala or Nicaragua, among the peasants, but there are so many unsavoury things about the Church's big business. It appals me.

I miss the security it offered. You know, like ... it sounds like a ticket to Paradise — I miss that, that certainty that if you do this you're right, do that and you're wrong.

I miss the metaphysics of it, because I think everyone needs that. I think it's why so many kids these days are turning to alternative religions, because I do believe there's ... well, I don't know whether you'd call it a soul, but I believe humans do have something inexplicable — otherwise I don't see how you can explain people like Mozart or Beethoven. And I think that the spiritual yearning in kids is determined to be fed somewhere. I mean they've made a god of pop, they make gods of rock stars, but I think because they're dissatisfied with the expression of Christianity in the twentieth century churches, that is why so many of them have turned to eastern meditative religions. It's got to be fed somewhere, this extra dimension of human make-up, the spirit, whatever you choose to call it, the intellect, or whatever it is that demands it. I think it's very sad, actually, because I think all mankind wants to worship something, even if it's only the races or the footballers, but they seem to me to be such boring gods to substitute.

When you are writing, do you feel a responsibility to try to alert people to different values?

No, I don't feel any responsibility. I just say what I feel.

Do you really think, then, that you write for yourself in the end?

Yes, yes, I guess you're right. You've now worked me round into an admission. I guess so. And there's always that vanity in all of us. If it's published it's a bit of a buzz, you know, and if it makes you some money it's even better.

Why do you keep writing?

Because I get amused by things, little things that happen, and I want to put them down, and I hope other people might be amused, or interested, or charmed, or revolted, or whatever.

So you want to share your experiences with other people?

Partly, which is terribly egotistical, actually, isn't it? But I mean I absolutely adore sharing what John Cheever has to offer of middle-class America. Thank God he was vain enough, or whatever it is, to put it down. I'm grateful. I mean, why else would I be raving about *The Home Girls*? All I could think of was, thank you, Olga Masters.

Do you enjoy writing?

Sometimes, when I feel I've lucked upon a reasonably original image, or a phrase, you know. But it's hard work mainly. It's hard work shaping it to your satisfaction. Especially comic things. I think it is very hard to be funny. But then I'll tell you another thing. It's a lot of effort, too. It's like ... say you do about 10,000 words and bits that are OK. You know when they're good. Sometimes you give yourself eight out of ten, and the rest is worth two or three, and you think, all right, I will rewrite, I'll fix it, and you've spent so many damn hours getting 10,000 words together, you think I'm buggered if I'm going to waste all that time. I'm going right through to the end. I know what the curve of the story is and I'm going to finish it, because I'm not going to waste this time. Maybe some publisher will dip into their pocket and give me $2000. Oh boy! It's not the money, believe me, it's just that you feel you want to be paid for the work, if it's reasonable. They make enormous profits, publishers, I'm sure. Bookshops do. The local newsagency sold seventeen hardback copies of *Hunting the Wild Pineapple* up here. It was ten dollars a copy. They made fifty-one dollars at the bookshop, just for selling them. I got a dollar a copy. I made seventeen. It's the pits. Maybe I made twenty, but there's a mark-up, thirty-three and a third per cent mark-up. It's automatic, just for having them in the ruddy shop. And by the time you've written 10,000 words a sort of plebeian rage excites you and you think, I'm going to finish this damn thing and I hope someone will take it and I hope I can get enough money for — what — a new fridge, or a new motor mower? *An Item from the Late News* got me a new pump, actually, which cost a thousand. The pump broke down just when *Item* was accepted. Something else went — the washing machine? Yes, you name my books and I'll tell you the household goodies. *An Item from the Late News*, Onga pump, suction rate: 2400 gallons per hour. Hitachi washing machine, never broken down.

What about Beachmasters?

Beachmasters. Beachmasters? Ah! Socked away so that I can move out of here. Three and a half thousand, socked away, waiting to be spent next month.

Are you working on something at the moment?

Yes, I'm working on a story at the moment. I've written one called 'Getting There', and now I'm writing one called 'Committing Sideways'. Sideways is a slang term for suicide up here. There's a wonderful character around town who talks about the number of people who commit sideways in Cooktown. It's a marvellous expression, isn't it? Committing sideways.

Cairns, October 1985

Select bibliography

Girl with a Monkey, Angus & Robertson, 1958; Nelson, 1977.
A Descant for Gossips, Angus & Robertson, 1960; University of Queensland Press, 1983.
The Well-dressed Explorer, Angus & Robertson, 1962; Nelson, 1977.
The Slow Natives, Angus & Robertson, 1965.
A Boat Load of Old Home Folk, Angus & Robertson, 1968; Penguin, 1983.
The Acolyte, Angus & Robertson, 1972; University of Queensland Press, 1980.
A Kindness Cup, Nelson, 1974.
Hunting the Wild Pineapple, Nelson, 1979; Penguin, 1981.
An Item from the Late News, University of Queensland Press, 1982; Penguin, 1984.
Beachmasters, Penguin, 1985.

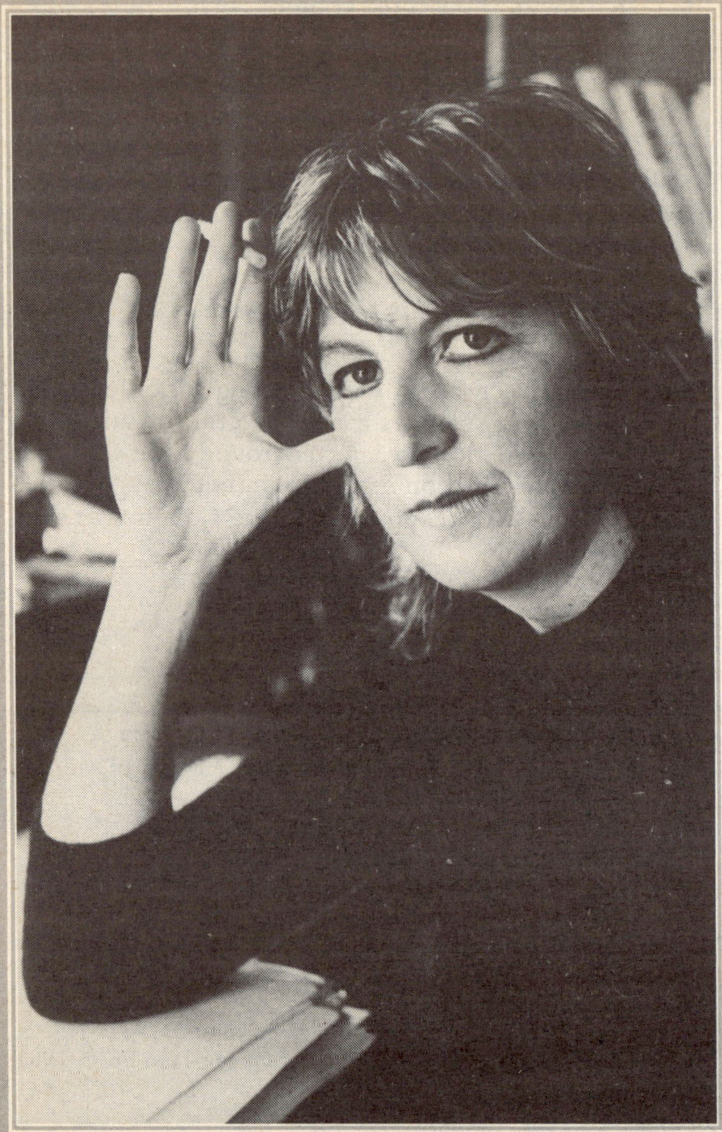

JEAN BEDFORD

'You want to do more than just tell a story. You want to tell the truth, and the way you see the truth is very political, always. I hope that my politics come out in what I choose to write about.'

When did you first start writing fiction?

When I was a child, I suppose, as everybody did. I used to write novels in those little blue dusty notebooks with the soft covers. They were all novels about girls who really turned out to be princesses, and their mothers had been fostering them, and there was always a handsome prince who came along and rescued them, and that sort of crap. I wrote fairly seriously when I was at high school, though I mostly wrote poetry then. I suppose I always tried to write. I've got a couple of novels that I started in my early twenties that are still very properly under the bed. I suppose it wasn't till my late twenties that I decided that if I was serious about it then I'd better start getting my writing into the market place.

But you had in your mind for some time that you wanted to be a writer?

Yes. I wanted initially to be a writer, and then in high school I got a bit seduced by acting, and that became what I wanted to do. But I had fairly old-fashioned, working-class parents who didn't think acting was a very good career for a girl, so I went to university on a teachers college scholarship. I did a bit of acting at university, and then when I left I acted for a year or two before I got married.

When did you first become interested in feminism?

Oh, right from the beginning, around 1967, '68, I think. As students we had all been involved in anti-Vietnam politics. I think for women of my generation it was a fairly natural slide from that into the early feminist groups.

You spent some time in Papua New Guinea in 1971. Why did you particularly want to go there?

Well, I was married at the time, and my husband got a job teaching Maths at the teachers college and, I don't know, our marriage was a bit shaky. I think we both thought that if we went away and did something else it might all be all right again.

And did Papua New Guinea leave you with any lasting impressions?

Oh yes. I loved it. I loved it. My next novel's going to be set in New Guinea, around that time.

What happened when you came back from Papua New Guinea?

Well, I came back because my marriage had split up, and I'd fallen in love with someone else who'd come back to Australia. So I came back to join him really, and I taught in Canberra at the CAE — English as a Second Language, which is what I'm trained to teach. I think it was about then that I really started writing seriously, thinking in terms of publication, thinking of writing as a professional (rather than an amateur) thing, as something you are going to let go of and let people see. Peter (Corris), who I'd returned to Australia to live with, was very helpful.

When we were living in Gippsland, we used to drive to Melbourne and on the way Peter would say, 'Tell me another story about when you were growing up', and I used to tell him all these stories about all these mad people I knew when I was growing up. I grew up in Red Hill, on the Mornington Peninsula. Peter started saying, 'Why don't you write some of these stories down? They're terrific.' I started to, and I finished a couple. *Nation Review* was running fiction every week at that point, and one week there was a story in it that I thought was absolutely ratshit. I thought mine would have to be better than that, or certainly as good, so I sent one to their literary editor and he really liked it. He rang and asked whether I had any more. I said I was actually working on a series of stories set in that place, and about those people; and he said he'd publish as many as I wanted to give him. So he published the first four stories that later became *Country Girl Again*. Then he got the sack, and the new literary editor didn't like my stuff at all, so I didn't get any more published. But that was just terrific, you know, to get your work published so quickly. It increased my confidence tremendously, and made me think I was a writer now, and that I could do it. It was just great luck that he'd liked them, and wanted to use them.

How did Country Girl Again *come to be published as a collection? Had you had other stories published elsewhere?*

No, I hadn't. I think I sent some out, to *Meanjin* and *Overland*, and they were rejected. I got grumpy, so I decided I wouldn't send any more out. I just kept plugging on with them.

McPhee Gribble had been going a year or two, I think, and Helen Garner's first book had been published by them. I sent some of my stories to them, saying that I was thinking of them as a collection, would they be interested? And they actually said the manuscript didn't fit into the McPhee Gribble publishing plan, but then about six months later they were instrumental in starting Sisters. Hilary McPhee rang me and said, 'If you've got a collection together we'd really be interested in looking at it for Sisters'. By then I did have about nine stories together, or eleven. I think Hilary rejected two of them, quite rightly. I sent them down and they said they'd do them for Sisters. That was 1979.

So in fact I was very lucky. My early publishing history was very easy compared with that of a lot of writers, because I didn't have an agent then.

Sister Kate *came out in 1982. What prompted you to write that particular novel?*

An American novel that Peter and I had both just read called *Desperadoes*. It wasn't at all like *Sister Kate;* it was a very funny book, and full of mad American Wild West stuff. Peter and I both were, still are, interested in American outlaws and gangsters and things, and we were on a walk one night, saying what a pity it was that Australian writers didn't do things with their myths in quite the same way the Americans have done. We were just talking idly about how really the only myth that you could do that with was the Kelly one, which had been done so often. Then I started thinking about the Kelly women. I did a major in Australian History at university and did quite a lot of work on the Kellys and that whole idea of social banditry, though we didn't call it that then, but the idea of outlaws as a product of the selector period.

I started thinking that it would be quite interesting to write the story from the point of view of the Kelly women, and I already had done quite a lot of work on it. Initially I was going to write it from Maggie's point of view, but I started doing some research, and the more research I did, the more I saw that Kate's life fell naturally into the pattern of the sort of novel I'm interested in writing. I mean, she was so young when it all happened, and then she had an unhappy marriage later. There were lots of rumours and songs about her, and then she clearly killed herself. That's why I concentrated on Kate.

Did you enjoy writing Sister Kate?

I don't know, I don't know if you ever enjoy writing things. I enjoyed thinking up the ideas and doing the research. I don't know if I enjoyed writing it. I had so much material. I could have written a historical monograph on Kate Kelly by the time I'd finished, and when I came to write the novel I could see that stacks and stacks of it was just irrelevant. That was very hard, because if you find out stuff that no one else has found out, you're really anal about it, you don't want to let it go. I just had to keep pruning and pruning all this irrelevant stuff that I'd found out. In the end, when Penguin got what I thought was the final draft, they wrote and said, there's something wrong with the beginning of this novel. I thought about it for months and couldn't see how to fix it, and then I realised that the first sixty pages didn't belong there at all. So I chopped another sixty pages off it. It was well on the way to becoming The Great Australian Paragraph by the time I'd finished.

How was the book received when it was published?

It was very well reviewed, I think, mostly. I can't think of a bad review of it. I'd gone to America by the time it was reviewed, which was quite nice. It felt like something that wasn't really happening to me — I was just getting the reviews sent to me.

You were at Stanford at that time?

Yes, I got the Australian Stanford Writers Fellowship to go there for three semesters to the Stanford writing program. But I didn't like the course. I left after two semesters. It wasn't what I'd expected it to be. It's very prestigious in America, and people like Ken Kesey and Raymond Carver have been through it. Because it was mostly for writers with some track record, even though not necessarily much published, I thought it would be much more about the mechanics of writing. I thought we would be really working out problems of narrative, or problems of voice, or stuff like that, and in fact it was much more like the undergraduate workshops I'd been teaching, where people were talking generally and theoretically about the pieces. It was fairly savage, too. It was the first time I'd come up against that American ambitiousness in writing. I didn't come in for much of that because, being Australian, I suppose I didn't matter very much, but some of the people in the class used to come out shattered after their pieces had been workshopped, saying they'd never write another word. There were a lot of young men in the class who were clearly scrabbling their way up the ladder. I was a bit appalled at that whole writing scene in America. Unlike the writing scene here, where most people are supportive of each other and helpful, it seemed to be a real dog-eat-dog thing there. But I made a lot of good friends there, and had a good time socially. In fact, I think that was one of the problems about Stanford, that I didn't have to do anything but write, and it drove me mad, so I played a lot of tennis. I think I've finally come to terms with the fact that I'm a very sporadic writer, that I'm not very disciplined, and I don't work consistently. I go for weeks without touching the typewriter. I'd started writing seriously when I was teaching, when I had young babies, so I always just crammed it into whatever time

I could find. I'd always thought I'd done that because I had to, but I think now that's the way I prefer to work anyway — that I don't work every day. When I've got nothing to do but write I sleep a lot, go out a lot.

So you don't see yourself as being a full-time writer in the sense that it's your only form of employment?

Well, I do actually, but it's very hard to make a living doing that. I would prefer not to have to do anything but write. I find doing anything else is very distracting, especially if you are working on something like a novel, because I think even if you're not at the typewriter it's going through your head all the time, and you are working, in a funny way, all the time. Having to do other work's very distracting, especially if it's related to writing. You feel that you are using up your energy.

Before I went to Stanford, I worked for the *National Times* as literary editor for about three years. I've also worked there as arts editor and a feature writer. I think journalism's immensely helpful, actually, to a writer. I think you very quickly learn not to be precious about what you've written. You very quickly learn that your immortal prose is very easily bluepencilled, and is usually a lot better off for it. The subs at the *National Times* are just fantastic, they're so professional and experienced. Also, editing stuff yourself, you quickly get an eye for what's extraneous, and what's necessary and what's not, and you get a very strong feeling that none of it's immutable, that there's always a simpler way, a different way, of putting it, that has an equal effect, if not a better effect.

Did you find it difficult to have a salaried job and to be working on your own writing as well?

Yes. Currently I'm working as a literary consultant at the Australian Film Commission. We put out a newsletter every two months, a précis of Australian books that have the potential to be made into film. But I think I'm coming to the point where I can only do one thing, and I don't know how you manage to live, and just write. I mean, you get grants, but you can't count on getting grants every year for the rest of your life, or having films made of every one of your books.

Do you find that job puts you in an odd position as far as other writers are concerned?

No. I don't think so. In the newsletter I do what I used to do when I was reviewing for newspapers. I don't put in notices of books I don't like. I only write about books I like.

So you have never written a bad review?

Not of an Australian writer. When I was literary editor there was no sense in running a bad review anyway, unless it was someone really well known and of general interest. There was just no point in wasting the limited space on books that weren't worth reading. If I was given an Australian book that I didn't like, I'd always give it back and tell them to give it to someone else to review, because I think it's very easy to be put in a position of looking as if you're in a clique, or as if it's jealousy or sour grapes.

Do you consult other writers about your own writing?

I don't know about consult any more. When I started writing, Peter used to read everything, and I used to read everything of his, so I suppose we used to help each other a lot when we were both starting to write fiction. I used to show Barry Hill my stories, and he used to send me his, but that was when he was more or less starting as a writer too. I don't know. Gabrielle Lord's a very good friend. We tend to read each other's stuff, and make comments. Helen Garner's a friend too. We tend to talk about problems, when we're together. We just hash out things we both think are problems in writing, rather than actually read each other's stuff in manuscript.

What effects do you think living with another writer had on your own writing?

Oh, I think it was terrific. I don't know what it would have been like if we'd both written the same sort of stuff. I mean, I used to get terribly offended with some of the perfectly accurate stuff Barry Hill used to write on my stories. But with Peter it was terrific, because he was writing detective stories, which is a genre I really enjoy reading, and know a lot about. I could read his work and just say 'Oh, it's sexist' or 'The plot doesn't work' and he wouldn't be offended, he wouldn't see it as a competitive remark. And he'd read my work and say 'It's too portentous' or 'It's too arty-farty here', and again, that wouldn't offend me, because I could see he was doing it from the outside, not from the point of view of someone who was also writing that sort of stuff. It was good, I think, for both of us, with our early work.

But how did you both manage your time, because to write you need to be alone?

Well, we both worked part time and we had very different methods. I mean, Peter writes all the time. He could take the spaces, and work in them. If he was in charge of the kids, he could put the baby down for her afternoon nap and then work while she slept. Then he'd get her up and play with her, and if she was amusing herself for half an hour he'd work again, whereas if I was in charge of the kids that was *all* I could do. I still can only work if I know I've got unlimited time, if my study's absolutely clean, if I've got a vase of flowers.

I used to really envy Peter's way of working and think, that's how I should be able to work too, but I now realise I just work differently. When I actually sit at the typewriter I write very quickly. I do ten or twelve pages a day. I think that's because I brood over it for so long before I sit down.

How did the republication of Country Girl Again *come about?*

I think it was because Sisters more or less folded. But Hilary and Di kept two of the Sisters titles — one was Beverley Farmer's *Alone*, and one was *Country Girl Again* — which they decided to re-issue under the McPhee Gribble imprint because those books had stayed in print, and kept being reprinted. I'd actually wanted *Country Girl Again* to come out again because I thought it would look as if I had a new book out. At that point I was despairing of ever finishing this bloody novel that I've just finished. And then Hilary said they wanted to republish it, so I was really pleased. I had about another six stories, two of which she didn't want to use in it, but I'm quite happy with the four she did use, the new ones.

Some of the recent reviews of it use words such as 'cruelty', 'repression', and 'oppression' — both sexual and female. Did you consciously focus on these things?

Yes. When I was picking the people I'd grown up with that I might like to write about, the one thing I thought they had in common was that they were trapped in lives or situations that they were mostly powerless to change. What interested me, when I was writing those stories, were the different ways women can get utterly trapped in domesticity or patterns of madness or patterns of oppression or unfairness, class, all that stuff. I get a bit cross with reviews that make it look as if you're trying to make too many polemical points. I'm writing from a fairly left-wing conviction about the world, probably a wishy-washy Marxist perspective, and I know where my sympathies are, but that isn't what I want to write *about*. I want to write stories, I suppose, in the end. And I suppose the stories do fall into a pattern, and the pattern means something, but I don't think they're as polemical as people seem to conclude, sometimes. If they are, then they've failed. Of course, you want to do more than just tell a story. You want to tell the truth, and I suppose the way you see the truth is very political, always. I hope that my politics come out in what I choose to write about. When *Country Girl Again* first came out I was quite severely attacked by some feminist friends for writing about women whose lives were failures, which I found extraordinary. I didn't actually think of the lives of those women in the stories as being failures. I thought the book was saying that within the situation in which they were trapped those women were being very courageous and strong, and that because you're victimised doesn't necessarily mean you're a failure.

Part of the reason I wrote those stories was, I think, a bit of class guilt. I'd come from a rural working class, and I'd been educated out of it into a sort of bohemian middle class, I suppose. I'd certainly been educated to a point where I had lots of choices, and women I grew up with didn't. Their choice was really whether or not to get married and have kids, and not much else. I think I also wanted to celebrate them, to retrieve their lives, in a way, to say that these lives are important, and these women are quite strong even though they're trapped.

I've still got some sort of distaste about writing about women like me who are middle class, who are highly educated and fairly affluent, who do have lots of choices and a lot of independence. I think there are people who can write about women like that, but for me it seemed like a bit of a wank. I think I've always been suspicious of that sort of middle class self-consciousness. You know, how articulate we all are, and can be, about every little nuance of unhappiness that we have. I think I'm changing, though. I used to think, oh, I'm not a real person any more because I've moved out of that class background.

So the only real people were the lower classes?

Yes, I suppose I had a bit of that. I really don't know. It's very confused. But then it seemed silly to say that sort of thing anyway, because most of the women I know — no matter how well off they are, or what terrific jobs they've got, or even often what terrific husbands, or male or female lovers, or how much choice they've got — are on the whole not happy. If you're going to be honest about women like us, I don't know that you'd be positing very optimistic role models anyway. And that was the argument: why aren't you giving women positive role models? Well I don't know that there are any.

I'm enough of an historian to think that you have to record what's gone before, before you can build new positive role models anyway, and I think we've lost a lot of women's lives.

They've been ignored in literature and history until recently, so I suppose I think it's important to record that stuff as well. But at the moment I'm writing a book of short stories with another woman. It's called *Colouring In* and it's subtitled *The Book of Ideologically Unsound Love Stories*. The stories are all very contemporary and about people like me, and they're mostly funny. And they're great fun to write. So I don't know. Perhaps I'm changing direction, though the novel I've just finished is a real downer. It was intended to be a novel based on my mother's life, which I've always been quite interested in and which I thought might be cathartic to write about, to get rid of some of my daughterly guilt. And it's ended up really being something else. I got interested in patterns, and how they could be repeated over two or three generations. You fall into the same patterns as your parents, particularly your mother, I think. Even when you spend most of your early adult life breaking away from the patterns, you find they're still there, and they're very easy to fall into, particularly emotional patterns, I think. This novel is called *Love Child* because it's also about love, which I'm very interested in. I'm interested in working out what love is and why it goes wrong for so many of us, what it is about it that makes it go wrong, what it is about our expectations and our patterns and our fantasies. I suppose in this novel I came to some sort of idea that I was really writing about false love. I was interested in looking at the difference between a romantic passion and real love that has to involve real generosity and a real understanding of what the other person is, and what they want.

Do you think the women's movement for a time overlooked love?

I don't know. In the first women's groups that I went to I think we were talking about love the whole time, really. We certainly talked a lot about love and oppression, and love and equality, and whether love was possible. Even when we were talking theory, or social practice, I think a lot of what people were really talking about was love, in the end.

I've spoken to a lot of women who at the beginning of the early feminist movements felt almost as though they'd been duped by love. Love seemed to be replaced by some bitterness, and almost a hardening of the heart.

Yes, I think that's so, and I think it led automatically to things like the radical lesbian movement, and those more radical fringes of gay feminism, where men are practically treated as if they don't exist. Which makes it very hard for feminists like me, who are heterosexual, and actually do like men. But I think we all felt we'd been duped, yes. Our generation was brought up on so much shit about love and marriage, the whole romantic dream.

Do you think there's a place for romance in feminism?

Yes, I do. But not the way we were given it, dished it out. We were encouraged to have fantasies about men, never to try to understand what they were like or what they wanted. I think men were pretty oppressed by that system, too, but I don't think men and women do understand each other very well. I think they do regard each other somehow as different species, and they romanticise each other in a destructive way. They make assumptions about each other, and the assumptions are not based on what people are really like. I think that's very damaging, and it's something I find very difficult to get out of. A lot of women were really disappointed when the men they took up with turned out not to be the Duke of Avon from Georgette Heyer, too — they just turned out to be fairly timid, ordinary, hesitant people like themselves, and they couldn't solve every problem, and they didn't know everything, and they couldn't look after you. Women were brought up to think men would look after them, and I think men were brought up to think they had to look after women, and it was a terrible strain on all of us.

Are you consciously trying to bring up your own daughters with a perspective that is different from the one you had?

Oh yes. Yes. Definitely. What I mostly hope for them is that they grow up centred in themselves. I think particularly women of my generation didn't. We were encouraged always to be centred somewhere else. I think we were brought up not to think very highly of our capabilities or our potential and we were brought up to think that what we were and what we did wasn't really very important. I think men escaped that a bit. They were at least brought up to think that what they did was important. We were encouraged to think that nothing was really important except attracting a chap and getting married, having babies. A lot of women still would drop everything for a love affair, in a way that men don't. I think men still have a stronger idea of themselves as people.

Do you feel that your writing is valued and that that has made you more centred in yourself?

No. I think I value it myself more. I think I've finally come to terms with the fact that this is what I actually do, that it's not just an accident.

My emotional life, I think, was always much more central to me than anything I did as work, and work's becoming much more central. Living by myself for the first time in my adult life has made a difference. I've come to see that I'm not as weak and hopeless as I always thought I was, that I'm actually quite a strong person, and that I quite like myself, and can live alone, happily.

When did you team up with your literary agent, Rose Creswell?

When I was writing *Sister Kate*. I think Peter went to her first then I thought it would be a good idea to have an agent, because although I'd been very lucky with Hilary and Di with the first book, I could see myself coming up to one of those awful things of hurling books at publishers. I approached Rose then and she took over everything to do with *Country Girl Again*, which was already published. She then did all the dealing with Penguin for *Sister Kate*, and she does everything for me now.

And does she have much of a hand in helping you with your work?

Yes, she does. She's unusual I think, for a literary agent, in that she's a very competent and experienced editor, too. She also has a PhD in literature, which most literary agents don't. I think with most of her clients she tends to go through stuff very thoroughly in the early stages, which is terribly helpful. She'd read every draft of *Sister Kate*, and made suggestions. She's read every draft of the new one, and made suggestions. She is someone you depend on a lot. She's probably a close friend of a lot of her clients too, which is terrific.

Have you had grants from the Literature Board, so far?

Yes, I've had one fellowship to write *Sister Kate*, and I've had one general writing grant, the year before last. That's all. Even though I keep getting attacked for being one of the people who always gets grants. I've only ever had two, from the Literature Board.

Do you think that it's important for writers to have grants?

Yes, I think it's essential. It's the only thing that comes close to an income for writers. It means you can take a year to write something, and you've got something like an income, which most artists don't have, and writers certainly don't have. They can't make a living from royalties, ever, in this country anyway.

The number of women writing seems to have increased in the last ten years. Do you feel any sense of competition with other female authors?

No, I don't think so. The only person I've had a twinge of that with lately is Kate Grenville. Reading *Lilian's Story*, which I thought was a wonderful, terrific first novel, I thought, this is the sort of novel I might have written — but nothing more serious than that. I don't feel that about Helen Garner. I think her stuff's very different, I really admire her writing too. Beverley Farmer, I think, is probably about the best female short-story writer we've got at the moment. I think Beverley's a consummate short-story writer. Some of the stories in *Milk* are almost classic examples of the perfect short story.

I think we all pick our different corners of whatever truth or obsession it is we're writing about. My experience has been that most of the writers I've met or had anything to do with since I've started writing have been really generous and pleased to welcome new writers, to help other writers and to encourage them. When I started out, there were a couple of really well-established writers who seemed to take an interest in what I was doing and helped to push it. I think writers who review other Australian writers' work are very generous, too, on the whole. I think most of us do think that if someone else has written a good book, then that can only be good for the rest of us, that it's increasing the market. Certainly all the women writers I know are very supportive of each other, very interested in each other's work, and it's terrific, I think. It's probably partly a provincial thing, that there are comparatively so few of us, that we feel a need to stick together and help each other.

Have any writers been particularly influential on you?

I think initially I wanted to write like Patrick White or D H Lawrence, and then I realised I couldn't do that, that no one else could write like them. I think Jean Rhys has probably been the biggest influence on me that I'm aware of. I often go back to her books and just look at how she does things, how she copes with the sorts of things I want to cope with. It's hard when you really admire other writers to know how much of an influence they've had. I've always admired Frank Moorhouse's stuff. I think he's a terrific short-story writer, and I read him a lot. I don't think my writing's really anything like his, but I suppose you hope that perhaps some of it rubs off if you read it all the time.

A lot of people have said that the second novel is more difficult to write than the first. Did you find it so?

It is in some ways. People are expecting the second one, that's the terrible thing. When you've written one and it's been published, you're suddenly not an anonymous person who's trying to see whether you can do the book or not. People are expecting the book, and it's a bit of added pressure on you. But I think my second novel was easier to write than the first. I think I had a clearer idea of what you can do in a novel, and get away with, and I had more confidence about being able to do it.

How do you know when a novel is finished?

I think there's a time when you're ready to finish it, when it starts to come together in your head, and even in your experience. Until that time you're not in a position to finish it. It's more instinctive than conscious. I think when I get near the end I know how it's going to finish, and it becomes a matter of stopping myself from bolting; of making sure I fill in the rest, before I get to the end.

Do you have any plans for what you want to achieve with your writing?

No, just to keep doing it, I suppose. I suppose everyone hopes they'll write The Book one day, the one they've always wanted to write. I was immensely cheered up by hearing Patrick White say a few years ago that whenever he's finished a book he thinks, oh well, that wasn't the one I meant to write, perhaps the next one will be. And I thought, oh God, does everyone feel like that?

When you write, are you conscious of being an Australian? Do you feel that you are creating something uniquely Australian in your writing?

Yes. I'm very chauvinistic about Australia. I think most Australian writers are. I think we're all very aware of where we live, and what it's like, and you do draw a lot of what you write about from it. For example, Peter Carey's *Illywhacker* couldn't have been written by anybody but an Australian. It's just a wonderful book. It's intensely Australian. I think of course there are nuances of grammar and sentence construction that are Australian. There are things inherent in the way you use the language that are distinctive, that are about where you're from, where you live.

Do you have any views about the function of literature, or how Australian literature relates to our cultural identity?

I believe in provincialism, but I don't believe in nationalism. I think that Australian writing relates to Australian culture in exactly the way that any provincial art relates to where it comes from. I don't see it as a nationalistic thing, I suppose. I think I just see it as a product of a place, and a particular sort of society. In general I think literature, all art, performs the necessary function of showing us ourselves, showing us other people and showing us how other people see things. The closest you can get to understanding other people properly is to read or see what people with a certain sort of insight want to tell you about the world and other people. I think that's really of primary importance. I think it's as important as anything else in a society. I don't think art is a special thing. I think it's inherent and necessary. Artists are as necessary as any other workers. They fulfil a function, just as a carpenter does, or anybody else who makes things. I think it's been very destructive, this whole idea that artists are special people. It runs both ways. It's like women being seen as either whores or nuns: you get the worst of both worlds. People think there's something mystical going on if you can make a piece of art, but at the same time they think that because it's special it's not part of society so they don't have to pay you to do it. I think it is a proper job, and it should be paid for properly, but I also think it should be demystified too.

The purpose of art is to extend our experience of life, I think. I believe it is good to understand as much as you possibly can about other people and the rest of the world, because I think the more you understand, the more generous you are to other people and the more you can imagine yourself in other people's positions, and so the more likely you are to see that other people being exploited or suffering is not good. And, I suppose, the more likely you are to build a better world of some sort.

When you're writing, are you conscious of the reader?

I am sometimes. I think I see myself as the audience mostly. I think I'm mostly trying to write what I like, mostly failing. I'm very wary of clichés, and I think that's because of some awareness of other people reading it, of thinking I don't want to say things the way they've always been said. I want to find a different way of saying things. I think part of the impulse of wanting to write, or make things that other people are going to look at, is some impulse to define things your way, and make people see how you see things.

You mean you want to make sure that people understand what you're trying to say?

Yes. I like writing that's accessible. I don't like much experimental writing, because a lot of it is only accessible to a very narrow group of people who have a clear linguistic understanding of what is being done. I think it's good that there is experimental writing, because often it breaks new ground, it changes the conventions, but I don't like reading it much myself, and I certainly wouldn't want to write in a way that was inaccessible to anyone who could physically read.

That's just talking technically. I mean, clearly the content wouldn't appeal to everybody. *Finnegan's Wake*, for example, is a great novel, but only a few people can read *Finnegan's Wake* and understand what Joyce is trying to do, or how well he's done it, and I personally dislike that. I don't like elites.

Sydney, June 1985

Select bibliography

Country Girl Again, Sisters, 1979; republished as *Country Girl Again and Other Stories*, McPhee Gribble/Penguin, 1985.
Sister Kate, Penguin, 1982.

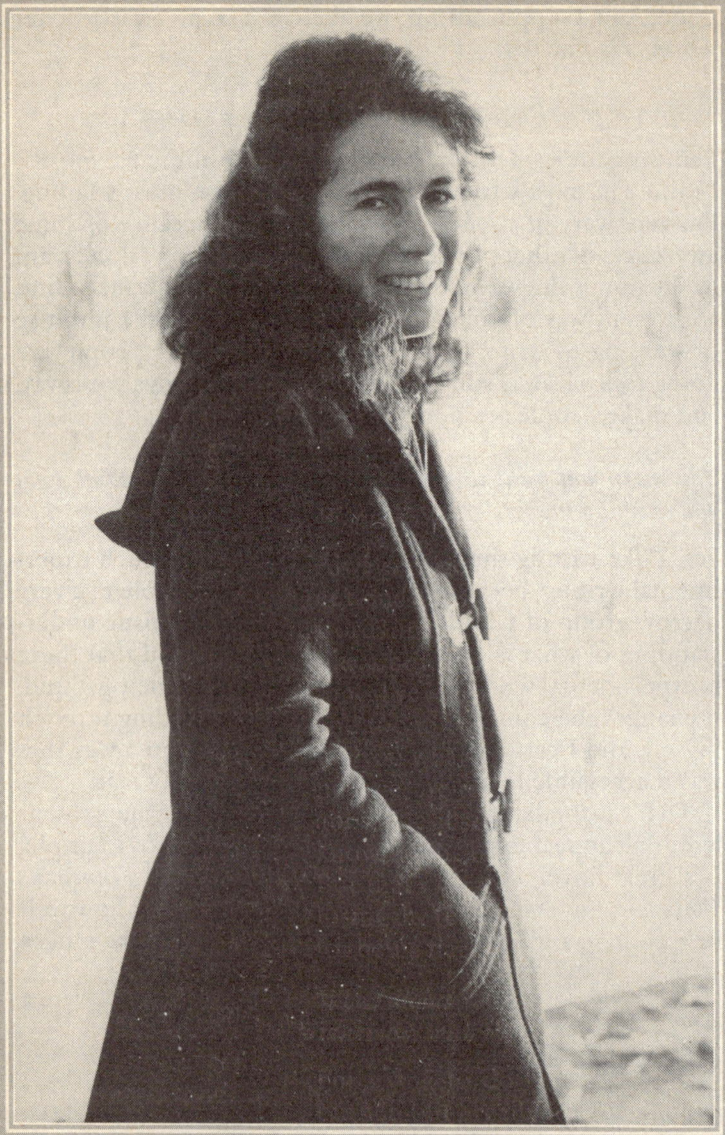

SARA DOWSE

'I'm very much drawn to writing about men. I think part of what makes a person a feminist is wanting to expand the feminine horizon and take in that realm of experience that has been denied us.'

When did you come to Australia?

I came in 1958 as a child bride. I was nineteen. I got pregnant in America to this Australian whom I married, and I was kind of disowned by my family. He couldn't get a job over there so we came out here. I was very, very heavy with child, as they say. We came out on the *Orcades*, which was an assisted migrant ship at the time, although we weren't assisted migrants. A month later I had my first child, and that just sort of implanted me in this country. I think if you have a child somewhere it's very hard to leave. When I arrived in Sydney I lost all my university credits from America, bar first-year History and English, so between having kids I used to take courses part time at Sydney University.

When did you move to Canberra?

In January 1968. By that time I had four children — the youngest was four months. I completed my degree at the Australian National University.

Did you come across any Australian literature then, or was it mainly English literature?

Well, I didn't know much Australian literature at all because it wasn't taught in the university English courses that I studied, and that's pretty typical for that time. So I didn't really know much about Australian literature, or indeed Australian culture. When I went to Sydney University, the world of English literature opened up to me. I was pretty ignorant as far as that went, because most of my literary studies consisted of American literature, and I still think that's the strongest influence on me.

What happened between coming to Canberra and writing West Block?

Well, I think the most exciting thing was that the women's movement got off the ground, and it was particularly strong here. I met a woman who told me about this women's liberation meeting and asked me to come along. And I went, fearful, as we all were, of what we'd find. I walked into the room, and for the first time since I'd been in Australia I just felt I was in the company of like-minded people.

What was it about them that made you feel that?

I think it was the lack of bullshit. I suppose it's hard to explain how different the fifties and the sixties were from the seventies and the eighties. I was a terrible prig myself, you know. I could no more have sworn than curl up and die. I had experienced an awful lot of repression. Well, I can only give this as an example. The first year I was here I read *Sons and Lovers*, and, you know, I was terribly, terribly involved in that book, because I identified very strongly with Mrs Morrell. She, too, was a middle-class woman who'd married a working-class man. It came to me as a great shock when I went to my lecture that she in fact was seen as the villain of the piece. And I think what the women's movement did for me was to validate all those immediate perceptions that I had had to reject. And there were all kinds of women in the movement who had read Mrs Morrell as a heroine of sorts, too. I mean, she wasn't the monster she was perceived to be by those people who were interpreting Lawrence to us. And I think it was just that shift of focus that allowed me, and so many other women, in fact, to say, well, this has been our experience, and it's just as true as anything else. And I thought that was an enormously powerful emotional and intellectual experience, to find oneself validated in that way.

Did your 'consciousness-raising', to use the old term, have any direct impact on the way you ran your life?

Oh, very much. I mean, fairly typically. Within two years I'd left my husband and, well, I just set out to re-acquaint myself with the person I'd left behind in America, more or less. I'm still getting to know her.

When did you join the Office of Women's Affairs?

I was first seconded from the Australian Information Service, where I'd been working as a journalist, to the office of Clyde Cameron, who was then the Minister for Labour. There were several platforms that the Labor Party adopted in relation to women in the 1973 conference, and three had to do with Cameron's portfolio: the adult minimum wage, part-time employment, and equal pay. So I was seconded to his office for a while and I wrote speeches in relation to those issues. Then Elizabeth Reid, who had been appointed Women's Adviser to Whitlam, wanted some departmental support, and so the Public Service Board created a section within the Prime Minister's Department, called the Women's Affairs Section. I went to head that, when it first began, in July '74. When Elizabeth resigned we were left without an adviser in the PM's office. Instead, the section became a branch and I was promoted to head the branch, and then the branch became an office, and I was promoted to head the office. I resigned in December 1977, after the 1977 election.

There was a connection between the two?

Oh, yes. It's very complicated actually, and I've written about this elsewhere. I may not wish to recount the whole bloody business, but anyway the Fraser Government was re-elected in '77 by a huge majority, and shortly after the election the office was taken out of the Prime Minister's Department and put into what was then the Department of Home Affairs. It was a department created to house a lot of things that the Government wasn't going to take much interest in, such as the environment, the arts and women. And there was little choice but to resign, because it was the only way I could make a public protest. If I had attempted to make a public protest at the demotion and still stayed in the office, who would have paid attention? But also I was looking for the moment when I could resign, because I felt that there was very little more that I could do in that job. I hung on after 1975 because it was important to stay there and look after some of the programmes that had been introduced for women, but after I'd done all I could, there was no point in staying. And besides, I wanted to be a writer.

When did you decide you wanted to be a writer?

Oh, I guess about twenty years before I actually did become one. But it wasn't possible. The first short story I ever wrote here I sent to the *Women's Weekly*. I mean, I was so out of it culturally, I had no idea that there was any other magazine that you could send things to. And of course it was rejected, and with good reason.

Once I started working all I could do was keep a diary, and write the occasional poem, and start (but never finish) novels. I really wasn't able to do anything. But when I went to work in the bureaucracy my desire became stronger and stronger, possibly because that experience gave me a lot more confidence than I'd ever had that I could actually do something I wanted to do. I mean, after being a housewife with four children, even though I did go to university, there were periods when I could speak only in monosyllables. I suffered the classic inferiority complex, feeling that I could never do anything. I can remember when I was in my twenties having fantasies of what I would be doing in my forties, and I thought, well, I suppose I should take up knitting, because then at least I could do nice things for people. That's the kind of crap I believed. The next thing I knew, I was in the second division of the Australian Public Service and that did a lot for my confidence.

But when I left in '77 I had lost belief. The experience took a hell of a lot out of me, it really did. It was about two years before I could really settle down to work on *West Block*. Actually, it was after I'd had a baby. I wrote several short stories, then I worked out several articles, you know, academic-type stuff, and I taught at ANU in the Women's Studies programme. But I was still finding a great deal of difficulty breaking from the 'official feminist' role, for both internal and external reasons. Externally, because people saw me that way, and responded to me in that way; and internally, because at least it *gave* me a role.

This is all with hindsight, of course, but it wasn't until I had this baby a little less than five years ago that people decided I was crazy enough to dispense with, and they left me alone to do what I wanted to do. I was forty-one when I had him, and on a deep, psychic level I felt that this child had something to do with my creativity.

So you started to write after the child was born?

I started writing *West Block* when he was three months old, and the first draft took me about fifteen months, because inevitably he got very sick. It went slowly, but the important thing was that every day I was doing it. Then I showed this wonderful draft — well, I didn't think it was wonderful, but I thought it was wonderful that I'd done it — to the publisher, and it was a terrible first draft. Absolutely terrible. He told me to redo it. So in seven months I rewrote it, and it was really white heat. I now realise that's the way I work, that I always write a terrible first draft, because the real problem for me is to actually do it and to not find a million and one reasons not to do it. If I learnt anything from the Public Service experience it was that, if you are going to do a draft, get it down, get anything down. Even if it's only thirty-six pages of the Canberra telephone directory, it doesn't matter, as long as it's on the page, and then you can rework it. *West Block* came out about three years after I started.

Did you work for set hours every day for fifteen months on the first draft?

Well, I did in a sense, because I needed to have day care, so I made good use of it. I'm a terrible procrastinator, and one good thing about having a child — and I don't make this as a prescription for anyone else — was that it provided me with a structure. Because I had so little time I had to decide for the first time in my life what my priorities were, and I just had to say no. The hardest thing in the world for me to do is say no. I'd have to say no to going to meetings, to a lot of social engagements and to writing things that I didn't really want to write. It's not as though I was ever a social hot dog but I hardly went out at all. I mean at all. It was just a very ascetic, hard, poor life, but I loved it, really loved it.

Do you think being an American, an outside observer, if you like, made it easier for you to write a book set in Canberra?

No. I think that an outsider can often see the things that the indigenes, if you like, don't, but that doesn't mean that what the outsider writes is any better accepted. In fact, it's often a little more difficult to accept what an outsider observes. I know Blanche d'Alpuget thinks it's easier, because she's written from the outside of a number of different societies. But my views on that are much more unsettled, perhaps more complex, because I really have been an outsider. And the older I get, the more I see myself as an outsider. I don't see any other place but Australia as home now, and, curiously enough, I feel very much at ease here. But, on the other hand, I will never be entirely comfortable with Australian people, comfortable in the sense that they will understand me. I know that. It's a funny thing. I've talked to other people from other cultures who've come to live in another place, and it seems to be a universal truth that, if you've formed certain patterns of responses, particularly emotional responses, in a certain place, in a certain cultural ambience at a certain time, that's stuck with you. There's very little that can change that. When I go to the States, which isn't very often, there are so many things there that appal, just appal, me. The politics of the place appal me. But, on the other hand, I never have any difficulty in making myself understood. There's a tremendous ease of communication when you're with people whose emotional responses are your own. It's almost a collective unconscious. But it doesn't happen to me here, and I often feel that it's a real struggle for me to be understood, in a very subtle kind of way. I think the fact that I'm American and we speak English compounds that, because Americans and Australians don't speak the same language.

I think one of the big ironies is that *West Block*, written by an American, by an outsider, is one recent Australian novel that's difficult to publish because it's so parochial. And I think that's infuriating because I worked so hard to get that idiom right, because it was foreign to me, and now people say to me, 'Well, it's too Australian'. It's very ironical. I think I'm sensitive to these questions because when you write fiction, you draw so heavily on your childhood. You draw on those really deep, spontaneous impulses that civilisation or adulthood haven't smothered. You need to. That's where your creativity comes from, if not your intellect. You're drawing on deep resources within yourself.

West Block *isn't structured as a novel in the traditional sense, in that it's a series of connected stories. How did it come to take that form?*

Well, them's fighting words. For months I hoped somebody would ask me that question, and no one ever did — that was what was so disappointing. You see, I dispute that a novel has to have a conventional beginning, middle and end. I dispute that a novel has to have a sequential, linear plot. I think that what a novel has to have is an internal, coherent vision. I think it has to have a unity, but I don't think it has to have the particular kind of formal unity that evidently a lot of people demand. The novel that I drew on mostly, in terms of form, was *USA*. *USA* is a series of interwoven episodes, and what Dos Passos was trying to do was to develop a picture of a society, not an individual in a society, not the moral universe as portrayed by individuals acting out different aspects of it, but the movement of twentieth-century mass society, and that's what inspired me. That's why I never thought *West Block* could have any other form. That's not the only reason, but that was an important reason formally.

The second reason had to do with truth, my apprehension of the true situation of that place and time — Canberra, 1977. The building was a metaphor of that society, and indeed, by extension in my own imagination, of Australia, Canberra being the symbol of Australia. It's the national capital, which was really shoving it down people's throats. But that was what I wanted to do, I wanted to shove it down their throats. We've got Canberra, because we've made it. It's what it is because it's what we are, although a lot of Australians don't want to see this. They think it's atypical, a mistake. I don't. And so that building was the structure of the novel. The building's a large, rambling building, with a special history, so that was my vision.

The third thing was that I knew, as a feminist myself, that feminists would want a novel in which the heroine, Cassie Armstrong, has an outright conflict with the baddies of the piece, for want of another way of putting it. That would be the novel's plot! But that would have altered the reality, for me, because the reality of the woman's position in the public arena is that it has been a marginal one, and the only thing that women have brought to those situations has been a new perspective, so that their battles are really existential ones of the highest order. So, I was trying to capture the essence of the time and place and a certain position, an existential position, of working in a modern bureaucracy and what that entailed, and I believe that to have done it in the conventional way would have been to distort the reality.

Cassie Armstrong's story seems to me to be one of a person who was overwhelmed and defeated by the odds. Does that relate very closely to your own experiences?

People seem to be reading that book in a way I didn't intend — which is my fault, not theirs. But the very last sentence of *West Block* is, 'She stepped down and Gina led her back.' And, to me, that meant she was going to go back and fight it out because of that daughter, because of the woman who was to come, and all those associative implications. So I didn't think she was defeated.

But attempting to commit suicide is a fairly strong statement of defeat, isn't it?

Well, that's a funny thing. People have funny ideas about suicide. What I was trying to say with the suicide attempt was that it was a measure of the distress she was experiencing.

I just felt it was a stereotypically 'feminine' thing to do.

Oh yes, but there was an irony in that. You see, there are a lot of clues in Cassie's section, and elsewhere, about Virginia Woolf. You know, her thing was following out Woolf's thing, but what I was saying was that Woolf drowned, but Cassie didn't. And the reason she didn't was because she had been saved by another woman. It was a kind of statement about where we are today in terms of the women's movement, and it was a symbolic rendering, I thought, of the difference between then and now. Suicide *is* the classic feminine response, diary writing is a classic feminine activity, but these things have been transmuted by feminism, and that was what I was saying there.

And the second answer to the question about being overwhelmed and defeated is that I didn't feel overwhelmed and defeated. I felt absolutely smashed... drained, smashed. I guess, in the parlance, I had a nervous breakdown afterwards. I'm sure that's what it was, although I didn't recognise it at the time. But what's defeat? If Cassie was defeated, or if I had been defeated, to me that's only a statement about the lack of human qualities in the society that defeated us. It's not necessarily a statement about the weakness in women. And that, I think, is a curious thing. I mean, there's all this emphasis on strong women. It kind of gives me the shits. Because what it's really saying is, 'We're going to take them on their own terms'. What I was trying to say was that Cassie's very weaknesses were her strengths, and, sure, it would be easy, it's easy for anybody to 'succeed', really, if you just jettison all your scruples, jettison all your humanity, your sensitivity, all the things that make it worthwhile being human. So there was a great dilemma there. Obviously we can't all go commit suicide, and we won't. What I was trying to say is that there's something deeply wrong with a society that will destroy, or try to destroy, Cassie Armstrongs. I wasn't saying, poor Cassie

Armstrong, because I didn't think that. I thought that she was truly good. And strong.

It must have been fairly autobiographical.

Yes and no. Lots of things about it were, but of course lots of things about lots of the characters were, and the male ones too. I think what Cassie and I had in common was that we occupied the same job, and that we had the same political views, basically. That's about it.

But it does invite that sort of connection.

I knew it would, but how else can you write? You put yourself into everything you write. You use whatever experience hands you in creating, and you can't shy away from that. In fact, if anything, I think my fault has been to shy away from myself in writing, and I want to get more involved in myself. I often think I've used fiction as a shelter, rather than as an expression. I think that's because so much of what I am I tried to escape from, and as I get older I'm better able to confront the things I was trying to escape. That's what I feel at the moment anyway.

With Cassie leaving, and you leaving too, does that mean—?

Cassie didn't leave. *I* did.

OK, Cassie went back. Does that mean she still has some faith in institutionalised change for women?

I don't think it's a question of faith. It's a question of necessity. Everybody has to fight where they are, that's my belief, and that's where Cassie was. I don't think you can say that some sorts of political action are more important than others. I think they all complement each other. I think mass action is the most important, but that alone is not going to create political change, in my opinion. I think you need people everywhere.

How do you feel about the women's movement now, in the mid-1980s?

That's a really hard question. A very, very hard question for me. I've become more and more detached from group action. I've become a solitary — it's a consequence of being a writer. I am a member of a writers group but that's about the extent of my group action, these days. So it's been a radical change for me. And I'm no longer qualified to say where the women's movement is at, because I don't participate in it in a formal way any more. I tend to think that the most important statements women have to make now are in relation to peace. That frightens me a little, because we've always been associated with peace, and I suppose there are some dangers in that. But the need for peace has become so imperative now that the world almost depends on women to make it happen.

Jonathan Rowe's story, in West Block, *seemed unusual for a couple of reasons. Firstly, because there was a man finding happiness in having a child, which is not a common view; and secondly because, to a greater degree than the other male characters, in the end, he seemed more preoccupied with his individual happiness than with public service life.*

Well, that's not quite the way I saw it. Jonathan's story was a story about an economist. It's filled with economic language and imagery. I was kind of sending up the neoclassicists, in my own impish way. Jonathan's own theories were turned inside out by the woman wanting to go ahead and have the baby because she had, in his terms, every right to do so. It showed the poverty of that conception of life as a sort of free market, with everybody acting in a vacuum. Because what one person does obviously has a very large effect on what another person does. It wasn't that he was concerned about his individual happiness so much as that he learned that he couldn't find any happiness as long as he believed his pursuit was one he could undertake on his own. It was a complex story in a way. There was a lot of me in that story, because I did have a child, although with a scientist, not an economist.

When I was writing it I wondered what it was that compelled me to keep going. And then I mentioned it quite casually to a friend about a year or so after the book came out. I said, 'I've often wondered why it was that I wrote that', and she said, 'Well, Sara, don't you know?' And she rattled off a list of eight women who'd had children in similar situations in Canberra. So it's obvious, although it wasn't obvious to me at the time, that women are making these choices, and by making them we're forcing men to examine the sorts of things that are really important to them. And I guess that happens in Canberra because Canberra is, relatively speaking, a middle-class society where there are a great number of economically independent women. Because they can afford to have children on their own, in a sense they're challenging the institution of marriage, and opening up the possibility of changed social relationships between the sexes. But there was also the possibility that Jonathan's child would become just like himself, because he, too, was a child of a single mother. You know, things just never change — *plus ça change* ... So there was an ambiguous ending, one with a multiple meaning. The last line is, 'One day, Jonathan guessed, much of it would be history.' That was supposed to indicate that his relationship with Bronwyn could fade and would become part of his personal history. But it also meant that whatever people do, however they create and re-create themselves, that's history. We make ourselves, not only as individuals, but by making other individuals, and through them, society. It's production and re-production. There are lots of resonances in that story.

The form lends itself to television and you are now doing the television scripts for 'West Block'. Was that something in the back of your mind when you were writing it?

Well, no. This is very interesting, incredibly interesting. When I started writing the first script I tried to remember just what I thought were really excellent television programmes, and I remembered a series called 'Talking to a

Stranger', which was screened here in 1972. It was a British series about a family, and each episode was taken from the perspective of a different member of the family. I had the Penguin book of scripts from years back and so I started reading them after I'd written the first draft of my own script, because I didn't want to be too slavishly copying. It struck me that I had kept that form in mind all those years, and when I went to write *West Block*, I was influenced by it, as I had been by Dos Passos. But I wasn't aware of it at the time.

What sort of difficulties, or challenges, are you finding in translating the written word into dialogue?

Most of television and film is not dialogue, it's visual. And the more I write, the more I think that a writer has a lot in common with an actor. Writers attempt to convey emotion through gesture and speech, and all those devices that an actor uses to communicate. My mother's an actress and I've come to respect her a lot. Good writing, like good acting, is just as much an absence of speech as it is speech itself. In the scripts you write in images and you're very conscious of what actors do and how they move. My fiction works that way, too. If anything, I leave out explanation, because I want what the characters say and do to convey what I want them to, rather than telling the reader. That's a risky way of going about it, and sometimes I err on the side of understatement, so that people might not pick up what I'm trying to say. But I would not want to write any other way.

It's interesting that the time span between novels being published and being translated into another medium is contracting. What's your feeling about that? Do you think there's any danger in it?

Look, I don't think there's anything that hasn't got its dangers. 'There's no such thing as a riskless policy', Noam Chomsky said. I think the fact that publishers are now publishing tie-in books for movies is a bit obvious. Maybe it's silly to try to cash in on that particular market, but publishers have to survive, and that doesn't necessarily mean this is the death of literature. On the contrary, it could mean more opportunities for writers. Writing a novelisation is one very good way for a writer to learn just what a novel is. When I wrote *Silver City*, which was a novel from a film script, I learned to appreciate what differences there really were between the two forms. It's hard to say of any kind of experience what is valuable and what isn't valuable. As a writer, I can't think of an experience that isn't valuable.

How did you feel about the general response to West Block?

It got a very mixed response. It was a polarising book. People either loved it, or they did not dig it. And that left me feeling very confused more than anything, because there was a period when I simply didn't know what my stengths were, and what my weaknesses were. There didn't seem to be any way of predicting, either, who would like it and who wouldn't. So I was left quite bewildered by the whole experience. I've heard through the grapevine that some people felt it was a bit flat. But there were other people who felt quite differently. Many people found the structure difficult, and other people found it marvellous, and you know they really did respond to that circular way of doing it.

Did you feel that it was misunderstood?

Oh yes, but I think that anybody, any writer, is bound to be misunderstood. The thing I learned was that the process of reading is such a subjective and selective experience that people will pick up things to which you intended to give a very minor emphasis, or they'll see things in it which you didn't see yourself, but which may be pefectly valid.

It's just an enormously complex business, and that was an important thing for me to learn as a writer, that no matter how hard you try, and God knows we all try, you're never going to be understood entirely, never. But I think the book, and the way I wrote it, runs against the grain of a lot of writing today in Australia, and I think that's what dissatisfied some people.

In what way does it run against the grain?

I don't think it's beautiful writing in the sense of being writing for effect, and I think there's a lot of writing for effect today. I eschewed that because I don't think that's honest. As a painter doesn't paint to paint beautiful things, but paints to paint the truth, a writer, I think, does likewise. In a sense it's more important to try to grate than soothe. Whether I failed or succeeded in that is another story, but I think I started out with that premise. But all this is speculation, because, you know, some people say the writing in *West Block* is beautiful, and I'd be the last person to be able to judge that, which is interesting. There, and even in *Silver City*, I did things with the language that I felt at times were pushing it, distorting it — like removing conjunctions, using words in different tenses.

What's in your mind when you're redrafting?

Always to get the focus sharper and sharper. To avoid repetition. When I redraft I really do rewrite, and I put in more words than I take out, because the drafting is really more like a blueprint, or a sketch, which I fill in. But, at the same time, I've learned to become suspicious of sonorous phrases, and too much explanation, so I cut. I think that writers who tell you what their characters' emotions are, down to the last nuance, are telling you too much — to get back to my point about the absence of speech. It's like syncopated rhythm, you know, it's the beats that you miss that are the interesting beats. But that's very risky, terribly risky, because you can end up losing the reader. I think that, when people criticise *West Block* for being flat, it's because they haven't picked up the nuances.

What about your next novel? Are you working on that simultaneously with the scripts, or is that aside for the time being?

I'm trying to do both. The novel's definitely on the back burner, but I really love it when I get to it, because it's more of myself than anything else I've done.

In what sense?

Well, it's about an Australian film maker who goes to Hollywood and then comes back again to participate in the great Australian film revival. But really, it's an inversion of my story, because I'm writing about Australia and I'm writing about LA, and I'm writing about people whom I've known and who have been important to me, but in such a way that it's turned inside out. All creative writing is enormously exciting and draining to me. As I said earlier, for so long I've been escaping things, but now I'm getting to the point where I'm beginning to confront them. This book is confronting me. This book is resurrecting bits of my childhood, resurrecting bits of my experiences when I came to Sydney. It'll take me years to write it because I'll never be satisfied with it, but it's like scraping away layers and layers and layers of paint and finding the grain of the wood underneath. I'm really loving it.

There are a lot of film connections in your work. How do you account for them? Have you been involved in the film business?

I love films. When I was a kid I used to go to the movies Friday night, Saturday morning, Saturday afternoon, Sunday afternoon and Sunday night. And, you know, my parents were horrified at this, of course, but it must have had some compensations for them. I grew up in Hollywood. My mother was an actress, my stepfather was a writer, my father was a lawyer who dealt with film stars and what have you. So, you know, my life was show business, and that's why I came to Australia. I thought the last thing I wanted to do was be a writer or an actress. I was really frightened of it, because I grew up in the fifties and my parents got into trouble with McCarthy, and all I wanted to do was be an average American girl. That was pretty impossible, so I fled. My mother had been a communist, my parents were divorced and Jewish, and they were in show business to boot. I didn't have a thing going for me, not a thing. At one stage I was going to be an actress, and shall I be so immodest as to say I was actually approached in a drugstore by a talent scout (that was when I was thirteen) and I was so excited. But my parents came down like a ton of bricks, all *four* of them, and said no, no, no, in no way shall this child ever be an actress.

Then at one stage I was going to be a singer, and I really would have loved to have done that. I was just about to cut my first record, and I got pregnant, and got married instead. So there were a lot of unconscious urges operating, a lot of conflicts in my life, which I was escaping, when I came to Australia. Part of the reason I ended up here was that I was a tremendous romantic, and still am, and there was nothing more exciting than running off to Australia with a football player. My parents were dumbfounded. They still haven't recovered from the shock of it all. Nor have I, really. To an American then, Australia was very exotic, until I arrived here and I found a nation full of men just like my husband. But I was a wilful child, so once I was here there was no way I was going to admit to anyone that I had made a mistake. Although it was a pretty unhappy marriage I stuck at it for as long as I had to. It wasn't until the women's movement that I saw any way out. I have a tremendous regard for my husband to this day, my ex-husband as he is now. He's a terrific bloke, but we were as different as chalk and cheese. It was almost tragic how different we were, and are, and the irony is that I've presented my children with the same dilemma that I had as a child. They've got two very different sorts of parents, and different value systems, and they've got to choose between them.

Do you find the loneliness of writing a problem?

Oh, sometimes, dreadfully, dreadfully. What I liked about the Public Service was working with colleagues, bouncing ideas off people. Oddly enough, there were many things about the Public Service that I enjoyed. I certainly enjoyed the Prime Minister's Department, because, hideous as it was in some respects, you really knew what was going on all the time. There was all this information, and sometimes I hunger for that, I honestly do. I feel very isolated. But I certainly would never have been happy doing that for the rest of my life, and I am happy now.

Do you expect to go on writing for the rest of your life?

Oh yes. Everything is in terms of, will I live to write? Will I be able to see to write? If you start in your forties, all these are very important considerations. Everything is measured, I find, in terms of writing. And there are so many things I want to write. Although I'm not particularly young any more myself, I feel young as a writer, probably because I have started late. Also, unlike some other writers, whom I envy, I think my approach is a lot more experimental, so I'm more liable to make mistakes. But like all of us I'd really like to be a Tolstoy.

That's another thing that interests me. I'm very much drawn to writing about men, and I think that's largely a masculine part of me finding its expression. Blanche said once that I have lived such a feminine life, and the only way I can correct that imbalance, if you like, is through my imagination. Both the main characters in the book I'm writing now are men, and so I wonder about that. Moreover, the writers that I really admire are men. Such as Dos Passos, Tolstoy, Fitzgerald. Sometimes when I sit down and read a woman writer I feel enormous comfort and relief. It's like, how nice it is to be home, sort of thing. But the vision that I get from male writers is something that has a much more powerful effect on me, and I find that very hard to explain in the context of being a feminist, except that I think part of what makes a person a feminist is wanting to expand the feminine horizon and take in that realm of experience that has been denied us. It seems more important to me to experience that through my imagination than it does to state my own experience.

Canberra, May 1985

Select bibliography

West Block, Penguin, 1983.
Silver City, Penguin, 1984.

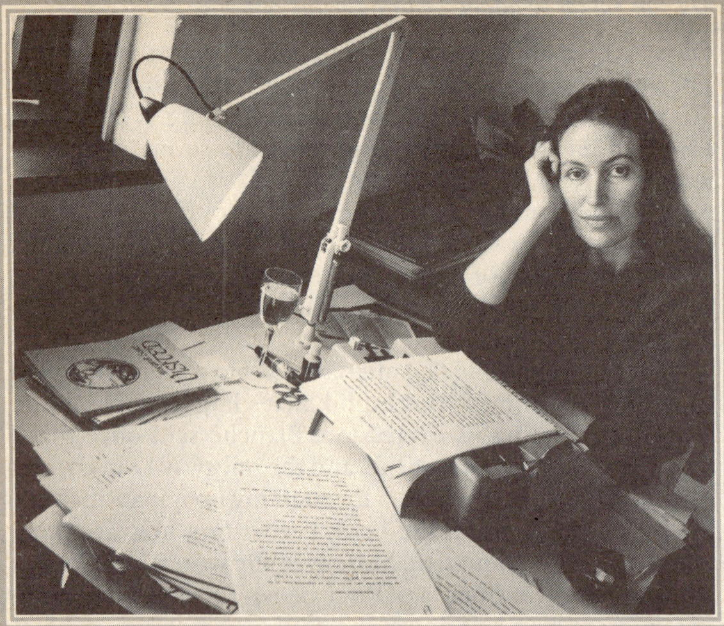

BEVERLEY FARMER

'When I'm writing I don't feel involved. The more emotional the thing you're writing about, the colder you have to be as you write it. First-person narrators are characters like any others.'

When did you first start writing?

I think when I was seven, you know how children do. I wrote little poems and things for my mother. She got me to send them to Corinella's page in the *Sun* and you'd get a certificate — blue, green or red, depending on how good Corinella thought it was. I suppose that's how I started.

Is it something you've continued to do ever since then?

I always *wanted* to write. There was a time when I thought I wouldn't dare to; that was after I left university. When I started teaching English at high school and had to teach the writings of Judith Wright and Kenneth Slessor, I read them for the first time (because we hadn't read them at university) and was fascinated by them. I really fell in love with Kenneth Slessor's work. It's like falling in love with a person: they fill your whole world for a time. Slessor did that for me, and then I started writing again.

Was it poetry that you were more interested in then?

It wasn't that I was more interested but that I felt it was more possible to construct a poem than a story or a novel at that stage.

At what stage, then, did you first start to write prose?

I first tried to write a novel in the vacation before my matric year and it was very ambitious — an allegorical thing about a modern Virgin Mary, a virgin birth and all the disruption that caused, and of course it was completely impossible. It couldn't be done. But I did a couple of chapters before I realised that, and then it was time to go back to school and I tore it up.

Alone was your first published novel. When was that written?

I'm not sure, by the way, that it's a novel, although we call it a novel in English.

What would you call it then?

Well, I suppose even novella sounds pretentious in English, but it isn't really a novel or even a novella. I've been reading in *Scripsi* about this man Michel Tournier talking about what he calls a *récit:* a narrative or a tale. He says, 'the appellation was made fashionable at the turn of the century by André Gide who used it to distinguish short, strongly autobiographical texts centred around an individual experience', which is exactly what *Alone* is. So really it's a *récit* if it's anything.

The structure of it is too simple for a novel. It's an extended short story — in fact, it was first published in *Westerly* (in 1968 I think) as a 1500-word short story. I took it off to Greece with me then (I went with my husband in 1969 to live in Greece for ever — such is fate) and just gradually began to do more work on it when I had time. Over the years that I spent in Greece it took its form as it is now and I suppose when I came back it was virtually finished, although I added a couple of chapters in '74.

It took a long time to write — probably too long — because I had a chance to stew over it. It's read at a much faster pace by the reader than the pace at which it was written, so it seems too dense, I think.

Why did you go back to it when it had already been published as a short story?

I think I felt that I'd only just touched the surface of something that I really wanted to work on. Perhaps not touched the surface, but opened a door, and I wanted to go much further than I had.

Was it a cathartic experience to write such a strongly autobiographical work?

No, because by the time I began writing it, so much time had passed since it had happened. It's set in 1959 and the events that it's based on were also events of '59. By then I'd taught for years. I'd been married. I was a different person. By then I could see it in the round, as an experience to be conveyed as somebody else's, that of another woman, not mine any more.

How did you come to get Alone *published?*

When Sisters Publishing was set up (I think it was 1977), I read about it in a newspaper or magazine and naturally thought there were possibilities there and sent it off. Hilary McPhee read it and liked it but there was a whole board of directors who had to read it and like it, so there were some months of nail biting before it was accepted in 1980.

Di Gribble was also a director and I trust Hilary and Di absolutely. They know what they are doing. I don't even have an agent: we negotiate directly. Hilary re-edited *Alone* with me in so far as it could be edited, because I'd written that a fair while ago. I remember Di doing the paste-up on *Alone* at nine o'clock one night. They were very shortstaffed at that stage, alone in this three-storey terrace house. They took so much trouble over it and they dedicated themselves so much to it that it's not just a business relationship for me.

Was it important to you that Alone *be published by a group like Sisters?*

I wanted it published. I didn't mind whether it was a feminist publisher or an ordinary publisher.

Do you have any feminist sympathies or do you define yourself as a feminist?

Oh sympathies, yes, but I'm not an activist. I'm in sympathy with equal rights and women's emancipation and all that, but the trouble is that women's liberation is such a flexible term. It means something different to everybody.

What does it mean to you?

I don't really want to give a definition of feminism but I expect people to consider women as equal to men and I'm astounded when they don't. But I'm not actually out there in the field battling against prejudice.

How did living in Greece, which is obviously a very male-dominated society, influence your views on the role of women and your views on 'feminism', for want of a better word?

I was only twenty-one when I met Chris, my ex-husband. We'd been together for seven years by the time we went to Greece and we'd adapted to each other in Australia. He had accepted that women are freer over here than he was used to. It was only when we went to Greece that we found that the compromise we'd worked out in Australia wasn't going to work in Greece because of family pressures and the scorn of other men, who thought he was hen-pecked if I was allowed to get away with what I took for granted in Australia. It was a very difficult time for us. I thought I was letting him down if I behaved with the freedom that I took for granted. Not sexual freedom, I should point out. And of course it's a generational thing too. His parents' generation were very shocked that I wore trousers, for example, as this was regarded as a radical act, but his brothers and sisters accepted me without question. His sisters were both working. They had had a good education. Now of course, with the socialist government, women's liberation is taking giant steps.

Do you still take an active interest in Greece?

Oh yes, yes. I only lived there for three years but we'd been married four years before then and we only went out with other Greeks. I lived in a totally Greek environment except for school. I had that split between my teaching life and coming home to a Greek household, Greek parties, Greek friends, Greek weddings, Greek books to read (even in Australia, in Melbourne); and then of course Greece itself, and then coming back here again into a Greek family. I suppose about twenty years of my life were spent in a Greek environment and I'm still loosely a part of the extended family because I'm still my son's mother. And I'm accepted. I went back there in 1983 after seven years away after the divorce, not knowing how I'd be received, but I was very lovingly received.

What sort of difficulties did you have as an Australian operating in a Greek culture? Did it make you more conscious of your 'Australianness', for example?

Yes, in a way it did. I realised that I had a fierce patriotism that I'd never suspected before. I got bitterly homesick for tea-tree and things like that. I think one of the strongest impressions when I came back was walking on a beach and it smelled right for the first time in three years. But that is more subconscious, I think, and it's only in encounters with individual people or incidents that offend you that you realise you're up against a cultural barrier. But you don't see it like that; you see it as Vassily being difficult or Stavros being difficult. It isn't the Greek male against the Australian female but person-to-person problems, just as they are here. That's how it is in the stories too — the conflict is from one person to another, because I'm more interested in the interaction between particular people. The cultural is sub-textual I think.

Was 'Alone' — the short story — the first work you'd had published?

No, the second. *Westerly* had published the first just before. It was called 'Evening' and was a Greek story: about Greeks in Australia.

So when did you start to write more short stories and get them published?

I hadn't really thought of the short story again for a long time until 1979. I wrote one — 'Gerontissa' — and sent it to *Tabloid Story*. Also I enrolled in a Creative Writing course at the Council for Adult Education. I did one of their short courses and I was interested enough to go on and do a semester at Prahran College of Advanced Education. We had to do short stories as assignments and I began fanatically to read every short story I could get hold of. I really fell in love with the form just as I had with Australian poetry before.

The first strong influence on me of Australian literature as literature — prose, I mean — apart from Mary Grant Bruce and Ethel Turner and all that in childhood, was a Patrick White short story in *Meanjin*, a Greek one too. It made me realise what could be done in Australia, that there were no rules. Coming out of university, I thought that writing anything and sending it out to an editor was more or less like sitting for an exam. Seeing this sort of work made me realise that a writer has to impose himself more or less, just by sheer force. By an 'inner force of conviction': I can't remember who said that, but it means that the writer who has the strength to impose his own view will be accepted — you don't write to please anyone; you just write what you have to.

There had been rules at university, categories and criteria, and this author was 'in' and this author was 'out', and I felt that I had allowed myself to be conned in a sense. I felt that university stifled any impulses to write. I felt we were being trained to be critics or lecturers, academics, and that this training was not only not going to help us write but possibly going to inhibit us and I ought to forget it and overcome it.

Did it take you some time to throw off that feeling?

Yes. And, of course, when you send work out and it comes back with a rejection slip, there's the humiliation of feeling that you've stuck your neck out and made a fool of yourself and that you're no good and you never will be. But you get hardened to it after a while. It's the first ones that kill you. I sent things out under false names, and addressed the return envelopes care of the post office so that they wouldn't come home and nobody would know that the thing had been rejected.

But there was something that made you persist?

Yes, obviously there was, but I don't know what, because for a long time there was no acceptance. Between the acceptance of the short story 'Alone' and the acceptance of the novel there was over ten years.

During that time had you been submitting short stories?

No, not until 1979. I don't write very many. I'm not prolific. Eight a year is good for me and six is about average.

Your stories strike me as being particularly well crafted. Is it a fairly meticulous process you go through before you feel you have a finished work?

Yes, it is. I do a lot of rewriting. At first I used to read each story on to tape to make sure that it sounded right, but I don't do that so often now. I think I can hear the inner voice without reading it aloud.

When you're writing are you conscious of audience?

Yes, I'm more conscious of the reader than I am of myself, I think. You're creating impressions in someone's mind, you're making them relive experiences and you want them to relive them in a certain way. You consciously leave things out that don't fit the image you want.

Do you follow any rituals when you write?

No. If I can't get started there's a tape I play for myself, an Indian tape of *veena* music. It tends to get me started. I can't write on to the typewriter straight away, so the first draft is always in longhand. And then I muck around with it and cut bits out of here and stick them in there or pin them together in a different order or something like that. When I can't make much sense of it I retype it in triple space and then muck it around again with a pen until I can't read it and then type it out again. This happens maybe ten times. Sometimes a story will come right almost at once, and then three or four drafts will do it.

Have there been any significant influences on your writing so far — people? Other writers?

Yes, but they come and go. It's a bit like people that you come close to and then you move away and then perhaps you come close again. It's the same with writers. Patrick White for a long time was immensely important to me because he was doing what nobody else had ever done in Australian writing. He was opening up new freedoms, I thought. Even if you didn't want to write like Patrick White, the fact that he had done this and been abused for it — 'verbal sludge' and all that — and had gone on doing it, that's what was brave.

What particularly are you referring to about Patrick White's work?

I think it's the imagery and the satire and the mixture of techniques and innovations in syntax, everything. It's a bit like abstract art, a bit like cubism. He was breaking up shapes, and he was abrupt and awkward and not smooth and not what you'd call a well-made writer at all. This was what was so wonderful about it. It was a bit like a Cézanne painting, doing the same thing with writing. And I've always felt, too, with my stories that I like the abruptness and the occasional awkwardness. I'm like that myself. I'm not smooth, I'm not easy. I'm impulsive, I'm jerky and awkward sometimes, and I feel it fits me that the stories are written in that way, that they're not smooth. On a rejection slip once the person said that my writing wasn't smooth and that it was awkward and jerky but the story gets told somehow.

Are there any other people who have been influences?

Yes, well, Slessor was an influence on *Alone*. I think you can tell with the water and the light, but I can't point to particular passages in my writing that were influenced by a particular writer. I think Chekhov has influenced me a very great deal over the last few years because I discovered him late, at exactly the right age. I discovered him and Katherine Mansfield almost in the same month. He's probably been the strongest influence on my stories, although I think it's less so now than it was maybe a year or two ago.

Do you read a lot?

Yes, about five books a week, I'd say. When I'm not writing I'm reading compulsively. Some writers affect you badly. I can't read Christina Stead because when I do, everything I write for the next fortnight turns out to be a pastiche of Christina Stead. She overwhelms me. She takes over. And the worst thing is, I don't realise it until I pick it up later and think, My God! How could I not have seen it? So when I'm writing myself I can't read Christina Stead, for example; and the same with Shirley Hazzard, although I admire their work.

Do you write every day?

No. I should probably, but I just can't concentrate on writing when things are not tranquil enough. I need a still centre, and when I haven't got it I may not write for a couple of months.

So you write in fits and starts, write intensively over a period of time and then leave it for a while?

Yes. I think a lot about a story and jot down notes and work my way towards it, almost looking in the other direction. You know what you want to do and you sleepwalk towards it, as someone once said. You know subconsciously that you're getting there, but you don't want to get there too deliberately because then you might lose it. And then when you've got the first draft down and you get to the end of it, you've got a story and you can work on it. Then I just can't drag myself away and I'm intolerable. Nobody can live with me then. I might spend ten hours at the typewriter every day until I've got all the drafts through and the story finished. So, yes, in fits and starts. I'm not saying this is a good work method; that's how it happens with me. I would like to be systematic like Virginia Woolf, who wrote from nine to one every day. And that was it. Put her pen down. But she had a settled life; I haven't yet. Maybe one day.

What sort of life would be ideal for you to be able to do that?

I don't know. I'm not worried about an ideal life. Again, I'll work my way toward that without looking at it, I think.

Are you able to live from your writing?

I've been living partly from an income that I had, an inheritance from my mother, a bit of money from writing and a few windfalls like a prize here and there — they help. I live very frugally. My expenses aren't high.

You mentioned teaching. Have you had any other jobs beside teaching and writing?

Waitressing, when I left university. I left somewhat in disgrace with a very poor degree because the events that were the basis of *Alone* actually happened at university and they were a crisis for me. I was supposed to teach. I was bonded to the Education Department and I was unable to go on with that. I was excused on grounds of mental illness, which was good in one way because I didn't have to pay back sixteen hundred pounds, but also I was labelled a schizophrenic. I'm still on file as having been on the edge of schizophrenia, maybe over the edge. I refused psychiatric 'help': I realise I had a lucky escape. It's alarming when you read a life story like Janet Frame's, for instance. She was labelled a schizophrenic and kept in a mental hospital for eight years. It was only because her book was published and she won a prize that they decided not to give her a leucotomy. They wasted eight years of her life in her twenties, the most important years. She wasn't even allowed to read. She had to hide her copy of Shakespeare and there was nothing else, not even newspapers. How she survived that, I don't know.

So I felt more or less branded, although not everyone knew. I met my husband working at Mount Buffalo Chalet: he was a cook. He had just migrated to Australia. I suppose it was he who persuaded me to give teaching a go, so I went back as a temporary. They must have looked up the file but nobody said anything about schizophrenia. I taught for six years in high schools. Then we went to live in Greece.

Some of your stories are written in the male voice. Is that something you find difficult to do?

No. I'm glad you asked that, because it isn't something that I feel is a great hurdle to be overcome. In fact, I never thought twice about it. For example, in 'Maria's Girl' I was thinking of telling the story from the point of view of the girl, and then of course I realised she knew too little, and the material of it just began to develop. It's a bit like Nadine Gordimer being tackled about how dare she write about black people. As she says, blacks and whites have lived side by side for so many generations that they know each other. It's like any two people who know each other, whether they're male or female, or of different generations. They *do* know and they empathise. It doesn't bother me if men write books from a female point of view or about women. Using a male voice doesn't frighten me in the least because, for one thing, I'm not necessarily aiming for psychological realism. It's not a naturalistic portrait, for example; it's a dramatic action in a sense.

What part, then, does imagination play in your writing?

Oh, it's hard to say. I think I'm almost deliberately not analytical about my writing. It's like the centipede wondering how it walks. I don't really want to analyse the process by which

I get a story together. Carlos Fuentes said somewhere, 'I am not interested in a slice of life, what I want is a slice of the imagination', and I like that. I love that. But I don't think, ah now I'm leaving naturalism and realism and entering the realms of the imagination. I don't think there's a dividing line.

So you don't think it's important to mirror life accurately in your stories?

I think it's almost more important not to mirror it accurately but to exaggerate just that little bit so that people are shocked into seeing something differently. Like in a painting: you make something slightly the wrong shape or the wrong aspect, like a Picasso profile, so that you jolt first yourself then other people into a different awareness by falsifying it. It's like metaphor: it has to be just that little bit wrong to make an impression. If it corresponded perfectly, it would just run through your mind without any friction at all. On the other hand, you can get it wrong and then you strike a real false note and people think, oh no, and they stop and you lose their trust. That's where the craft comes in.

Do you try to convey through your writing any of your own conclusions about life?

If you get the idea of some people and something happening to them and between them, I think that more or less includes your view of what life is about. That you've chosen this particular action is significant, the mere fact that you have isolated it.

Does that mean that you're not concerned about your characters?

When I'm writing I don't feel involved. I think Chekhov said the more emotional the thing you're writing about, the colder you have to be as you write it. Katherine Anne Porter called it 'a calculated coldness', and even Joyce said the same thing: that the artist remains 'indifferent, paring his fingernails'. It's true that all you're trying to do at the time of writing is refine an experience so that it comes across to the reader with the utmost intensity. Whatever morality it contains, it's too late to do anything about it by that stage. Conclusions can probably be drawn from my stories, but I don't draw them myself. Colin Wilson says in his book about the novel that each writer's offering is a bit like that of the grocer who gives you a slice of cheese to taste on the assumption that the rest of the cheese will taste like that; you're giving someone a slice of life, so to speak, on the assumption that this is what life is like. Morality in fiction is implicit these days. My characters might make moral statements, my first-person narrators especially might, but that's not me. First-person narrators are characters like any others.

What about the narrator in Alone — *that's you, isn't it?*

When I wrote *Alone* I felt I was revealing not myself but Shirley, who was a creation based very largely on me, but I changed a lot about that. And it helped me to change it. The mother was perhaps a bit like my mother but the father wasn't, and I haven't a sister, and I hadn't walked out of my matric exams (it was at university that the affair happened), and various other changes that I made helped to distance her from me. So that I could create her as a separate person. But what did bother me on publication was that everyone would assume that this was an effusion and that I was just spilling my guts out in the confessional. Worse, in public.

But that wasn't enough to stop you wanting it published?

No. I don't think the fear of how people might receive it ever stops you wanting something published. Because I knew it wasn't just a gush of confession. It was a rounded experience. It was one night in a lifetime — very much a ritualised night. She ritualised it herself, and she had it all planned and she acted it out. Part of being on the borderline of schizophrenia is that you feel you're acting a part all the time: living in mirrors.

How important are reviews to you?

To a career, of course, they're important; they make a big difference to your reputation, to your sales. And a good opinion from people whose opinion I respect is wonderful of course. Getting letters from readers is good too. In any other sort of job you have people you can have a coffee break with. You work with other people all the time. But in writing there aren't many chances for contact over the work and it's good to get responses from people and know that they are reading you. You're not just a book in a shop that nobody takes off the shelf. As I said, you write for the reader. If there's no reader, there's no point in writing. In fact, I don't think a story exists until it's published. I feel it's in embryonic form, it's not born, until it's in print. So I'm very anxious between when a story is finished and when it's in print, and this can be for a year or more.

Have you ever sent any of your work overseas to be published?

A couple of pieces now and then, but I don't really care about overseas publication.

Why not?

Why should I? I suppose it's because that's not my environment. Those magazines are just names to me in an author's guide or something. It would be different if I was living there and reading the magazines and wanting to be in them.

Do you feel happy with your writing career so far?

It's not a question I ask myself really. I'm more or less looking to the future rather than the past. I've been very lucky, I think.

Why do you feel you've been lucky?

The path has been fairly smooth since *Alone* came out. This is a good time to be writing in Australia. If you have talent and you are prepared to work I think this is a good time. Australian writing is being supported by the Literature Board, by the publishers, by the readers. It's not the way it was twenty years ago.

Do you have any thoughts on why that might be so?

I suppose it's because of the devoted and dedicated work of a few editors, publishers, writers, behind the scenes. It didn't just happen by chance. But this isn't really my field, the growth of Australian literature over the last twenty years. I've just been an onlooker. I think I'm a beneficiary rather than a participant.

That sounds so modest.

I'm not modest. Not at all. I hate that word. Writers have immense egos, otherwise they could never keep going.

Why do you think that you're a beneficiary then, rather than a participant?

Well, I feel I've been looked after really, by publishers, by editors, I've been accepted, I've been given chances. I got a grant from the Literature Board. What have I done to deserve this? I haven't edited a magazine. I haven't worked for the development of Australian literature. I haven't been an academic pushing Australian literature in the universities, and that's very important — what is being taught, and taken seriously.

Are they the sort of people who create a receptive climate for Australian literature?

Yes. Roland Barthes said, 'Literature is what is taught'. He might have been being cynical but I think he was just being truthful. That's how it is. If it's not being taught the assumption is, it's not worth much. Australian literature wasn't taught, twenty years ago. 'What Australian literature?' people said.

Are you quite happy being a writer? Is there nothing else that you really wanted to do?

No. I always wanted to be a writer. I didn't think it would be possible to live as a writer. I thought this was an impossible dream. You couldn't in Australia, unless you were Neville Shute or Ion Idriess or Morris West. In fact, hardly anybody writing now makes enough to live on, but I've just been lucky that my mother's property appreciated in value and I can manage with writing income and other income, and I think if I'm sensible with money probably I can go on like this forever. It is good. It's a dream come true.

When did you realise that you were living a dream come true?

Well, only recently. The last couple of years I suppose. It's only recently that I have been, because we had the restaurant in Lorne for a long time with my ex-husband and then after I left I had no money, no income, and I was waitressing at the Southern Cross Hotel. I was much too exhausted to write, although I had thought I'd come home and write.

How would you describe the passage from beginning to write to considering yourself as a writer?

I think it was imperceptible. You just, at one stage, without knowing how it happened, realise that you now consider yourself no longer an apprentice. You know what you're doing. You know what the rules are and that you're going to break them if you decide to, and if other people disapprove of that, well, you'll listen to them courteously but you'll still go on doing it because now you're a writer. You know your job now and you want to take risks.

Well, how important was the fact that you won the New South Wales Premier's Literary Award?

That was lovely, very important, needless to say. But that happened outside me. You don't consider yourself a writer because other people consider you one. It's something internal, I think. You know when you're doing it right, I think. And when you're not. There's a sense of mastery, like in any other trade.

What about the mechanics of writing: the editing, the redrafting, writing from different perspectives, have you virtually taught yourself all that?

Chekhov taught me and Patrick White taught me. Anything wonderful that you have read is a lesson. There are whole passages, for example, in *A Fringe Of Leaves* where I could feel myself going green, not with envy, but because the blood was draining out of me. The intensity of what he was doing was so wonderful.

So you sat down and consciously analysed what was working?

No, not consciously analysed, just read and re-read it and re-read it until I saw. I don't mean that I could ever do anything like that, but when you see somebody else doing something wonderfully you've got to see how they did it. I don't think you can analyse how it's done. Critics can, but writers don't approach things in that way.

What about the issue of structure — is it something you have fairly ordered in your mind before you start, or is it more like the point you made about coming to a story with your head turned in the other direction?

It's a bit like a piece of music I think. The tempo has to feel right, and the key, but probably the tempo has to be pretty much the same all the way through. You can't vary it as you can in music, otherwise the reader is just too thrown and disconcerted. It's a hard question to answer because it's one of those things you refine as you do draft after draft. You feel that somehow it's too bulky here and it's too straggly and wordy there, and you tighten it up or you take that bit out.

The trouble is, I feel myself very much at the beginning. I feel I've only just begun, and I'm still experimenting (though a bit more competently than when I first started, but it's still experimenting) and finding my way. I'd like myself more if I could be bolder. I can't really offer you the rightness of my own experiences of writing yet. If I'd written ten books, if I had a body of work behind me, I'd be able to answer these questions much better. I learn as I go.

Do you feel it's difficult being a female writer?

This is the big question, isn't it? I don't know. If I were a man, would you be sitting here and asking,'Do you feel it's difficult being a male writer?'

No, I probably wouldn't, because it seems to have always been expected that if men want *to be writers, they* can *be writers.*

It has for centuries for women, too. I mean, Jane Austen, George Eliot, George Sand — oh, it goes a long way back, doesn't it, that women have been accepted as writers. It's almost like actors and actresses, that writers were emancipated long before the average woman was.

Except that, of course, George Eliot wrote under a male name.

And so did Henry Handel Richardson. If it was required of them, then, it certainly didn't stop them writing. Writing under a pseudonym might even have helped them to distance themselves from the material and the female role, to be the omniscient author. A pseudonym is a mask. There have been men who have used pen names too, like Stendhal. Perhaps not female pen names, though.

I think Dorothy Hewett was terrific on the subject of being 'women writers' in Adelaide in 1980, when she gave a speech about how ambivalent she felt about this feminist ghetto that we risk walling ourselves up in, and all the defensiveness and hostility and self-justification that follows from that. You build the wall yourself, and you create your own prison. We shouldn't be doing that. The point of fiction is that it leaps over walls; it turns them into panes of glass.

But it's almost become obligatory to address gender as a point of difference.

I don't like the feeling that men writers are still regarded as more ordered and more cerebral, whereas women are instinctive and confessional and impulsive. Who could be more of those things than D H Lawrence when he was worked up, for example? And George Eliot was as cerebral, and, you know, ordered, as any man. There's really no point in going by these stereotypes; there never has been.

Do you feel that there are any sort of sacrifices that you have had to make to become a writer?

I think I was the sort of person who was born to be a writer, and a solitary life isn't a sacrifice for me. It comes naturally, and I'm naturally frugal too, and so it doesn't worry me that I don't splash money around, and what other sacrifices have I made?

It sounds as if you feel you've done something noble if you've made a 'sacrifice'. After all, I've done what I wanted to do. It seems to me that the people of whom the sacrifice is demanded are those who are close to the writers. They're the ones who are neglected, and left alone. It's the others who suffer if anyone suffers, not the artist or writer.

So do you think it's a more selfish thing to pursue what you feel is important to you?

I don't know that it's selfish to pursue what's important to you. I think that's a reasonable thing to do in life. What else are you going to pursue? Something that's important to someone else?

Something you feel you should pursue perhaps.

I think the only thing I believe in — I'm quoting Blake now — is 'the holiness of the heart's affections'. I love that quote.

Do you enjoy living alone?

I'm used to it, I suppose. Fifteen years of my adult life I've lived alone. I'm very used to it. Ideally I suppose I would like a nice big house down on the coast, the surf coast, the west coast. Big enough for me to work in and live in, and have visitors down to stay and still go on working, and they could cook, play music, and walk on the beach and everything, and keep company with me when . . . you know, when that was the thing to do, and go off on their own when they wanted to, so that there'd be people there. Big enough to have a room only for writing.

An inner sanctum?

No. I see myself as being on the upper floor somehow, above everything, so let's say an upper sanctum. I think that'd be ideal. That's what I think today would be ideal. But I don't know . . . I'll have to see.

Melbourne, February 1985

Select bibliography

Alone, Sisters, 1980; McPhee Gribble/Penguin, 1984.
Milk, McPhee Gribble/Penguin, 1983.

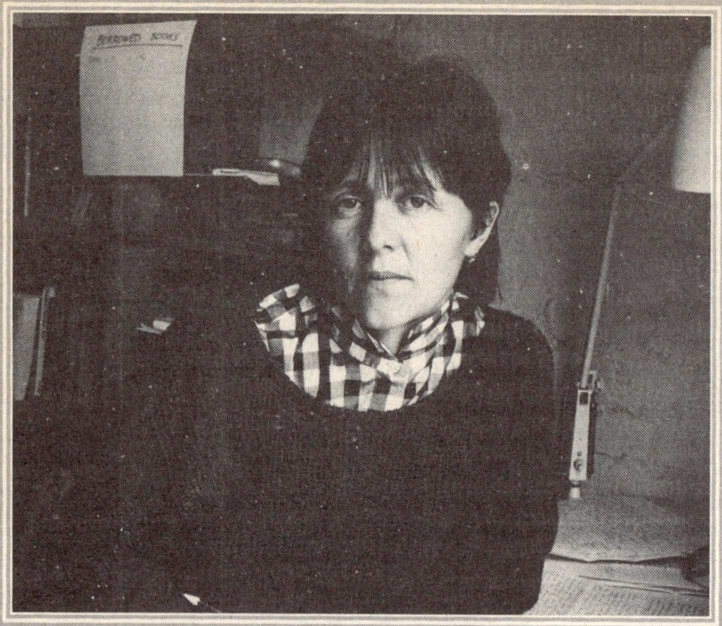

HELEN GARNER

'I don't know why anyone else reads novels but I'm interested in how the hell people make decisions in their lives, on what basis, and how people draw a line between responsibility and freedom, and also what happens to people who don't.'

It was your first book, Monkey Grip, *that put you on the literary map. Can you outline your development as a writer leading up to the publication of that book?*

Well, I'm probably one of those quite rare and lucky people who haven't had to bear a lot of rejection of work. I was something like thirty-five years old when my first book was published. It was the first novel I'd ever written, and my first attempt at one. Before that, one short story which was only slightly fictionalised from real life was published in a women's liberation newspaper called *Vashti's Voice*. I'd also had stuff published in *Digger* magazine, which was how I made a living after I got the sack from the Education Department, but I never really tried to write fiction.

A lot of people talk about how they spent their childhood writing stories, or trying to. I'd never written stories, except for school essays and stuff, but I'd done an enormous amount of writing. I'd written a diary for God knows how long. When I left Geelong to come to Melbourne University (that was when I was nineteen), I burnt volume after volume of those diaries and I'm still not sorry. I suppose I've written every day for as long as I can remember. I'm a prolific letter writer, too.

So what made you attempt to write a novel?

It's hard to say. One thing was that I'd seen a story in my own life that was big enough to be a novel, and the other thing was that I had some time to do it. I was living on a Supporting Parents Benefit for four years and it was during that time that I wrote *Monkey Grip*. It was the first time in my life that I'd had a lot of time each day and a bit of money coming in.

So you virtually wrote full time when you were writing Monkey Grip?

Well, not really, because I used to read a lot. That was a wonderful thing, to have so much time. I read Proust and I read Tolstoy and all those huge things that you can't get a grip on when you've got a job. It took me about a year to write *Monkey Grip*, so there were lots of other things I did over that period. When I was writing *Monkey Grip* I went to the State Library every morning. The doors would open at ten and I'd burst in and work there till after lunch, and then I'd go home and lie on the bed and read all afternoon. To me this didn't seem like work, it seemed like pure pleasure and happiness. I knew a lot of other people who wrote or who were on the dole or on Supporting Parents Benefits and they used to say, 'Gee you work hard at it'. But to me it didn't seem like work. I was really happy.

Did any of the writers you were reading at that time have any particular influence on you?

Oh, it's hard to say. I always find it hard to say which writers have influenced me. I can probably talk about that more now than I could back then, because *Monkey Grip* is to some extent an unconscious piece of work. I didn't know what I was doing with *Monkey Grip*. I thought, here's a story (and I knew about these people because one of them was me, so I could speak with authority). I thought, I'll slog away at this. It's based on a diary and that's why it's got that rather broken-up structure. Its sense of immediacy has come precisely from the fact that it's a diary-based thing. But I didn't think of myself as a writer then. I was just messing around.

Now that I think of myself as a writer, I can think more clearly. I can actually go to a particular writer if I'm stuck, and think, now how would this be solved by Chekhov or whoever? I might go and have a look and see how he finishes a story. Actually that isn't something that I thought of myself. I'd heard people talk about influence and I never knew what they meant. To me it was mysterious. But now I can identify two main sorts of influence. One is the huge and blurred influence that comes to you from the moral world of the kind of writer that you're attracted to. For example, I've been watching 'War and Peace' on TV and I remember with a great rush how much I love the Russians — Tolstoy in particular, and Chekhov. Their work is big and at the same time they're not ashamed to talk about really small things that you don't understand. They can do the battle of Borodino on the one hand and the tiny things on the other hand, like how Natasha feels when she's talking to herself in the night, saying, 'How wonderful it is that I'm so intelligent!' — that kind of youthful boasting.

So that's one sort of influence: the world picture that comes to you when you're reading. And the other sort of influence is a purely technical influence and that's something that at the beginning you absorb unthinkingly. For example, people often remark on the fact that I write in a rather conservative way; maybe what they mean is that my sentences are grammatically correct. That's something that can be absorbed by reading perhaps nineteenth-century writers rather than modern writers, who tend to fracture things more. But it's also to do with having been taught grammar and syntax at school.

This sort of influence is what you can go out and look for on purpose. For example, I once wrote a story for a newspaper. I knew that at the end of it I'd gone mushy and I didn't know what to do about it. I took it to a friend of mine (he's not a writer but he's a terrific reader) and I said, 'What am I going to do with this?' He was able to point out immediately where I'd gone off the rails, the exact word at which it had turned soft, and he said, 'Why don't you go and look at how somebody else ends a story? Why don't you go and have a look at Chekhov?' He said Chekhov would do this and Turgenev would do that and Dickens would do something else. That was the first time that it really hit me that you could go to somebody with a specific question about a technique and get an answer just by looking at how they'd done it. I don't think I could have done that when I was writing *Monkey Grip* because I was too ignorant and too naïve. But to some extent that's why *Monkey Grip* has got some kind of crude appeal. That's obviously one thing people like about it.

Were you surprised by the book's success?

Yes. I was absolutely staggered. The very first review of it that ever came out was in *Nation Review*. I hadn't seen it but Hilary McPhee, my publisher, rang me and said, 'There's a ghastly review of the book. It's about as bad as it can be so I'm warning you.' Naturally I masochistically rushed out and bought a copy and it was horrible. After that, everything was up. It got some other horrible reviews but it got some good ones as well. I was amazed.

Do you think the success had anything to do with the period of time during which it was published?

Yes, oh yes, absolutely.

Do you think the state of publishing or the way Australia was just starting to develop an identity were partially accountable for the success of the book?

It's hard for me to say. At the time when I wrote *Monkey Grip* (that is, the time that it described, which now seems to me to be over) I had lived inside a comfortable ghetto-like world for quite a few years. One thing that surprised me very much when the book came out was how shocked some people were by it. And so I suppose what I'm saying is that I had lived in a rather sheltered way. Oviously a lot of people would think *Monkey Grip* was not about a sheltered life. They'd think it was a life full of toughness and cruelty and horribleness. It's hard for me to see what was going on then, outside that ghetto.

I don't know if most writers are like this, but, although I read stuff that's being written by my contemporaries, I don't think I could give you a clear picture at any stage of what was going on. I wouldn't be able to tell you what the trends were. If you're functioning in a particular field yourself you've got a funny feeling towards your colleagues: partly envy, partly fear, and all sorts of competitiveness which is repellent, morally repellent to one, but one still feels it. Your approach to your contemporaries' work is often coloured by those feelings and you can't really get a clear picture of what's going on. But I suppose there must have been a lot of people who were starting to live in the way that's described in *Monkey Grip*. And the fact that the women characters are to the fore in that book and in everything I write (or most things I write) — I think that attracted a lot of people, a lot of women anyway.

What sort of influence did the success of Monkey Grip *have on you in terms of your next work,* Honour and Other People's Children?

It took me three years to get *Honour and Other People's Children* together. Although it's a small book and it's two stories, it was originally a novel and it was awful. You see, I went to Paris and I didn't know where I was. I put my daughter into the local school and started to go to the local library there and write again. I was just fumbling around in the dark, not quite knowing what I wanted to do. It took me about eight or nine months to produce something and then Hilary McPhee and Diana Gribble came to Paris on their way to somewhere else. They said, 'Look, this is no good, it's terrible. You'll have to sit down and redo it.'

Was that a shock to you?

I already had a fat head, and by then *Monkey Grip* had won the National Book Council Award, so I thought I was pretty hot shit. Yes, it was a shock. Of course they were right and that was an excellent thing to have happened to me. I got one sleepless night out of it and then I started to hack away. I came back to Australia and it took me another year after that to knock it into any sort of shape, because I realised I wasn't going to be able to do another *Monkey Grip*. I was trying to do another *Monkey Grip*, not consciously, but I was learning to write in the third person which already made it more difficult. I had to learn to get myself off centre stage; that was the hardest part.

Were you happy with Honour and Other People's Children *when it was finally published?*

Yes, I like it. I like the first story very much, because it's about things that are important to me. The second story has got a lot of loose ends hanging but they don't matter. Tim Winton remarked to me once that he thought I'd never been allowed to serve an apprenticeship, and I think that's true. I see those first two works, in a sense, as being apprentice works. Tim was very young when his first work was published; his remark struck me as interesting because I was a late starter. I'd never tried to write a novel before. I don't think people should ask for special treatment because they publish apprentice works. You can expect to be criticised. I feel OK about that.

I believe you've said The Children's Bach *is the best work you've done so far. Why do you feel particularly pleased with that novel?*

I like it because I think it works formally. Reviewers liked it. Reviews are useful, especially when you get on in your career and people start to take you more seriously. They might look more carefully at *how* you've done it rather than just at the *fact that* you've done it. I suppose also your book is given to more experienced critics or people who are interested in looking at the prose style or the structure. I've been glad to see that critics have actually had a look at those things, because those are the things I worked on the hardest. There are things that I bunged in there without knowing why they were there. I did them entirely by feel. Critics have said that the book is held together by all sorts of resonances and links and I thought, Hooray — it's worked!

Compared to your previous works would you say you were far more conscious of structure and form in The Children's Bach?

Yes, yes, much more, but it's hard to say in what way. I find it hard to talk about my own work because I work on instinct and feel to a certain extent; but I've learnt to trust my instincts.

You use them in an early stage to get the stuff out on paper and then you start cutting back. It's as if your instincts and your feel become more finely honed.

What's the most important thing to you in the craft of writing? What gives you most pleasure or satisfaction?

The physical is always very important to me. I didn't think very carefully about that until the other day when a friend of mine sent me a couple of her stories. I liked them but I noticed that the physical world was almost totally absent from them. I want to make physical things do a lot of work, to carry a lot of weight. I'm very keen on sentences that are rhythmical and also grammatically pleasing. That's important to me. I like doing dialogue too, but it's getting the physical thing right that counts. If I can get the physical right, the other stuff often comes out of that.

Within the broader theme of domesticity which seems to inform all your work, there seem to be two recurring motifs: children and music. Are you conscious of these?

Children are terribly important. Gerard Windsor said in his review of *The Children's Bach* that the characters are judged by their attitudes towards children. This is true but I hadn't done it consciously. Children are wondrous; they strike me with awe. And they're so tough, and funny.

Music is always there too. I never thought about it, until *The Children's Bach* — it was just there, like air, as it is in everyone's life in the modern world.

In *The Children's Bach* the music works as some kind of moral or ordering principle. It's a cliché but nevertheless true that art tries to impose order on experience which is not orderly, on a universe full of terrifying and demoralising things. I've tried to make music do that job.

Are you then addressing explicitly 'moral' issues in your writing?

Yes. I suppose so. Two things got me out of a big mess at

a certain point in my life. One was feminism and the other one was the whole ethos of collective households. That's the sort of thing that people who don't live like that were attracted to in *Monkey Grip* — the fact that there were those open households where people actually cared about each other and tried to create some kind of alternative to a family, some social organisation that would contain the good things about a family and minimise the bad things, the awful neurotic thing that happens in families. It certainly happened in mine.

'Honour' has a moral title and it's a moral story. It's about people trying to behave in ways that are open and generous. The two women are trying to learn to confront each other, and to confront the fact that one's the first wife and the other's the second wife; they're not going to let themselves get slotted into social roles that have been created for them. They're going to try and approach it in some more open way. I think you could say that was a moral story. And *The Children's Bach* is a moral story because the woman comes back — and by that I don't mean that all women should go back to marriage. I think a lot of people probably interpreted it that way, you know; they thought, here's Helen Garner recanting. Of course, I think it is possible for people to walk out of a marriage. There's a period of sadness and suffering and so forth, but some of the kids I know who are products of broken marriages are the most extraordinary children. They're children who've got resilience and knowledge and sense. People talk about kids of broken marriages being traumatised, but how many people are traumatised by marriages that *don't* break up?

Would you say you are very conscious of the female characters and the whole issue of feminism in your work?

Of course. Some people think my men characters are drips; they don't know how the women in the stories can be bothered with the men. But I think that's a function of the fact that the women are centre stage and the men are slightly to one side. It might also be because my work shows the flip side of what feminists have grumbled about for all those years, that women weren't very well observed, that male writers didn't know what they thought or how they felt. I always feel conscious of taking a risk when I say 'This is what this man's thinking', because I don't know. But then I don't know what other women are thinking either! I'm only guessing. You can only guess and go by hints and try to listen carefully.

Are you particularly interested in finding out more about male characters? Would you like to write more about male characters?

Yes, yes, I would, and in fact am doing so now. I've always had a very difficult relationship with my father. I think a lot of amateur psychologists would have spotted this already in my work. My relationship with my father has been the chief drama in my life and still is. It's going to be a job for me to understand my relationship with my father. He rejected me for many years and I behaved in such a way that he could only reject me. It was a tremendous battle and it's only now, in my forties, that I'm starting to be able to see him as separate from me, and not this force of nature breathing down my neck and saying 'No, no, no.' The other thing that happens to women like me, who have had such a difficult relationship with their fathers, is that you tend to be attracted to men who aren't going to love you as much as you want them to; it's because you've got unfinished business with your father. You want to recreate that situation with other men. Why would someone like me fall in love with a hopeless junkie? Because he's the sort of person who's unable to express love and so I can continue this battle to get him to love me, which is what the whole thing is with my father. That might seem like a rather crude analysis but I think it's true.

It's taken me a long time to understand this about the male characters in my work, how many of them are unable to love. People have said they're weak or they're boring, but that's not the point. The point about them is that they're incapable of love. That's why, for me, this character of Dexter is such a huge advance: Dexter can *love*. He may be slightly clownish still and a lot of people have written to me and said 'What a dill this Dexter is, I really couldn't stand him', but to me Dexter is a wonderful character. In terms of my personal emotional development separately from my work (if the two can be separated, which I doubt) that's a bit of an advance.

How did feminism directly influence your writing?

It directly influenced my writing in the sense that I felt that it was all right for me to be writing in the first place. I still have trouble even now with the thought that I'm not as worthy as a man. I have to put on a bit of bravado sometimes to get past that. I mean as a writer. It's the kind of female cringe that we recognised in ourselves when feminism gave us a way of looking at ourselves usefully. An act of will isn't enough to break out of female conditioning. You can't just bounce on the sofa drawing attention to yourself, saying 'Look at me! I'm terrific!' You have to believe it, quite quietly, right inside you. That's a lifelong process.

But the reception that *The Children's Bach* got certainly helped. Don Anderson's review in the *National Times*, the first one that came out, I'll never forget. I thought, Phew — nothing can touch me now.

The idea of feeling less worthy is a hard one to examine. It's hard to distinguish between some form of not wanting to be up oneself, and the objective nature of people's responses to you. Every time somebody in a magazine or a newspaper says 'Australian writers, like . . .' and then gives a list of names, if I'm not on that list I feel mortified. And when I feel like this I stop and I think, now what's happening here? I think, is this just my screaming ego wanting to be among the top of the class, or am I really looking out to see if I'm being excluded from some sort of category because I'm a woman? If you really wanted to answer that question in a specific case you'd have to go and read everything that person's ever written, and why bother?

Also, I think that even people who like my work, and who think it's good, are probably waiting for me to write about something else. They seem, almost in spite of themselves, still to think of it as small beer because it's about domesticity and what happens in kitchens and bedrooms. I used to think, why can't I have a war or a revolution or something? And then I'd think, but I don't know anything about those things, and I won't be able to write about them until I do, and I may not ever, and I can't go out and look for them. There's a lot of that in it, the feeling that women's concerns are small or less important or secondary in some way. I don't think that myself. I think they're really crucial. I love novels about families. I suppose everybody does. Look at *War and Peace* — that's about a family as well as being about war. When I was writing *The Children's Bach* I felt very strange and anxious from time to time because the scope of it was so small and domestic. And one day I was walking home from my room where I'd been working, and I went past a print shop. In the window of the shop was a print of a Van Gogh painting, that famous one of the chair in his bedroom. I looked at it and I thought, this is a wonderful painting, a painting that fills you with hope and life. And I thought, what is it? It's a painting of the inside of his bedroom and there's not even a person in it!

Do you think generally women writers do need to fight for recognition in Australia in a way that men don't?

That's a hard question to answer. I don't have the chip on my shoulder that I would have once had about this sort of thing. And, besides, I haven't had to deal with men in the business because I've got women publishers.

Has that been important to you?

Oh God, it's been crucial. If I'd had to take *Monkey Grip* to a male publishing company, either it would have been thrown out immediately as being too emotional, et cetera, or I would have had to hack at it and change it in lots of ways. It may be that the structure of it wouldn't have been acceptable to male publishers. I'm not saying that this is definitely the case — it may not be true — but I think it probably is.

Hilary McPhee and Diana Gribble are wonderful to work with. They're the sort of people whose opinions I really care about. When they came to Paris and told me my second novel was shit I knew it was shit because I trusted their judgement. They're the sort of people I can take something to when it's only half done and say, 'Am I on the right track here?' and they'll say yes or no; I trust them to that extent. I don't really trust anyone else to that extent. *Anyone.*

Do you think they're rare publishers in that respect, that you can discuss the work with them?

I think they might be. I haven't had experience with any others. I did a job once for Thomas Nelson but that was just a novelisation of the film *Moving Out*. I did that with Jenny Giles. It was really a piece of hack work. We did it in five weeks and made a bit of money. It was nice. I haven't had to be humiliated by men publishers. I'm sure that's made an enormous difference. I really haven't had any experience of what it's like working with men publishers except before I actually wrote *Monkey Grip*. I was messing around with the idea of writing a novel, and I knew these guys who ran a publishing company so I thought, I'll type up a bit of this stuff that's in my diary and I'll show it to them. They returned it to me some days later looking *very* embarrassed and said it was over-emotional — that was the main word. That stuck in my mind and I was mortified with embarrassment at having shown it to them. I had so little idea of what my stuff was worth that the slightest breath of criticism could completely demolish me. I'm not like that any more but I'm still potentially like it. It still kind of sticks in my throat, for example, that *Meanjin* was not impressed with me for such a long time. It's ridiculous to be concerned about that kind of thing, but there it is.

What gave you the impression that Meanjin *was not impressed with you?*

They'd only ever published one review of anything I'd done and that was of *Honour*. It was a horrible review. It said, 'Helen

Garner talks dirty and passes it off as realism.' Some things are hard to forgive. However, the pendulum's swung wildly the other way since *The Children's Bach* came out.

You seem to be a fairly ambitious writer.

I suppose I am. Look, Simone de Beauvoir said, 'I write to be loved'. She came right out and said it. When I first read it, a long time ago, I didn't understand what she meant. Now I do. You want to be loved by a large number of people and love is a name for what? For praise? Or?

Respect?

Respect, yes. I suppose I'm ambitious for that. I'm not ambitious to be Colleen McCulloch and make a million dollars. That'll never happen. It won't. And I don't care. I think I've come to terms with the fact that I'm never going to make much money out of writing. It's fairly clear that I'm not going to be so famous that when I walk into a room everyone will know who I am. You like to think that people will read your stuff and know what you mean. You hope that your nuttings-out of things and the way you express them in the book are going to be useful to people. That's what it is. It comes back to what I was talking about before, about moral things. I don't know why anyone else reads novels but I'm interested in how the hell people make decisions in their lives, on what basis, and how people draw a line between responsibility and freedom, and also what happens to people who don't. Greek tragedies show you what happens when you don't obey the rules.

Do you see yourself as a successful writer?

My idea of myself as a writer changes every day. Some days I think, I'm quite good at this; and other days I think, I'm a beginner and I'm narrow in my experience. There's an outside feeling and an inside feeling. Most of the time, inside I feel I'm probably OK, that what I do is worth doing and that I do it reasonably well; but you never do it as well as you hope and dream that you will. I spend a lot of time thinking about what I'm going to write. If I had to be locked in a room for the rest of my life I would have enough material in my head to write at least another five novels. Sometimes I start to despair that my life is empty of incident and that I don't know anything and haven't got enough experience to write anything else. When I stop trying to think up grandiose plots I realise that the stuff's all there, you just have to find it and dig in.

Did you ever have a sense that you were destined to become a writer?

I don't know if people are destined to be anything really but I always did it. I never had any idea that my stuff would be published or read. But now I think that might have something to do with being a woman. What strikes me about men writers I know is that having an idea of themselves as a writer doesn't really present a problem to them. Like Tim Winton, for example. It's not that he thinks he's terrific as a writer, it's just that he thinks of himself as A Writer without feeling that it's audacious of him. I remember when I was finishing *The Children's Bach* I wrote a letter to my sister saying, 'If I can pull this off, I can really call myself a writer.' And now I can. After *Monkey Grip* I thought maybe it was just a flash in the pan, but now if someone asks me what I do, I say 'I write books' and I *do* write books. I feel that it's no longer audacious of me to say that.

Do you think a distinctively Australian literature has developed over the last few years?

Yes, distinctively Australian in the sense that it calmly, but not nationalistically, puts Australia at the centre of things rather than on the periphery. I'm ashamed to admit that my reading of Australian literature is very haphazard. When I was at university, Australian literature was a tiny unit that was tacked on in the last year of English, so that was the only time I ever studied it. There's a lot of nineteenth-century Australian stuff that I haven't read at all. I mostly read things that I think are going to be useful to me technically so I get impatient with things that are long-winded. Also, I'm not very interested in reading things about the outback although I still think I should read *Capricornia*.

Are you very conscious of being an Australian?

Yes, I am, and I become more conscious the more my stuff gets published elsewhere. *Monkey Grip* has been published in England and the United States and *Honour and Other People's Children* has been published in the United States. *Monkey Grip* is being translated into French and it's going to be published by Des Femmes, a feminist publishing firm in Paris. I got a lot of reviews for *Honour and Other People's Children* from the United States — I was staggered, something like twenty, all extremely favourable. It got a paragraph in the *New Yorker* — very flattering! But all sorts of provincial papers wrote quite glowing reviews. Many of them were struck by what they called the 'exotic' nature of the stuff. I thought, how extraordinary. What struck them was that the characters had outside dunnies, for example. That's unknown to them, or it's really quaint, and the fact that people can ride through the park at night and not get mugged. They see Australia in my books as being like the America of twenty years ago, and that makes me feel very Australian.

When you read people like Kundera and other eastern-European writers or South American writers, there's a depth of experience of horribleness that we just don't have, I mean big, national, political horribleness. We don't have that kind of stuff. In Aboriginal writers' work, of course, you get a kind of despair and grief and rage that people like me are just not acquainted with. To me, the ghastly and terrible things are death, which everybody has to think about, or distorted relationships between generations. Those are things that all writers have in common, but when you read Kundera writing about his country being overrun, what do I know about that? Nothing. I suppose it's just the period in which I've lived, and the country I've lived in, and the class I was born into. I've had a remarkably sunny life by comparison with the sort of thing you read about from eastern Europe.

Do you think grants from the Australia Council are important?

Yes. Funding is necessary, here. Very few writers can live on their work in a country with our small population. I'm a member of the Literature Board now. There's never enough money, and terrible decisions have to be made. We come out of those working parties white-faced. Seeing funding from the inside has been a strange experience. I've been generously treated myself in the past: I've had four fellowships and two residencies. But I dread becoming hooked on grants. One's urge is to sit in a room and push the pen. I like to be obliged to get out in the world — well, I don't *like* it, but I need to. That's why I'm starting to write screenplays. At least you get a decent wage.

It took me a long time to learn how to use a grant, to develop proper work habits. I know that if you want to write a book you have to go and sit in front of a piece of paper. That's something you'd think a person would know, after they'd written their first book. But they don't.

So it's basically about discipline?

Yes, and having faith in your own method of doing things. During periods when I can't write, when I'm working at something else for money, I keep a notebook all the time. I keep notes blindly, without a conscious purpose. And when my time comes around again, I get out those notepads and type them up, and the patterns begin to emerge: I know from this that there's a level of my imagination which works doggedly and faithfully all the time, whether I'm directing it or not.

Do you see your short stories as keeping your hand in for novels?

No. They're quite different. In a story I can take bigger risks. You can do anything in a short story. It's wide open. It's a very difficult form though; you've got to whack the stuff into a very small space. It's the right form for a smallish idea or a small incident that means something. You can do all sorts of technical things that they probably teach you in creative writing courses if only I'd ever done one. Sometimes you can see the end of it before you begin. It's wonderful to be able to finish something in a few days. When you're writing a novel it's a tremendous haul, so *long* — you're inside it for months and months and months. Some of the time it's exciting and terrific, of course; but it's like a marriage. A short story is more like a one-night stand. I'm sure Frank Moorhouse said that!

Are you more committed to or concerned with novels than short stories?

No. I enjoy both of them a lot. Until now it's been hard to sell a book of short stories in Australia, but I think that's changing. There haven't been, till recently, many magazines in Australia that will publish decent short stories, and they don't pay you very much money for them even if they do accept them. The only place you can get a lot of money for a short story is in something like *Playboy* or *Penthouse* and you have to sell them the copyright which I would never do.

Having been an English teacher yourself, do you think writing is something that can be taught?

There's no point trying to teach someone if they don't want to do it, and then there's a lot of people who want to very much and can't. No, I don't think you can. Someone asked Anne Sexton how big an influence Lowell had been on her poetry. She said, 'He never told me what to put in. He told me what to leave out.' I think that's as far as I'd go in teaching the thing. When I was Writer in Residence I wasn't interested in working with people who weren't bringing me stuff all the time, who weren't already driving themselves. The main thing you can hope to teach them is to edit their own stuff intelligently. To me the difference between the artist and the non-artist is that the artist is the one who does it. Almost everybody thinks they can write a novel. When a writer comes to a university they all think, maybe some of it will rub off on me and I can go home and write a novel. But either they're not obsessed enough, or they're too lazy, or they're too busy, or they just don't really want to. People don't realise what an incredible slog it is to write a book. They think they're just going to sit down and let it come pouring out of their pen. Then, when they start, when they realise, they get bored and put it aside, because they're not really a writer.

Then you don't think artists, including writers, are particularly born with a gift?

I don't know where the gift comes from — whether they're born with it or whether it's something that happens to them in their early life. I don't know whether I'd even call it a gift. It's some longing or desire. I've got a niece of nine who's very talented with her hands. She's got terrific spatial sense and is always busy. She never gets bored, and she hardly ever watches TV. She came up to me once with that glazed, absorbed look and said, 'Do you like making things? I *love* making things. I lie in bed and think about all the things I'm going to make.' It's that longing to make and shape and preserve, and to show people the thing. I once saw some marvellous drawings by a Melbourne artist called Irene Barberis. They were drawings of things on her kitchen table. They were *beautiful.* In the exhibition catalogue each artist had made a little statement; most of the blokes had written high-flown, polysyllabic statements about life, art and politics, but she'd written, 'I'm sitting at the kitchen table. *I feel like doing something.*' I think that's what it's all about.

Melbourne, January 1985

Select bibliography

(Helen Garner)
Monkey Grip, McPhee Gribble, 1977; Penguin, 1978.
Honour and Other People's Children, McPhee Gribble, 1980; Penguin, 1982.
Moving Out, with J Giles, Sphere, 1983.
The Children's Bach, McPhee Gribble, 1984; McPhee Gribble/ Penguin, 1985.

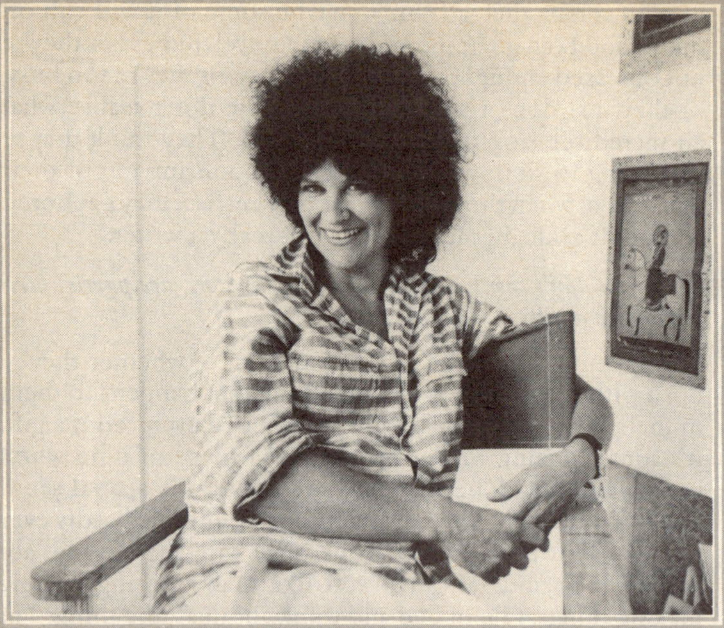

KATE GRENVILLE

'Fiction ought to be allowed to do absolutely anything at all, but the fiction I like is that which makes the world look slightly different afterwards. It's like living through it to find experience.'

Why do you think people decide to become writers?

Well, in my case it was because I was always a bit shy and inarticulate. I come from a family of big talkers and I could never keep up with them. Writing was like a private revenge: you could go away and get it all down on paper, and no one could interrupt you, and if they read it they sort of had to listen to you. But the irony is, of course, that if you have any success at all as a writer you then are called on to perform in public, and to talk into tape recorders and things.

Do you think that reason might be common among writers?

It's hard to generalise. I think it's quite often true of women writers. I mean, 'inarticulate' would be the wrong word. But I can't think of any women writers that I know who are really brash performer types. I do know a lot of male writers who are performer types though. So it might be true of women. It's sort of the underground river of fiction rising to the surface.

When did you first start writing fiction?

I had several false starts. When I was about seven or eight I wrote a composition at school called 'Trapped by the Tide', which was a wonderful piece of melodrama. It was read out to the class, and this was a moment of great glory for me. The other thing about it was that we had to write it over two weeks. I got them trapped the first week, and the second week I had to untrap them. I said to this teacher, I have no idea what's going to happen. How am I going to rescue them? And she said, like Hitchcock said to the actress, 'Fake it, baby, just make it up!' And it was like a revelation to me, that I could actually invent. So of course I went overboard and invented a fleet of helicopters or some mad thing. But it was an incredible freedom, that anything could happen in fiction, whereas all sorts of things couldn't happen in life.

That was one start. And then, when I was sixteen or so, I wrote a story about betrayal — melodramatic and cliché-filled, totally lacking in any kind of talent — which I sent to the *Women's Weekly* because it was the only magazine I knew. And I think I got one of those horrible little flimsy pieces: 'Thank you, we read it with interest, but...' Then, in the long vacation between finishing high school and going to university, I started a novel. I mustn't have been sufficiently cast down by the *Women's Weekly* to stop writing. So I wrote a fragment of a novel, which is the most atrocious stuff. I was about seventy pages into that when I started uni. I did an English Degree, and the effect of all that analysis, and all that criticism — and I've spoken to so many other people who've had that same thing — is that your tiny nervous tendrils of wanting to write just get crushed by that heavy load of 'Is it Art?' and, you know, 'Would it make the Leavis top ten?' So I stopped writing completely and absolutely for about eight years.

During that time I worked in film. I went into it very consciously, because I hadn't ever read any film theory. I thought, here is an art form that's related closely enough to what I'm interested in but somehow hasn't been sullied by the great thumb print of academia. I started writing when I left London for Paris, where I knew nobody. Nobody was there who would say to me 'What are you doing?' and 'Can I look at this?' It was like taking myself out of my life and saying, you can have six months or so, just try it, and nobody need ever know that you did it. It seemed necessary for me to do that really secretive, anonymous, ashamed sort of thing, to give myself the courage to try it. And at the end of six months of writing I was really hooked and I realised that this was what I wanted to do.

Why did you decide to leave Australia?

For a lot of reasons. I'd always meant to do 'the tour' — you know how people do, in Australia, and I kept postponing it. I knew that there was a larger life than mine in Australia.

I knew that there was more. I knew that there would be somewhere that would be totally baffling all the time, and I wanted that experience, of not knowing where I was, or how things worked. It wasn't just a series of things I wanted to see, or know about, or have done; it was suddenly a whole lot of parts of myself that I wanted to allow to happen.

Did you live in London and Paris or were you on the move all the time?

Basically I lived in London. My pattern would be to live there for, say, six months and work at whatever I could do — sometimes film or sometimes being a temp typist — and then go to Europe for a while and write on the money I'd earned. After about four years of that I moved to America for two years.

Did you begin to have stories published while you were away?

In Paris I had a story published in a little American English-language weekly, and that gave me a lot of encouragement. And then I wasn't published again for about eighteen months. It was in 1979, the year before I left London, when I suddenly had a whole spate of things published. I had started to send stuff back to Australian magazines and had things published in *Southerly* and *Quadrant*, and in England in *Forum* magazine and a few little ones. And all that was just enough to keep the fires burning.

Were you sending out stories to everybody?

Yes. In London I had it down to a real system. I had them constantly circulating like birds in the air. I had a logbook, and the minute a manuscript came back I would just check what magazine hadn't yet seen it, and send it off again. What kept me going, I think, were a lot of very encouraging rejection letters — they didn't want them but, you know, they'd like me to send more, or there was some degree of personal interest. There was just enough encouragement to make me think it was worth going on. Actually it was a funny thing: the more rejection slips I got, in a way the better I felt, because I had always wondered whether I wanted *to be a writer*, rather than *to write*, whether it was the lure of fame and that whole image of being a writer that I was really attracted to. And I thought, if I just keep getting rejection slips and I still want to go on writing, then it means that I actually want to write. So they didn't depress me but they did make me rewrite my work endlessly. There's nothing like a rejection slip for making you re-read something in very cold blood, and it's a good way to learn really. I'd just take the stories apart and do them again.

When did you begin to feel that you were a writer?

About a year or two ago, I suppose. In 1980 I went to America to do an MA in Creative Writing at the University of Colorado and, by the time I left, I suppose I was starting to think of myself as a writer. I'd learned so much about it in those two years, and I'd finally started to write things I thought were better than beginners' efforts.

What sort of things did you learn?

We had fiction workshops each week. One of us would have a story completely taken apart by the whole class and then rewrite it and bring it back. That is an excellent way to learn to write. At the same time we were doing conventional academic courses — the same as the PhD students were doing. But we were coming to read the books as a writer, thinking all the time about the problems of how to tell a story. Because of that, I was reading Wordsworth and Willa Cather and Gertrude Stein with a completely different eye. I was seeing how they were solving the same problems that I was trying to solve. Also, every week I taught four classes of undergraduate students who were learning to do creative writing. I had to workshop their stories, which meant I had to learn to read them and see what the author was trying to do (and why it didn't work if it didn't), and be constructive about what could be done to improve it. All of which is a lot easier to do with someone else's work than your own. But if you're doing it often enough with other people's work you learn a hell of a lot about your own, and about getting distance and perspective on your own. So those three things about it made it a learning experience.

When I left America I had written a novel called *Dreamhouse* which is going to be published next year. In fact, by then I'd written three novels, but only one of them I confess to, because the others were terrible stuff. I had this idea, and I still do actually, that you have a certain amount of trash within you, and the quicker you get it all out, the quicker you get to the good stuff. When I came back to Australia I had those three novels (one of which I thought was publishable) and a lot of short stories, some of which were published in America. So I was starting to feel that it was possible.

How did Bearded Ladies, *your collection of short stories, come about?*

When I got back to Australia I realised that if I put together all the short stories that I thought were any good, there were just about enough for a collection. I sent them to the University of Queensland Press because I knew that they published interesting short stories and could cope with slightly unconventional writing, and they accepted them.

Why did you decide to come back to Australia?

I was on the point of migrating permanently to America, because in spite of everything that's wrong with it I loved America, and I thought, before I do that I should just go back and see whether I've changed, or whether Australia's changed — how I feel about my own culture. I'd been away for about five years, and just before I left I thought, I'm going to hit Australia and the culture shock after so long away will be traumatic. If I haven't started another book there'll be a long gap before I can get my head around to starting something. I thought, I want to write a book about a woman, and I want to write a book about somebody I like (because I had just written a book about some awful people), and I want to write a book about somebody eccentric (because in the novel that I wrote in America I'd had great difficulty motivating people). I got really hung up on the need to make it convincing. I thought, if I have somebody who's a bit crazy I don't have to worry about motivation. And somehow, over there in Boulder, Colorado, the image of Bea Miles floated into my mind. So I wrote about thirty or forty pages of *Lilian's Story* before I left America.

Did you ever meet Bea Miles?

I saw her, when I was a student. She was pretty old then. I was such an inhibited little middle-class girl that the sight of this enormous, fat, sweating, loud woman in the middle of the street just shrivelled my soul. So I never talked to her, which I regret now. But if you grew up in Sydney you knew of her. She's one of those urban myths, and I knew a dozen things about her, which were enough to start writing a novel. I wasn't writing a biography of her, just using her as a starting point, a springboard.

Did the things you knew become incorporated into the story?

Yes. They're things she's famous for, like jumping into people's taxis, and quoting from Shakespeare. And I knew there was something odd about her, that she had been a brilliant student and a beautiful young woman and had somehow ended up as this rather sad street person. I was very interested in how you make that transition. But I didn't really know much about her at all.

Did you think out the story before you started? How did you decide on, or create, that transition for her?

I didn't think it out at all. I never had any idea how it was going to end. It was a really exhilarating book to write. The first two novels I wrote, which were such a disaster, I'd planned really carefully, with chapter headings. I knew exactly what each chapter was going to do, and it just died on the page. I got bored writing it, I think, because I knew what was going to happen. But with *Lilian's Story* I felt like a reader. I didn't know what was going to happen on the next page. I had to keep writing to find out what would emerge.

How does Dreamhouse *differ from* Lilian's Story?

It's a bit more like the stories, I think. It's much snakier in tone. The person telling the story is a woman, and she's not a very pleasant person. She's in a sort of marriage of convenience. She doesn't leave, because she's too lazy and too greedy, basically, until the end of the book. It's a rather malevolent and cruel book in some ways. Which is a truth of the world. Part of the world is like that. But I think of *Lilian's Story* as a much more benign, compassionate, happy sort of book, because I think I've changed in that time and those positive things are the other part of the truth of the world.

I'm interested in your reasons for choosing to write about someone like Lilian, who's not a typical heroine. Would you say feminism has had a direct influence on you and your work?

Well, it's a big subject. I grew up a real tomboy, having two brothers, and then suddenly hit that puberty thing that Germaine Greer talks about, when at fourteen you have to put behind you everything that you've ever enjoyed, and everything you've ever been good at, like physical things. Suddenly you have to masquerade, pose as this creature called woman, which involves all kinds of things you don't want to know about. So, like so many women of my age, I think, I went through that tortured adolescence of trying to do it right, to be a woman, and failing miserably. Then I hit the women's movement, which was just getting into its stride when I was at uni. I remember reading *The Female Eunuch* and I thought, this book is dynamite; if I go on reading it and allow myself to actually think about it, I will have to change my whole life, because this book is saying there's something radically wrong with this whole thing of trying to be a woman. I just wasn't prepared to make that huge rethink of attitude, so I put it away. But on the other hand I was willing to nibble around the edges of things like not wanting to be married, and not feeling I should have children, and wanting a career. I knew all those things were OK.

Then, in London, I started to read again about feminism and to get involved with the women's movement, in a timid sort of way. And I got to know a lot of feminists in London, and I realised that they weren't as frightening as I'd thought. I'd been a part of that classic thing of not having made any women friends, all that conventional fifties wisdom that women don't trust each other. Suddenly, in London, I was meeting women that I trusted and felt good about, much more than any man I'd met.

As far as the fiction goes, one of the reasons I started to write was that I wanted to read about my own experiences, the experiences of being a woman of my generation. And I found a few things, but nothing was quite right. Of course I'd read Virginia Woolf, who's still the model of a woman writer for me. But that was all older stuff: Elizabeth Taylor, Elizabeth Bowen — it was a generation that wasn't mine. There was all that American stuff, like Erica Jong, but that didn't seem right either, because those women were so confident. They *knew* they were liberated.

My experience was one of confusion and uncertainty, and I couldn't find any fiction that reflected that. And also a lot of anger. I couldn't find that either. So I felt that there was this huge gap in women's fiction. I got a certain amount of flak when I started to show my stories to people in London, men, literary people. They'd meet me and think, oh, what a sweet little thing, and then they'd read these furious stories and hand them back at arm's length, visibly thinking, she's crazy, and she's so angry, and she hates men so much, have nothing to do with her. There were a few terrific men, though, who were extremely generous and encouraging — Peter Porter especially. So there was that on the one hand; but on the other hand I was also sending my stories to very feminist places, and they were sending them back saying they're not feminist enough. So I really did feel that I was between two stools. And one of the things that kept me writing was the feeling that there were a lot of women like me between those two stools, and that's where the writing wasn't happening. That was the writing I wasn't finding, to read, when I went into the libraries.

So that's why those stories in *Bearded Ladies* are the way they are. I was terribly angry a lot of the time in London about men, and I think that a lot of women have to go through that period of terrible fury, which is fury at yourself too, but men are also...often...culpable. But that anger doesn't dominate me now, because obviously there's a huge difference in tone between *Bearded Ladies* and *Lilian's Story*. I suppose I resolved the anger that had to do with myself, and so I can cope with being angry with men who are deadshits. My attitude now is, that's their problem, not mine, and I have other things to do with my energy than spend it getting angry all the time.

Also, I think I've realised, knowing more genuinely good men, the problems that men have. In fact, one of the books I'm writing now is about a man, a fairly unsympathetic character, and I'm writing it from his point of view and trying to understand what makes him do pretty terrible things, and that's a very interesting exercise for a feminist.

Are you confronted by writing that?

Very, yes. Because in a way I have to put aside all my feminist clichés and try to understand the scenario in his head which makes his actions perfectly OK. But it is confronting, because I'm realising how little I understand, really, about men, or let's say about classic macho men.

Do you lack confidence about writing from a male point of view?

Well, I do, yes. I've actually set this book aside at the moment, so I don't have to deal with the problem of men reading it. Nobody's read it. But if it gets finished or published I will have to deal with that whole argument about whether you can write well about the opposite sex. Tolstoy did it, and George Eliot did it, but how good is it really?

You don't believe that because you're a writer you can automatically write from a male perspective?

No, that brings up a whole thing that I'm not quite sure about. You can say men are just people, and you should be able to write about a man just as well as you could write about a woman other than yourself, like Lilian Singer. But perhaps men are so foreign that it is too difficult. Perhaps you bring too many prejudices to the subject. Still, writers aren't scientists, striving for objectivity, and it's enough for me to say I'm writing my idea of what such a man might be like.

You said before that Virginia Woolf was your ideal image of a woman writer. What do you mean by that?

First of all, I think her books are magnificent works of genius. And then, she had an idea that women would write differently from men, about different things and in a different style. And her style, that very musical, allusive, impressionistic style, is really like saying, here is the female sensibility finding its own language. I also really admire the fact that she could theorise about not only feminism but also women and writing.

You've mentioned that you weren't sure whether you wanted 'to be a writer' or whether you wanted 'to write'. Now that you 'are a writer', how does the reality match up with the image?

It doesn't really, as I suppose I knew it never would. When I was in London, getting all those rejection slips, I sometimes used to walk along the street feeling cold and depressed, fantasising about giving interviews just like this, and how wonderfully clever and brilliant I would be, and also how I would revenge myself on all these philistines who were rejecting me. But of course the reality is that in the interviews you are not quite so certain. I think the more I write, the less certain I get. I used to be terribly dogmatic in my theories about fiction, and I'm not at all any more. And the desire for revenge has left me completely. Other things, too. I used to hear people say 'Oh, you know, a writer's life is so solitary', and I'd think, oh, nonsense, it'd be wonderful. But in fact I suppose I am feeling that that's true. It really is very difficult because the isolation lets you lose perspective, that's what I didn't realise would happen. I don't like to show people work in progress, so you really are locked up with your problem, and no one can help you with it.

In other ways, though, it's wonderful. And of course there's the thrill of being published. I suppose the biggest thrill, and the one that I hadn't ever expected, is getting letters from complete strangers, telling you that your writing has actually moved them in some way. The fact that something I wrote was able to reach somebody in that way, I find astonishing, and slightly spooky, and wonderful, but it's also a responsibility. There is actually a power in the written word, and you have some sort of responsibility to do something with it that's going to be positive.

Were you conscious of trying to do something positive when you wrote Lilian's Story?

No, not really. I knew that there were a lot of things I wanted to say about a reject woman — you know, a woman who is fat and ugly and doesn't do any of the things that a woman should do. What interested me about Bea Miles first of all was being a woman at that time. If Bea Miles had been a man she probably wouldn't have had to become so eccentric, because she seems to me to have been somebody with an enormous appetite for getting out there and encountering life, and having a huge theatrical experience. And I think that's always been a lot easier for men. I mean, they become explorers or prime ministers — all those larger-than-life things.

How did you go about writing Lilian's Story, *in that unusual form of short pieces with headings?*

I wrote it in those short chunks. Because I never quite knew what was going to come next, I didn't write it in consecutive order. The very first thing I wrote was a scene right at the end of the book as it is now, and every day when I went down to the shed to write I would have no idea whether I was going to write about Lilian as a child or as an adult. Then when I went to type it out I thought, OK, now we put it in a coherent narrative, and I did that, and it just died on the page. When I looked at that typescript — which was a very coherent narrative, because the bits actually fitted together beautifully — it was just really dull. So I chopped it back up again into more or less the same fragments. I think perhaps also working in film was a model for that, because I see those little sequences as like a film sequence, and then you fade to black or just cut to the next thing. People have learned to read films like that, and it's another sort of choice that a writer now has, to pinch that bit of grammar from film.

Why didn't you use quotation marks?

Ah! Well, I have always hated quotation marks. Quotation marks and semicolons I have always loathed. I think it's because, for me, quotation marks are associated with a certain kind of writing where this god-like narrator tells you what everybody's thinking and what they're saying. What life really is, is events happening and people talking, all just going on at once, in a seamless sort of way, and I wanted to find some device that could make it seamless again in fiction instead of: new line, indent, double quotes. And the italics worked in *Lilian's Story*, because there wasn't much dialogue.

Were you conscious of not having a lot of dialogue?

I think part of that was my trying to get away from anything resembling social realism, or realism at an elementary level.

And also, you can have stylised dialogue, like in *Lilian's Story*, only for very short patches, otherwise it sounds wooden, I suspect. I didn't want realistic dialogue, because it wasn't a realistic story.

Do you have disciplined working habits?

In theory, yes. Until a few weeks ago, I was working three days a week at SBS television. I've just stopped working because I received a Bicentennial grant, so I'm actually much more disciplined now. I work in the mornings from about eight till about twelve-thirty or one, and I make myself sit at the desk. Flannery O'Connor is a writer I really admire. She said that she made herself sit at the desk for four or five hours every morning, and didn't allow herself to do anything but write. She wasn't allowed to read, or daydream, and in the end she got so bored she would write out of sheer boredom. And I find that works quite well. So, yes, I try to keep the mornings to write.

Do you find your current writing situation ideal?

Well, I've never had a grant to work full time for a year, which is what this enables me to do. The longest I've ever been able to afford is a couple of months, and there were five months once when I was on the dole. So I don't really know, and sometimes I get nervous that I'll become paralysed. Having complained about my lack of time to write all those years, when actually presented with it on a platter I was afraid I might sit there with not a word coming out. But that doesn't seem to be happening. I think it's good, actually.

What ambitions do you have for your writing?

I would like to be able to keep writing. If I can still keep writing when I'm in my fifties, and still be thinking of new things, I have a feeling that those extra years of life might enable me to write something richer and thicker and more humane than I feel I'm writing at the moment. There's something about maturity, I think, and a lot of life experience. I would love to write a book like *The Tree of Man*, or *Mrs Dalloway*, which are just packed with a sort of wisdom.

Did the publication and acclaim of Lilian's Story *have any dramatic effect on your life?*

Yes, actually. My professor in America always used to say, 'You shouldn't worry too much about getting published, because it won't change your life overnight, the way you think it will.' But it did, in a way. The biggest change, I suppose, is that I feel more able to take myself seriously as a writer, and it's really nice for me to think, well, I've written something that a lot of people actually enjoy reading. And that's terrific, because you can worry that you're just wanking away in an ivory tower, being terribly self-indulgent and silly, not doing anything useful. The fact that it frees me to write very much more is the other huge thing. And I suppose for all writers, but especially if you write in the sort of exploratory way that I do, you really need a lot of time, because you don't know what you're going to write next. You can't just sit down and take it up for an hour and put it down again. So that's made a huge difference.

Do you have any views about the function of literature in relation to society?

I think it should be an addition to life, an additional experience of some enlarging kind, which is why I don't believe in any kind of preaching, because I don't think that's a new sort of experience, it's just a new didacticism. To feel compassion, for example, for a character in fiction that you almost certainly wouldn't like in real life seems to me a genuine kind of enlarging, because when you're reading a book you're in a special state of mind. You allow yourself to become open to things that you would never be in real life. That's also why I don't like social realism, because all that does, it seems to me, is to try to mirror life, to re-create it exactly, point for point, rather than enlarge it. Well, there seems to me no point in doing that. I mean we've got life. We can live that ourselves.

So fiction, I think, ought to be allowed to do absolutely anything at all, including social realism and including propaganda, but the fiction I like is that which makes the world look slightly different afterwards. It's like living through it to find experience. And I suppose what that means is a kind of tolerance, in terms of bringing it back to society. I suppose fiction ought to be able to say something like, here are these infinite numbers of ways of living, infinite kinds of being a human being, and they are all life. When you read a book by Conrad or someone, you are briefly an adventurer, or, you know, some madman in Malaya, and you've got to come back to your real life slightly enlarged by that experience.

Why do you think being enlarged is a good thing?

The trite answer would be that it's what keeps life alive. I suppose it's because I think people have infinite capabilities in all kinds of ways, including imagination, and we limit ourselves all the time. It's one of the reasons I was interested in Lilian Singer: she didn't want to be limited. If you have infinite possibility, and you're only using one tiny little corner of it, somehow that is wrong. I don't quite know why, but it's the parable of the talents or something. You know, life ought to be lived absolutely fully, even if only through the pages of a book. And I suppose that does have a social effect, in that if you feel that sort of tolerance that comes from realising that you yourself could be a mass murderer or a madman in Malaya, then you are much less dogmatic about how people should live. The sort of infinite complexity and mystery of life is a good thing to acknowledge as a society, I think.

What sort of difficulties, or stumbling blocks, do you encounter in your writing?

Oh, lack of imagination, lack of talent, stupidity, total obtuseness about life and people. Small problems like that. I just constantly come up against my own limitations, I suppose. I just think, oh, how shallow this is, how trite my understanding of life really is. And, you know, I meet people whose humanity I respect, and I feel so tiny and puny and trivial, and that my mind's locked on all these terribly boring, mundane sorts of levels, when it should be soaring into the stratosphere.

What exactly do you mean by someone being 'filled with humanity'?

I'm not sure what I mean there. It's actually a fairly recent discovery for me, that that's a quality you even look for in people. I used to look for qualities like, are they interesting, and do I have anything in common with them, but I'm starting to believe in good and evil, I think, or something resembling that. Words like compassion and tolerance sound terribly mealy-mouthed, and I don't mean anything like that. But kindness and all those things, they matter a lot.

Do you ever fear that you'll run out of material?

I suppose so. I guess every writer does. But I also think most novelists don't write that many great novels in their life. You don't really have to churn them out, so you can take some time and live in between times. I have faith in that as a way of filling up the banks again with new ideas. I have a feeling that if I was just writing at home for five years I'd really run very dry. Because again it's the haphazard, it's the random things that happen to you; in work places where you're forced to be with people that you dislike, for example, doing things you would never choose to do, that's actually a very rich source of good things happening in your mind, and they don't happen when you're sitting at home doing what you want to do.

Do you think, though, that there are any costs involved in being a writer?

Oh yes, definitely. The isolation is the biggest one, in the sense that you're not forced to deal with people most of your day, and so you can get a bit paranoid, and you can lose perspective. You can get very insecure about yourself — a lot of writers do. And you can lose that very quality that I've been preaching about, that quality of humanity and tolerance, because you forget that out there are people whose lives are dominated by the need to make a living and support their families. And there's also sometimes a sense that you're being very self-indulgent, just spinning this web out of your own entrails and holding it up to admire, when in fact again out there in the world are those terrible and very real problems that maybe you should be doing something about, like starvation, and people living in misery. It's a terribly privileged life, and that has its own cost in terms of, not quite guilt, but something like that.

And then, in terms of personal life, I suppose there are prices to pay; perhaps there are for any kind of life. Certainly when you begin to write you pay a high price. I wasn't involved with anybody very seriously when I started to write. If I had been it would have been really difficult, because you have to spend so much time on your writing, and become really obsessed with it. You're very boring and withdrawn, I would think, and if you were living with somebody, it would be extremely hard on them.

And of course you do pay the literal price of not making much money. So you have to recognise very early on that materially you're not going to be terribly well off.

So has writing influenced the way you run your life for some time now?

Very much so. I've chosen jobs for the last ten years on the basis of whether they would give me time to write, either because I could make enough money short-term to then take some time off, or because they were part time, like SBS. Architecturally, a lot of thought has to go in to the space that I live in. Can I write there? Is it going to be quiet enough? And if I share the house with other people, can I get on with it without feeling self-conscious?

What physical things do you need to be able to write?

Ideally, a bit of sun in the room where I'm working, and to be able to look at something, like a garden, where the eye can wander a bit. But apart from that, I can work almost anywhere, I think. In fact, I have worked in rooms with absolutely no views and no sun, in very noisy houses, so I suppose you can do anything if you have to.

Are you happy being a writer?

Yes, I suppose I am. Although sometimes I think, at what point do I actually enjoy this process? Is it when I'm thinking about what I'm going to write next? I suppose that really is the best bit, when you're sitting around and the novel's all there, in its beautiful perfection, in your head. I suppose that's the most fun. But I do also enjoy the actual writing. I sit there giggling away, or getting angry, at whatever I might be writing about. And seeing it in print is a terrific pleasure. Yes, I suppose I do enjoy it.

There's nothing else you'd rather be doing?

No. Isn't that good? What a good thing to be able to say.

Sydney, September 1985

Select bibliography

Bearded Ladies, University of Queensland Press, 1984.
Lilian's Story, George Allen & Unwin, 1985.

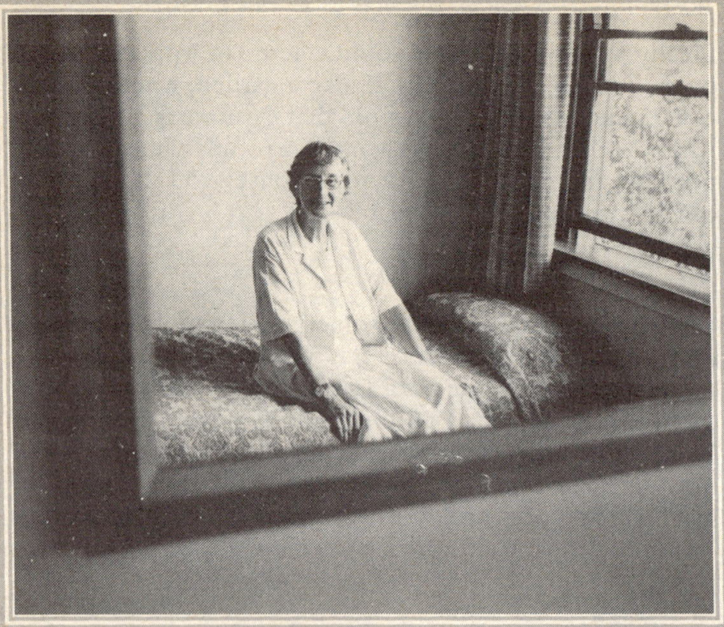

ELIZABETH JOLLEY

'I really think that to get emotional about women writers is a mistake. It's well-intentioned but I think that a writer should be a writer, and a perceptive man is as perceptive as a perceptive woman.'

How do you see your latest book, Foxybaby, *in relation to your body of work?*

Foxybaby has been written in a more compact way. With the other books, I was writing more than one at a time. They go over a certain number of years. I concentrated on *Foxybaby* — just wrote it and finished it. Everything in the book has to come through Miss Porch. I've not written like that before. Because the book is a kind of visionary nightmare, Miss Porch has to be there for every single thing. Nothing can take place without her being there, because the book is actually through her mind, in a way.

Did you challenge yourself to do that?

Well, put it this way: I started doing the book and it kept falling flat, and it kept being very wooden. Then I made a complication by trying to work it through her, and then it began to work. It's as though I made a kind of complication, or the book made a complication for me. It was much harder to do this, but I hope that the material is more satisfactory in this way.

You have a repertoire of characters who recur through your works, and certain recurring motifs. How have these developed?

They seem to develop from each other. Peycroft, in *Foxybaby*, is a version of Miss Thorne. I don't intend to do that, but I find that I go on exploring a character in yet another situation, and it's a different person. Very often there'll be a rather level-headed person who makes a balanced view, and Mrs Viggars, in *Foxybaby*, does something of that sort. I think Miss Snowdon, in *Miss Peabody's Inheritance*, is the kind of little line of balance, do you see? And I suppose I see the world in layers of people: those who are very ambitious and try to initiate people, or take life with both hands, and those who see things in a rather more balanced or even way. Some of my men characters tend to be the more reliable. Perhaps I see characters in various ways. They're not all one thing or another. They will have their frail bit, and their ridiculous bit, you know, which I think is human.

Do your characters live on in your mind?

Yes, yes indeed they do, and I often feel Miss Thorne wincing at my clichés, you know. They are with me rather. It's a nuisance in a way, but I feel very affectionate towards them, and fond, humble in the presence of them, and feel sometimes I'm not good enough to portray what they are, and that again is another form of exploration and challenge. I suppose anyone hacking their way through a jungle feels they could have done it better.

I would describe a lot of your characters as fringe dwellers, people who for one reason or another find themselves on the edge of society. Would you agree with that?

Yes, well, I think people are on the edge of something, and some people who even seem to be in the thick of things are on the edge in another sense. It has been said that I don't have any straight sex in my stories, that everything's bizarre and grotesque. I think that what I really see is the individual, and the particular aspect of loneliness, or fear, that that individual has, which puts him immediately on a fringe of some sort. And I think most people are like that, though they do have a little structure that keeps them going. If the structure is taken away then they really become very much on the fringe. And I don't intend to write about sexual perversion at all. It just is that certain things drive people to certain relationships, or they snatch at certain relationships.

What do you think is the function of that bizarre sexuality?

It seems to me that there's a sort of ridiculous side to life, to living. And I don't quite know what is meant by a straight sexual relationship, because even that has its ridiculous side. I suppose it is indeed to show the ends to which people are driven, though none of my people does anything evil. I mean, it's all harmless, and possibly they fulfil various needs or emptinesses in life.

But some of them are cruel to each other, don't you think?

Well, don't you think people are cruel to each other? I think they are. I think there's nothing so cruel to a human being as another human being — the rejection, anger, or irritation with a person, revenge. Even remorse is a cruel thing, it brings out cruelty. People pursue happiness very often at the cost of somebody else. Well, take publishing, for example. If you're in, somebody else is out. You know, it's all very highly competitive. And people are kind, and maybe they're kind for their own ends sometimes. The fight for survival, which starts from birth, or from before birth, is indeed a strenuous fight for survival. If ever you've taken part in, or watched, it, you're amazed that a baby lives, very often. I think it goes on from there. I suppose I'm interested to explore the inside of people's survival.

Another strong motif throughout your work is the land. Can you trace that association?

Well, in a personal way, I have a great wish to have land. My own father came from a family of farmers in the south of England. They were not very well off. My father became a teacher; so did my aunt, but my father always had a great yearning for land and he had what is called an allotment. I don't know whether you know what that is, but as well as having a garden with the house you could rent a piece of land — just, oh, quarter of an acre or something like that, a strip with a whole lot of other strips. My father would work the allotment and grow vegetables. When I married, my husband and I also had a house and a small garden, but wherever we lived we rented an allotment and grew vegetables and things. Well, in Western Australia there aren't any allotments, but as soon as we felt able to, we purchased five acres of land forty miles out of Perth. Territory matters very much to me. I'm a sort of territorial person, perhaps a bit grasping over land. It matters enormously to me to have my own place, and on the whole I think I'm happier not leaving it. I can get homesick by the time I get to the airport.

Was the idea of purchasing some land one of your reasons for coming to Australia?

Oh no, no, not at all. Never dreamt that I'd be able to. Never even thought about it. We came out, you know, with the realisation that we possibly wouldn't manage to go back, but we loved it and I wished that we'd come before. It just has this freedom of movement, so that you have an enormous range of possibilities in a country like Western Australia. You can do things that you couldn't do in England. We could not have afforded, in England, to live in the kind of place where we could have bought something to go to.

What image did you have of Australia before you arrived?

I had an absolutely blank mind. I knew very little, I regret to say, about the country. I looked up the rainfall, and found that it was much the same as Glasgow, but in Western Australia it all falls at once, instead of the year round. I knew that the population was small, but I don't go in for figures, and I knew it was a long way away. But there was a kind of challenge about it, and I knew that Leonard wanted to come. I think we're very glad that we did.

It's amusing that you refer to Western Australia as a country. Do you feel that it is quite distinct from the rest of Australia?

It is a separate country in a way, and if you live there and write, and you want your writing to get published, you really have got to cross, as though from one end of the world to the other, to get to Sydney, to Melbourne, to get to London, to New York. You could live and write there and never get over, but obviously the writer wants his work seen ultimately, and this is one of the things that you're very much aware of. Your work has to spring from where you are, and it's got to take tremendous leaps. But people in Sydney won't have that feeling. They don't feel they have to get across to Western Australia. And I quite understand that.

When did you first start writing?

I've been writing since I was a child. All sorts of diaries and stories. But I didn't start to offer for publication till the 1960s, when I came to Western Australia. I had a bank of material. A lot of the books that have been published in the last few years I have been writing over a long period.

What prompted you to start submitting your work to publishers?

I started submitting because around then I wondered if I was mad, and whether my writing was readable by anybody else. You see, you're very alone, and you can't give your writing to your friends, really. I started to submit in a very tentative way, and of course everything came back. But the BBC World Service was a good market, and the ABC did take some short stories, and I gradually began to break into the journals, but very, very slowly. It was a very slow, painful thing. I've had as many as thirty-nine rejections in one year. But everything that was rejected has now been accepted. Some pieces I reworked. Others are just as they were. I think that often the writer is writing things that are not acceptable because perhaps the writer is aware of things in life around him that publishers' editors feel the reader is not ready for. Also, I think, editors really want to know whether you are serious as a writer, and perhaps they want to see a lot of things before anything is taken.

How did you feel during that period when your work was rejected?

Oh, well, I used to get very down. I can be very, very depressed and low. I can get like that even now. It's a fearful thing, and

I wonder sometimes why I do write. Once you start to get accepted, of course, you have to follow up with other things. It's no good just selling one story. If you want to be published, you've just got to keep going. I must have a streak of optimism in me, and it was a sort of challenge really. Perhaps it's like gambling — send three stories off and see if one will get accepted. You know, a kind of horrible excitement.

But you must have had a certain belief in your writing, to persist?

Well, I couldn't believe that the writing that was rejected was so much worse than what was being accepted. I took a strong look at it and I read contemporary fiction to try to see and learn. I do read a great deal anyway, because I'm interested in reading, and because it excites and pleases me, and I read all sorts of writers. I did wonder if there was something hopelessly wrong with my work. You see, you don't know yourself, you aren't always your own best judge.

During that period, were you writing virtually full time? Or how did you manage to write?

Oh no, it's only in the last two years that I've written full time. I was doing eighteen hours' teaching before. Before that I did other jobs. As a housewife and mother you don't have a lot of time for writing. But I would squeeze in the time. I've been used to making time, because that's what I wanted to do, you know. I would often write late at night and early in the morning. I still do that — that habit still hangs on. You have to make time, for anything. If you want to weave, or make pottery, you've simply got to hurry up with shopping and cooking or whatever.

When did you decide that you wanted to be a writer?

Well, I never decided, and I never called myself a writer, until I was called 'writer' from outside. I would never have put it as my occupation. I was a nurse by training. But I'd never called myself a writer. It would have felt as though I was claiming something that I wasn't, and I wouldn't want to do that, you know.

Why do you think you had difficulty claiming that, when you were writing?

Well, I suppose because I wasn't published. And I suppose even when I had the first book and then the second book published, although in one sense I was the author of those books, I still hesitated. I suppose one doesn't want to set oneself up to be in the position that one perhaps has longed to be in. One is a bit afraid of the knife in the back. Mind, everyone's been most affectionate and loving towards me, I don't know why I worry. I suppose it is just lack of confidence. One is terribly afraid of people saying, 'Oh, calls herself a writer, does she? And that's all she's done.' Because, of course, this is part of the cruelty of the world, that people are cruel about each other, especially in a competitive world, aren't they? And maybe you shrink from putting yourself forward, because if you do that then somebody else can knock you down. I think there's a famous line: 'He that is down can fall no further', or something like that.

Do you find it helpful to meet with other writers?

I think it's very helpful to see people, though you can't fit the writer to the work. I often think that people are disappointed when they meet a writer. They might read a book and find it really fascinating and perhaps a bit glamorous or something, and then what turns up is an ageing woman with a woollen shawl round her shoulders. But a kind of affection can spring up between people of the same profession, and I suppose there could be jealousies, too, that you have to overcome. You know that jealousy is a very strange thing, and it goes back to childhood. It wouldn't be a normal person who wasn't jealous or envious. I think jealousy is a very interesting emotion, and one of the themes of *Peabody's Inheritance* is jealousy — the pain of it, and the revenge that somebody might take because of it.

So you don't necessarily see jealousy, or competition, among writers as a negative thing?

No, not necessarily. If I feel jealous of someone it might be because I'm feeling insecure. In a way, at my age now I don't feel jealous, but I might if I was only thirty-two or thirty-three. But I'm not, I'm sixty-two, and I feel very fortunate the way things have turned out for me, you see. I think it's much harder for the writer in his twenties or early thirties, who gets a run of publications and then has to maintain something, or else turn to something different.

Do you think about readers when you're writing?

Oh yes, I do, but not when I'm first writing. I am just the reader by myself. I'm reader and writer. And then in subsequent writings I rearrange and craft, and think, what will a reader make of this? But you can't think of a reader too much, because there are so many different kinds of readers. And I don't really know quite what sort of person I'm trying to reach. I don't think I can think about that. But I do want to try to be entertaining, and to put things in a kind of order so that you suspend things a bit. You know, have a little sense of drama. Even though my books are not dramatic, there is a little inward drama, as it were, and I do really consciously consider that in the craft. I think there is a craft you have to study, by reading other people, to see how they achieve things.

A lot of the central relationships in your books are about women. Can you tell me about the importance of women in your work?

Yes. I'm very interested in women, overbearing women, and the kind of headmistress type of woman, the matron type, the secretary who's in a muddle. I suppose I've seen these people in operation in different organisations and institutions, and I suppose I'm interested to explore what's behind the white blouse and the jacket. And of course in the world of nursing you meet a great many women, and a nurses home is a hotbed, in a sense. At the age of seventeen I left school and I did training in two different places. It must be that I became aware of large numbers of women and their relationships and their interests, and my imagination just got off on them. I was at a mixed boarding school. We had masters and mistresses. Even then, I was aware of relationships between males and females in the school, and between women staff.

Is there any guiding principle behind your work?

I'm not trying to reform or judge. I'd like to interest people. I would like to entertain people, and I would like people perhaps to go with me in the exploration of human beings, but one can only explore really, and put one's exploration forward. If anything in my writing should inadvertently hurt someone, I would feel terrible. There would be no point in writing and being published. And if anyone thought I was cruel in my writing, that would upset me too. I don't intend to be cruel. I do see a ridiculous side in human nature because I don't think we can live without it; and if I've portrayed that, it isn't out of cruelty, it is just that I think it helps us to get through. I don't ever want to write anything cheap or sensational. I would hate to do that, and sometimes in my first writing I do just that, and I hope that some of that doesn't get left in by mistake. But I suppose you put things down in the quickest, most cliché-ridden way that you can, to get it down, and I'm sometimes horrified at some of the scenes that I might write. And then I rewrite, and craft that. In *Miss Peabody*, you see, I did really quite a terrible scene between Edgely and Thorne before Gwenda comes around and knocks on the door, and then I do a very slight picture there, and at one book club where I was a woman said, 'How could you write such a filthy scene?' What she's done is to see what I wrote in my early writing, but I only imply something, you see. There's nothing really filthy written there at all. So I thought that was very interesting, that even though I had removed the whole thing, but just made an implication, it still was there.

What about the process of writing Milk and Honey?

I'm interested in the exile, and again the survivor, the suffocating relationship and the over-devotion which produces unnatural behaviour, I think. In my teens, people were leaving Europe and coming through my parents' house, because they were pacificists and my mother was a Viennese. They helped an enormous number of refugees who left in 1937, 1938, before the war broke out in 1939, you see. People were pouring out from Germany and Austria, and a lot of them stayed with us in a small house, and when I went home from school for the holidays I always had to sleep on the floor. People would be in a little knot whispering and crying and moaning — you know, they'd left behind a relative and they didn't know how they could find that relative, or they'd made an unhappy marriage in order to get out. All those sorts of things.

I was fifteen then, and it really made a great impression on me. And you have no idea: these people were dressed in a very sombre way, and were almost like migrant birds who had lost half their feathers. If those people could be brought together, which my parents did try to do, they would almost suffocate each other with devotion. And they also had to do all sorts of work that wasn't right for them. Some very aristocratic woman would have to be a housekeeper for people who were very vulgar and rich just because they were in some kind of industry. It was very painful, and *Milk and Honey* really sprang from that experience, though it's an entirely fictitious story, and it's set in Australia. Some people liked the book and some people hated it, and of course it has no humour in it at all.

No. It's most unusual and disturbing.

Yes, disturbing to write too. And Jacob is entirely unable to consummate his marriage. He is quite warped. He can only manage when he's rescued from outside by something. And then at the end he is still in a structure, but he has discovered that life really depends on service. It's a bit of a golden dawn at the end.

Yes. I wondered, with that book particularly, whether dreaming is important to you, or imagination or fantasy, because Milk and Honey *has a strong dream-like quality, particularly in the first sections.*

Yes, it is like a sort of nightmarish dream, isn't it? I think I found myself writing it like that because when I was about fifteen these people seemed to come and go, to be whispering in a corner one minute, and then they'd be gone. And then another time I'd come, there'd be another lot of people. But certainly imagination and fantasy are a great part of my life. I often imagine far too much, and suffer because of that.

You've spoken at a lot of functions over the years, and a lot is written about your work, and about you. How do you deal with being a public figure?

Well, I don't really feel much of a public figure, so I don't have anything to deal with, in a way. When I'm somewhere, like at a conference, I just feel really that I'm a tiny speck in a large city, and I don't feel a public figure at all. I guess if my picture was on every lamp post like Salman Rushdie's was at the Adelaide Festival, I would feel a bit different, but really I feel very small, and perhaps that's a good thing.

Can you identify any particular qualities you think someone needs to be able to write?

Well, I think you've got to be able to make time. You've got to be quite strong physically, and quite strong emotionally in that you've got to be a receiver of emotion, and be emotional and imaginative, but you've got to be able to control. It often annoys me when people say, 'Ah, yes, you know, one's characters take over'. They don't take over at all. They're there, and you create them, and you are in charge of them. It's quite true, as I said earlier, that Miss Thorne is wincing, but that's because I've created her. She's still my creation, and I tell her to shut up, you know.

The thing is that imagination can run away with you, and

ruin your work. I think discipline is enormously important. You've got to be disciplined also in saying, no, I won't go out to dinner this week, I'm working on something. I won't go to morning tea with so-and-so, and I won't spend three hours of the day at a lunch, do you see? And this tends to give you a lonely life. So that's why I'm glad of my teaching, because I'm with students, and if I wasn't I'd never see any young people.

You have to be persistent. You have to sit down and write, when it's the last thing you want to do. But I do recommend that people who want to write make little notes during the day, so that when they come to the time that they've got, there is actually something enticing them there. Because if you go to a blank page, and you're a bit tired, and you're going to try to force yourself through that tiredness, the thought of writing is appalling. You've also got to have a family who will respect that you need the solitude.

Do you have fixed working methods, or times of the day when you write?

My method of writing is unchanging. I still make my little pictures on bits of paper and then write to a certain point, then go back to the beginning and start again. I keep working up to that point and then go past it. I do an awful lot of rewriting. I usually take my current novel wherever I go. I'm very good at using the time to get something done.

Do you feel you can teach people to write?

Well, what you can do is to teach them how to split up and structure something. You can teach them how to look at their own work and see where they've repeated themselves, because we all do that to start with. You can't teach people to have imagination, but you can show them how to be aware, and how to keep notes, and how to cut something down, or how to expand, or to write a parallel, or how to approach drama so that they can put a little peak of drama which leads up to a bigger peak of drama. You can show them how a writer has done that, you see, and then they can craft their own work. I think writing is a craft. It isn't just an outpouring. You *can* teach. After all, people who can sing have had to learn. They may have a beautiful voice, but they've still got to learn how to use it.

What do you think is the function of literature in society?

Once I had a very profound sentence on that, but I can't remember it. If literature has any function, could it be to explore and present human feelings and emotions and actions as they are, but without any kind of judgement, and without any kind of resentment? I know that some poetry and some stories are full of resentment, and hurt, but possibly it's necessary to present them. My answer would be to present human life, I think, but at the same time, to craft it in such a way that you present the essentials that will tell the story, or be an entertainment, and when I say entertainment I mean interesting, not just something to make people laugh. Entertainment means to interest people, doesn't it, to engross them? Yes. And I think perhaps it's important for people to make some kind of identification with the lives that are being presented. That goes all through children's literature, too, because you become an explorer when you read about an explorer, as a child.

Do you think that writers, by their craft or their profession, transcend issues like gender and perhaps also nationality, that there is an international community or unity?

Yes, a sort of universal thing, yes. I think of writers as people, and it doesn't worry me, man or woman writer. The thing is that it's quite true that in some feminist writing there's a tremendous gushing of the menstruation, as it were. But I think that a man writer could write the same thing, if he wanted to. A man writer would have the same awareness and perceptions and imagination that a woman writer will have, and he will know certain things. A man watching his wife in childbirth will see more of the childbirth than the woman will. He will even experience with his own imagination and awareness, and his own tenderness if he has it, her feelings, I think. Certainly he'll see the colour of the amniotic fluid, and the placenta, which the woman who is giving birth won't see. Many women like to write about childbirth, when they've experienced it. Others write about it without experience. I don't think you need to experience — you can make the implications, or you can leave it. You can leave what I call a sophisticated space on the page, and the reader will create for himself, or herself.

I really do think that to get emotional about women writers is a mistake. It's well-intentioned, but I think that a writer should be a writer, and a perceptive man is as perceptive as a perceptive woman. Somebody who is unaware, man or woman, will remain unaware. I think a man can be aware of a woman's sexuality, very much so, because after all there isn't all that much difference between male and female sexuality. Resentment can be felt equally. Suppose it's an unsatisfactory sexual relationship: both can feel resentment, and it would be the same sort of feeling. Why should a woman feel that her resentment is the thing that matters, when a man might be feeling that his is, do you see?

Have you been particularly involved in, or affected by, feminism?

Well, I can see the cause. A woman married to the wrong man, submitting to sexual caresses that she doesn't like and that she wants to get away from but doesn't know how — I think she needs liberating. But I don't know whether the feminist movement, as such, will ever reach that particular woman in a suburb.

This kind of thing has gone on forever. Some men really prefer not to be married, but were expected to marry. They're breadwinners, and they've got to caress their woman when they don't really want to. I think the sexual side of the unhappiness of people marrying when they shouldn't be married will go on. Not many people are brave enough to withstand marriage and children if they're under pressure for this conventional social behaviour, you see. I think it's better than it was, but it still does exist, and I don't know what the answer to that is. I'm glad if women have their movement, and I'm sorry if I disappoint them by not being a feminist writer.

Do you have any theories about the increasing number of women writers being published?

I think that the women writers are writing well now, and if they're writing well then they deserve to be published; and I don't know that they were kept down. I felt when I was being rejected that I was being kept down, but that may just have been a personal paranoia, you see. It never occurred to me that it was because I was a woman. I don't think it was. I think it would be because some of the stuff wasn't quite ready, and that it is just very hard to break into publishing anyway, whether you are a man or a woman, isn't it? I mean, I meet as many men that would like to get published and aren't.

Do you find reviews of your work helpful to your writing?

Yes, they should be, they should be. I find them painful and difficult. I worry about a review very much, you know, and I think reviewing is very hard to do. I've done some myself, and I think it is one of the hardest things in writing, to read someone's book and then, in a short space, deal with it. I think reviewers can be helpful if they pick on some fault. The only trouble is that no two reviewers pick on the same fault, or very rarely.

So you could end up thinking you've got a very faulty book!

Well, yes, you could, and that would be the devastating thing. I can get very distressed reading reviews — reviews about anybody's work, not just about my own. It's a kind of writing that bothers me, you know.

Why does it bother you?

It has to be written in a particular kind of style. It's clinical, and has to be efficient, and the reviewer can't use his imagination. It's factual, it's direct, it's got a bit of authority, you know, and it's all the things that one might be afraid of in life, really, like a dental examination or a medical test or something. I think that I'm a bit afraid. I'm frightened of writing a review, and frightened of reading one.

What do you think makes a good review, though?

Well, I think the reviewer needs to give a little picture of what the book is, and if he finds a fault I think he should be able to substantiate the fault, with a quotation, or something like that. When I'm reviewing, I take the idea that when I write the review I would like to make somebody feel they want to read the book, so that if I can find phrases that show how the writer makes pictures, or captures something, I would like to quote them. If I find there's some grave fault in the book that I really can't take, then I have to bear in mind that somebody else might not think that was a fault, but at the same time I may want to draw attention to it in some way. Of course, a severe criticism, if it's done in a particular way, can still encourage a reader to have a look for himself. But I think any statement should be supported. And, of course, a reviewer is quite free to give his personal opinion. That is the whole idea. It is his personal opinion. And that is important too.

What about literary awards? Do you think they serve a useful purpose?

Oh yes, I do. I think even if you don't win one you might think, oh, it would have been nice to win that, all that money slipped through my fingers, you know. But I do think prizes help because we live in this competitive world and, after all, publishing is a business. Anything that will help the sale of books I think is a good thing. I think if people are generous enough to present prizes, then we should be grateful. However much you dislike publicity, and you don't regard yourself as a public person, you understand that you've simply got to go along with certain things. You sign a contract to that effect, in a way, with the publishers, that you will do things, you won't object to publicity and so on. They've got to make their living, and employ their people.

Are you happy being a writer?

I'm just about to say I'm never happy. Put it this way: I can forget all the worries of family life, and the world, except for the bit of world I'm dealing with in my novel. When I'm writing I go into the world of the novel, and the characters, and I like that. It is happy in a way. It's fascinating. Happiness is a difficult thing. I'm almost the kind of person who doesn't know she's been happy till she's unhappy. No, that's not true. I'm a very optimistic person, and I try to make the best of things. I like to write, though I find it terribly hard. Put it this way, if I wasn't writing I don't know what I would do.

The thing about writing is that you do several things alongside, and that writing is only one part of your life. If you made it your whole life, you might go entirely mad, especially if you didn't succeed, because it would be so devastating. I have my orchard and my goose farm, the family, and the teaching, and of course I was nursing before, and I also did things like door-to-door selling. I've done lots of different things. And I was writing all the time. I took the writing alongside, and I really did make a conscious decision that I would never just do writing and nothing else, because I could see that, if it was no good, and if I never got published, then the disappointment would be so devastating. So, you see, I love the orchard, and that's very soothing, and even if a book doesn't get accepted, well I've got my fruit trees and I've got my poultry, and the slope of the land and all that. You know, I think that's important.

I wonder, now that you have had nine books published, and you've been to lots of places and experienced lots of emotions through your work, do you feel wise?

Oh, I don't think I'll ever be wise. I'm the biggest fool on earth. I'm capable of making the same mistakes over and over again. You know this thing, the rite of passage, where you go through a little private ceremony of awareness, so that you are a changed person. It seems as if I have to keep going through these little enlightenments. I make the same mistakes over and over again. Isn't it strange? I don't know that I have any wisdom, but this is where I think perhaps Something may watch over me. They say God watches over drunks and little children. Well, I'm not a drunk and I'm not a child, but perhaps He also looks after people who blunder through things.

But you must feel that you've learned an incredible amount.

Yes, but it seems to run off me, you know, like water off a duck's back. What an awful cliché. Miss Thorne is wincing ...

Melbourne, September 1985

Select bibliography

Five Acre Virgin and Other Stories, Fremantle Arts Centre Press, 1976.
The Travelling Entertainer and Other Stories, Fremantle Arts Centre Press, 1979; republished with *Five Acre Virgin*, Fremantle Arts Centre Press, 1984.
Palomino, Outback Press, 1980; University of Queensland Press, 1984.
The Newspaper of Claremont Street, Fremantle Arts Centre Press, 1981.
Woman in a Lampshade, Penguin, 1982.
Miss Peabody's Inheritance, University of Queensland Press, 1983.
Mr Scobie's Riddle, Penguin, 1983.
Milk and Honey, Fremantle Arts Centre Press, 1984.
Foxybaby, University of Queensland Press, 1985.

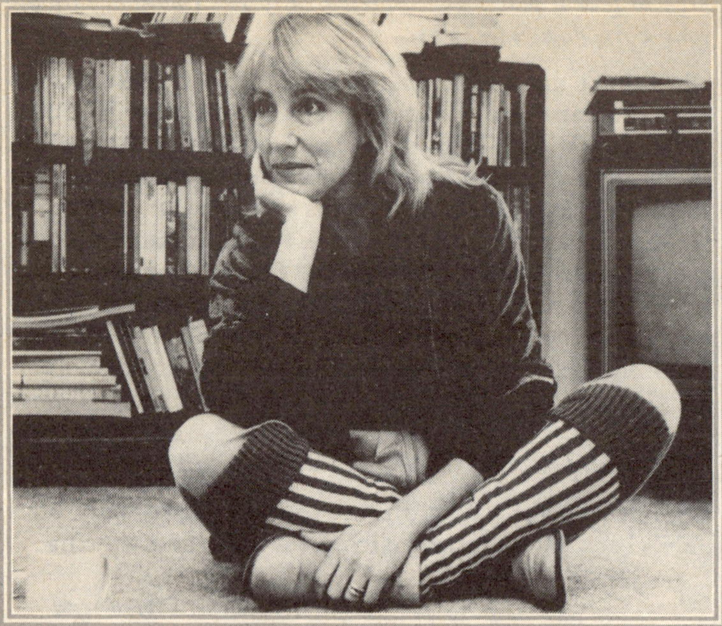

GABRIELLE LORD

'Writers re-examine and rewrite the myths of the culture in which they live. Good writers turn the myths on their heads and, without losing any of the mythological qualities, make people take notice of what they're doing.'

Your novel Fortress *is an extraordinary story. What prompted you to write it?*

Well, I'd been haunted for years by the Faraday kidnapping, or rather by the fact that almost at the same time Richard Speck had bound and murdered those nine nurses in Chicago. Do you remember the Chicago slayings? And they'd all allowed each other to be tied up, you know, nine healthy young women, and he only had a knife. I suppose that had got to me, and the fact that Mary Gibbs (I think that was her name) had not done as she was told by the men, that she'd decided to try to get the kids away. I think she must have really battled over whether it would have been better to be a good girl and do what she was told so that no one would get hurt. It used to horrify me imagining what would have happened if those guys had come back while they were getting away, and seen this young chick and a bunch of kids thwarting them. The police found what the kidnappers had prepared for them later. It was a hole in the ground with a few packets of chips in it, and they were going to cover it with corrugated iron and then just put brush on top. The coppers reckoned they never would have found them, and they reckon the youngest kids would have died that afternoon from heat exhaustion.

Did you do much research on that case?

Not at all. Nothing. I relied on my memory of it. I didn't want to be confused by the facts, like the judge said. I just wanted to have the feel of it.

The pace in that sort of novel is important, and you seemed to have a sure grip on it. Did you consciously work on pace?

No. I knew already what made a good thriller. I knew pace was very important, and I probably wouldn't even, at that stage, have consciously thought of pace. You sort of learn the technicalities as you go along. But I was a reasonably practised novelist by then, with unpublished stuff. *Fortress* was, I think, my third novel and its pace was instinctive. I wrote it in three weeks, at red-hot speed and with the rage that I felt while I was writing it. I was absolutely obsessed. I've never worked like that before — or since, praise the Lord. The first draft was pretty well the final draft. I think it was boiling away for a long time before it actually came out.

What was the rage to do with?

The destruction of innocence, I think, basically. The reaction to the bully, and the hopelessness of fighting violence with violence. The fact that it appears to be the only way to cope sometimes, and yet it's an impossible solution. Dorothy Day's pacifism is something that I'm becoming more and more attracted to, realising that in the long run *I* don't have to use violence, that I can allow myself to be slaughtered rather than harm another human being. It's just not workable for me at the moment, because I doubt very much that I'd have the courage to do that anyway, but I'm starting to see that there are no answers in violence.

Was part of your rage based on being female?

Probably. Yes, I think so. I think there was a conscious feeling of 'THE BASTARDS, rotten bastards'. But that of course was because of my own personal failings with men. I have been bullied myself, by men, or by a couple of men, and it's a slavish response just to get angry and mutter, I wish the bastard was dead, you know, that sort of thing, instead of doing something about extracting yourself. So I think there was a lot of anger directed towards myself, too.

Would you describe yourself as a feminist?

I would describe myself as a feminist, heavens yes. I think anybody who thinks would have to be a feminist. I don't belong to a group or anything. I think feminism, like Christianity, covers a huge range of definitions, from the sublime to the ridiculous. But if feminism means treating equal cases equally, oh yes, of course, I'm a feminist, yes.

I notice Fortress *is being made into a film. Have you had much involvement with that?*

No. None at all. I got paid a lot of money for them to do what they liked with it, and I'd sort of lost interest in it. It was something I had done quite some time ago, and if they wanted to have a bash at it, good on 'em. I just knew I knew nothing about film, and that I'd only upset myself if I hung around, so I decided to keep right away from it. But I'm becoming increasingly interested in film.

Tooth and Claw *is also about a woman under siege. I wonder why you were drawn back to that theme?*

Oh, look, I've got the feeling that I'll probably only ever write one novel under various guises. I think *Tooth and Claw* is very similar to *Fortress*. Most people don't notice that, because it's decked out in a different way, but it's still the same story. They are both very similar in construction; there's even the similarity at the end of the chase, where Beth hides in that ferny cleft. I started to see that it's really the *vagina dentata* that I'm writing about, which actually chews them up in *Fortress*. But in *Tooth and Claw* she hides in there, regains her strength, and comes out and bops them. So maybe I've finished with the *vagina dentata*. I don't know. It just occurred to me one night, that that's really what the plot of *Fortress* was all about. You know, the cleft in the rock, and the womb, and the ferns around the entrance, and this poor crazed man charging in. Poor bastard.

Do you think that's true of other writers, that they've really only one story to tell?

It has been said. I don't know how true it is. Possibly you

do really only have one story to tell, because there's only one of you telling it. I'd hate to make that as a claim, because I think you could probably very easily disprove it. But I think I'm moving away from that sort of siege mentality. I think I just had to write it out, get rid of it, or grow through it or something.

Do you feel with Fortress *and* Tooth and Claw *that you are creating a new genre in Australian fiction?*

Mistress of the Macabre, somebody called me. Well, I don't know. They're certainly different from the stuff that anyone else is doing. But that's understandable, because I'm different from other people. What I'd like to do would be to use humour much more, because I've seen how devastating it can be, correctly used with tension and suspense. Magnificent. Whether to give them a real fright, or a false fright, or a funny fright. It's great stuff. I always felt sort of uncomfortable because my work was different, and I used to wish I could write a book like Blanche d'Alpuget, a proper grown-up book, about grown-up people. And then I used to think, well, I'm not grown-up. How can I? I'm just a clever child. So I might as well do what I'm good at. But as I do grow up more, I hope I can use that sort of enthusiastic, sharp-edged, fast-moving story to talk about grown-ups, and what grown-ups do, when I find out.

Do you think you will find out, one day, when you've grown up?

Yes, I'm looking forward to puberty. And a nice bride's outfit.

Both books are very dramatic in their focus and intent. Do you consider that element necessary for a good novel?

No. I think a good novel can contain very little action or drama, and yet still be very gripping and un-put-downable. But I'm not good enough yet to write that sort of book. I might never be. I'm a good storyteller. I love stories, I've always loved stories, and I enjoy telling them in writing. If

I mature as a novelist, I should think I'll always have a soft spot for the suspense and the drama of it all, even if I just use that as a sort of hook, to get other things said.

What about your next novel? Do you feel that you've developed as a writer through that?

Yes. It's funny. You don't know until you look back. I mean, you can't tell in advance where you're going. But I re-read *Jumbo* recently for final editing, and I thought, this is all right, you know, this is OK. And I've never really felt that about the other two. There was always that awful wince, except for bits that you were pleased with, that you felt worked. *Jumbo* is a thriller, but it's much, much wider and deeper. I've moved away from an isolated settlement. I've come out a bit, and there are more characters. I've tried more stuff on. It's more complicated. There's a very brief and unsatisfactory look at male-female relationships, but at least I put them in as a possibility, whereas they don't exist in the other two, really.

Why have you started to put those in?

Oh well, because we do it, I mean it's part of life. We actually have a bit to do with the buggers. A lot of people have pointed out that the other two books are, in a sense, hostile towards men. There's that underlying feeling that, you know, they're only good for one thing, and that they're not very good at that, and so they go around stamping their feet and killing people. And that's very unfair and very childish of me to regard fifty per cent of the world's population like that. Some of my best friends are men.

You said you'd written two novels before Fortress *was published. When did you become serious about writing?*

Well, I'd read something when I was about twenty-two or twenty-three. I'd picked up a biography of Gertrude Stein, and I'd just opened it at a page where she was quoted as saying, 'When I'm thirty I will write'. She'd decided. And I thought, what a good idea. I'd always scribbled, you know, I'd written short stories and very bad poetry. It was almost like a hypnotic suggestion. On my thirtieth birthday I walked up to the paper shop, bought a great big pad and a new biro, and off I went.

Did you continue to have other employment?

Oh yes. I worked all the time, in the CES, as an employment officer — an unemployment officer, as the kids used to call us. But now I'm writing full time. I'm staring at walls full time, which I think is writing full time.

Do you tend to work set hours?

I would like to be able to tend to work set hours. I try to work from nine to eleven every day, and I get terribly envious of the people who can do that sort of routine. But I've come to just accept my pattern, which is erratic. That's just the way I do it.

Are you always working on a particular project?

Yes. At the moment I'm doing a screenplay. I drafted it out as a novel actually, in 1978, the year I got a New Writers Fellowship. I drafted *Tooth and Claw* in that year, too. I was very, very busy in that year, because I knew how important it was to do as much work as I could in that wonderful time off from the dole office. I started to rework it as a novel when *Jumbo* was finished, and I thought, this is crazy. It might make $5000 as a novel, and I knew what people were paid for screenplays (between $100,000 and $150,000) and I thought, a woman's a mug. I could see that it would make a ripper film, and I'd seen that my work could make good films — I've got a producer very interested in *Jumbo* at the moment, still in manuscript — so I thought, it's silly for me to be doing all that bloody hard yakka, novel writing, when I could come up with the original idea, do the original screenplay, get paid a heap of bloody money, and then do what I like for a while, without any financial worries.

Would you sooner be writing for films than writing novels?

I think I like writing prose best, and I think I probably always will. It reminds me of, say, the difference between playing the piano and playing the guitar. With a novel, I think, you've got all your notes there, whereas with the guitar or the violin you've only got so many strings and you've got to make them all work; and there's all that awful fretting — fretting, good word, fretting. So I've been fretting at the screenplay, and I'm finding it very interesting, a very different year from prose writing. But I think for my own personal satisfaction I somehow enjoy the larger scope of prose.

You don't feel more conscious with the novel that you're creating a work of art?

Oh shit, no. I ain't creating no works of art. I'm only telling stories. Beguiling ones.

A good story's a work of art.

Oh, I suppose it is a work of art. But in a sense so much of your work's already done for you, because you're appealing to the resonating things in other people, you know, fairytale stuff they've always known — baddies have to get DONE, you know, PUNISHED — so that in a sense people are prepared for it. They know already what's going to happen.

Do you find that the processes involved in writing the screenplay are different from those in writing novels?

No. I find what I'm doing is actually short cutting. Instead of working, as in prose, from an image in my head to a description on the page, and then having it read, I'm working straight from the pictures that are in my head. So it's really a closer operation altogether.

So when you write prose you work very much from pictures?

Oh yes. I'm working from a film in my head to start with.

And I think this shows up in my writing. A lot of people have said, 'Oh, you obviously wrote that so that a film producer would be interested in it', and of course this was the furthest thing from my head. But on re-reading some of the stuff, I can see where I do write in that sort of clear, cinematographic, descriptive way. Maybe I've just got a film head, or something. I don't know.

Have you always been interested in films?

Not at all. I don't like them. I'm very hard to get out to go to a film. I like a good thriller, a good horror movie, because I know there's no disappointment in it. So often you go to a film that's been lauded, and it's just so disappointing, and so second-rate, you realise that people are being had a lend of all over the place, and I get despondent about that. I just don't go where I will be disappointed.

Do you feel the same about reading books?

Often. I used to read promiscuously, but now I'm more selective, because I know time's running out. I did a lot of junk reading in my youth, though, which was good. I was always a voracious reader.

Did you study literature at university?

Yes. I did an Honours Degree in the Victorians. I also did an enormous amount of work in Old Norse, Old English. I'm very interested in words, the magic and the power of the word.

In my writing, I'm very conscious of getting the right word, getting the word that still has magical qualities. I've got a theory that everybody knows about the magical qualities of certain words. I mean this is fairytale, I know, this is madness, but remember those ridiculous letters that came in to the press when poor Lindy Chamberlain was going through her ordeal, and there was some nonsense about 'Azaria' meaning 'sacrifice'? I thought, people are so bloody ignorant. Any of the blessing words means 'sacrifice', because at the oldest level of the word, 'blessing' was a sacrificial word. It meant something that you achieved through blood sacrifice, a blessing. It's the same root as 'blot', 'blotch', 'blood', 'bless', 'blotsian' (Old English: 'blotsian'); to get a blessing you made a blood sacrifice. Many of those biblical names are going to have that sacrificial quality. And I thought, this is the sort of ignorance that really irritates me, that they can then make a case, using some sort of nonsense about her being a blessed sacrifice in the desert. A lot of people will tear me down for saying this, they'll say it's absolute bullshit. But I'm not so sure. And that's just one example. But there's millions of them around. I know lots of them, and I like them, and I'll play with them. And if there's people out there who have that kind of sixth sense about the word, they'll know when I'm getting menacing, because of those sorts of qualities. Other readers might miss out. But I'm playing with people who like my games. It's my right.

I like the sharp Saxon words, the Norse words, and instinctively avoid going for the Romance, the Latinate word. I write a hard, bitter English. But I didn't know that until I'd read over what I've written, because it certainly wasn't conscious.

George Orwell said, 'Distrust any writing that doesn't make pictures in your head.' And I think that is a terrifically good rule. I think if you look at bad writing, particularly scientific writing, or any of that jargon stuff, you just get nothing in your head, nothing, no picture. And this is why it's incomprehensible.

You had a year off in 1978 to write on the New Writers Fellowship. When did you begin to write full time again?

I resigned from the CES towards the end of '83, when the film rights money for *Fortress* came through finally. I looked at my bank account, and I looked at the office, and I thought, what am I still doing here? And I left. It was wonderful. Then I had the guilts again — as we all do, I realise — because I thought, oh, I'm not really a writer, I've just had a fluke. I'm starting to believe now that in fact I am a writer, and I'm getting more and more comfortable with that feeling. But it's taken a long time, because of images in the head, illusions of what a writer really is.

What sort of illusions do you think you had?

Well, obviously ones that I didn't measure up to, so that I couldn't put myself in the same box: hard working, brilliant. I certainly knew I wasn't either of those two.

Was it something to do with the belief that writers were perhaps special people?

Yes, probably. And that I would be excluded, so I was always very sheepish when people asked me what I did, even for ages after I left the CES. Even though writing was my passion, my real living, in every sense of that phrase, I'd say, 'Oh, I'm a clerk in the CES.' I'd never mention the other. And this was when I had two published books. But I'm getting used to saying I'm a writer, although I still look around for where she is. But I believe that's common. I've spoken to a lot of other women writers. Something to do with low self-esteem.

You don't really strike me as someone with low self-esteem.

Oh, people with really low self-esteem never strike you that way. They've learned the tricks. They know how to stand up on their back legs. My self-esteem is improving a lot, has done enormously over the last year, and not really because of any change in my writing at all, just that I think I'm starting to accept myself. I think maturity is starting to happen finally, and with that goes acceptance of the sort of person I am. Once you come to terms with yourself, and you stop wanting to be something else, or wishing you were better, I think you stop fussing so much about where you've failed.

Do you feel a part of a literary community?

No, not really. See, I was always very isolated from anyone

else who was writing, and I was always a bit suspicious of people who talked a lot about writing and didn't actually do it. I suppose I thought, if I start talking about it maybe I won't do it, so I'd better shut up and get on with it. I'm starting now to see the importance of writers for the society and the culture from which they spring, but I was never game enough to even look at that because, remember, I didn't even think I was a writer, so it's been fairly new. Now, I'd be prepared to say that writers re-examine and rewrite the myths of the culture in which they live. I think good writers turn the myths on their heads and, without losing any of the mythological qualities, make people take notice of what they're doing. I'm starting to feel now that writers are custodians of the culture, that they're vocal, and that they can shock and they can check. They can present a picture of the society which is so close to the one that the society enjoys looking at and patting itself on the back about, but they can give it a little bit of savagery, and make people see it in a new light, and make them go away feeling very bloody uncomfortable. And then perhaps from that feeling of dis-ease, a direction might not be taken that would have been taken. I mean, this is fantasy, but I wonder if it does sometimes happen.

Has that made you feel more aware, then, of what you can do with your writing?

Yes. I'm passionate about the ghastly things that are happening in science. You know, the whole in-vitro thing gives me the shivers. I've got to work out why. I think it's because of a deep-seated suspicion that ninety-nine per cent of it has very little to do with making mummies happy with the baby in their arms. I think ninety-nine per cent of that's to do with very, very unpleasant stuff indeed. But because I'm ignorant, and I don't think these sorts of things are made freely available, I don't really know what the buggers are up to with all this stuff, but I don't think it's nice. I'm deeply suspicious of it. I don't think such a huge project would exist if it were to make mothers smile as they see their impossible baby in their arms. I just disbelieve.

And they're the sorts of things you feel you want to deal with in your writing?

Yes. In fact, I'd like to write a musical called *Come On, Ned, Come On*, in which Ned Kelly rides Phar Lap across Anzac Beach and beats the Americans. Now I reckon that'd be an absolute winner, with Ned wearing a nice tennis outfit or something. You know, I'm just revolted by that sort of superficial stuff that people seem to flock to, and that constant self-congratulation that doesn't examine anything, doesn't strip anything away, just always trots out the old stuff: the British were bastards, they misused the nice, naïve, lovely Australian sportsperson boys, and isn't it all terrible, and wank, wank, wank. And nothing's ever looked at, so that gets me enormously irritated.

So while you work with myths you feel you don't just re-create them?

Well, see, until actually talking now, I've never really talked about myths or working with myths — that's just occurred to me now. I was thinking of 'The Little Mermaid', Andersen's story, and why a good fairytale works, and why some of the modern writing for children doesn't work, and it occurred to me that this little mermaid is a wonderful warning story: don't try to be something you ain't. Against all the odds, motivated by sheer self-will, the mermaid sees a pretty prince sitting up there. She goes through hell because she wants that. Now, she forgets she's a fish and he's a chap, she goes down to the witch, she gets the wherewithal, she has to walk on knives, she is mute, so communication can never happen. She should have seen that at the beginning. She'd be blowing bubbles, and he'd be telling rude jokes. I mean, it's a wonderful story, because it's a warning to young women not to pursue a man who will make them desperately unhappy. Try to find a nice mer-person, which in the long run she should have done, because he of course marries another land princess, who is his natural partner, and she just topples over the edge of the boat and goes back into air. You know, it's a wonderful warning. And they're the sorts of things that I'm interested in examining. I mean the Phar Lap myth, say: the Great Horse, the Great Spirit of Australia, once again being killed by the dirty Americans — it's just re-run. Why not have a look at the horse, why not have a look at the horse in Australia, the gambling, the whole idea of something for nothing, you know, and how that reflects something about Australians. What is the horse to them? Why do they love their horses more than their wives? Why will a man spend seven hours in the TAB rather than half an hour with his family? These are the sorts of things that I'd want to look at.

How did you come to be published by The Bodley Head?

Well, John Cody of Australasian Publishing, the Australian publisher, wrote to the placegetters of that year's New Writers Fellowship, asking to look at any work that resulted, which I thought was a good move. And that's how I got on to them. I sent *Fortress* to him, and that was snapped up very quickly, so I've been with them ever since. I've got a wonderful editor there, in London. She's an awful long way away but I trust her. She's enthusiastic about my work, even stuff that some people don't like. I think she knows what I'm doing, and I'd love to work more closely with her.

Do you talk to other writers?

I'm self-conscious about doing that. I feel I don't like to waste their time. It'd be wonderful to have some sort of confidante to whom you could talk, who would be interested in it. I suppose my belief that things would not be interesting to anybody else holds me back from ever taking up someone's time like that. It must be wonderful to be a man, have a lovely wife to hang on your every word.

Does the solitariness of the work bother you at all?

Yes, I think it's very destructive of your relationships with other people, and I think it can be a retreat in a negative sort of way, and it can be a hidey-hole. And there must be a balance between retreat and being in, and of, the world; otherwise you'll lose touch. Because of the preoccupation, you can neglect people badly, you can't see clearly what other people can see, because you're wandering around bemused. Unless you've got friends around you (and I've been very lucky in my friends) who understand that, I think it can be hurtful to other people. I think you can get a bit precious, and think, oh, I've got to keep away, keep safe. I think it can be a bolthole, instead of a truly creative retreat.

I think it's very hard to sustain a relationship, full stop. And if you're writing, you might tend to blame the writing for that. But if you had another high-powered job anywhere you'd probably blame that, and if you had ten kids you'd probably blame that. I think writing might be scapegoated. Although there does seem almost to be a mutual exclusiveness, doesn't there, about whether you're a woman in the normal terms of society, or whether you're a creative woman. The women who combine both, to me, are just magnificent. I don't know how they do it. Or I don't know if they should have to do it. My belief is that everybody's creative. Everybody's a writer, or a painter, or a something; but some just suffer from worse writer's block. There's something about people who do produce the goods that has enabled them to knock down the normal inhibiting factors that cover up everybody's creative processes. Now whether this makes for a person who's trickier to get along with, perhaps because they are a bit clearer sighted in some ways, or they have seen through certain levels in themselves to be able to pull out the stuff to write it, I don't know. It might make them seem formidable to others in some way.

What sort of things do you think inhibit creativity?

The illusions that our heads are filled with, most of the time, that we're brought up on. You see, I was lucky, I wasn't brought up on a negative illusion. I had a wonderful mother. I still have a wonderful mother, who used to say things like, 'Gabrielle could do anything', and that was an illusion I believed in, because my mother had said it, and it was a very sustaining one, even though she was sometimes very cross when she said it. I think those sorts of things are very powerful, and if you've got a mother who says, 'You're hopeless, you'll never be any good', you won't. Or a father. But mothers are more powerful, and therefore cop more of the blame. I can't imagine growing up with expectations on me to be a particular way, because for one reason or another it didn't happen. All that was expected of me was that I'd do something, and I'd do it very well.

Do you think the world would be better if there were more creators?

I think it's amazing that there are any at all sometimes, given the way people are crippled, and the way the crippling process is just spun out in families, down through the generations. But somewhere something breaks down, and someone gets out and escapes. It's not as if I think the creating of literature or art is any more important or less important than the creating of anything. It's just that cakes don't get put in libraries. But so much wonderful stuff is relegated to the craft level. I think mostly because you can't refrigerate it, or something. You can't keep it like you can a painting or a book. The ephemeral sort of stuff, that mostly women do, even housework itself, that just gets kicked down every day. All that's creating, and maybe they are exhausted or somehow satisfied, or somehow that forms their creative area. So it probably doesn't have to be books. I mean in the long run a book goes. It's no more permanent, in the long term, than a dress or a cake.

Do you feel that making books is really only a short-term thing, too?

I don't really look at it like that. I enjoy the making of it. I'm terribly bored once it's finished. It's time to get on with another one, and so I don't really see it in terms of making a long-lasting piece, at all. There's that lovely samurai thing that 'he who dwells on the outcome loses the cutting edge'. I think if you are looking past what you are doing, you've spoilt what you're doing.

Do you see yourself as a spiritual person?

I'm starting to have to accept the fact that, yes, I am a spiritual person. I've rejected it all my life. I suppose because of the unpleasant avenues it takes, like organised religion, and vile occultism and all that junk, and I think I've been so firmly set against all of that sort of nonsense that I've thrown out the baby with the bath water a bit.

I suppose man does not live by bread alone, as the Bible says; that there are things that are much more important than physical comfort; that there are ideals that are in us, from somewhere; and that Western civilisation is discovering now that wall-to-wall televisions don't make you happy, and that the concept of harmony and brother- and sisterhood of people is a wonderful ideal and one that might never be realised, or not by this race of humans. God knows what might come next. We might just be a mistake. There's a wonderful story in one of the Talmudic scripts, very, very early stuff, that says this is actually the twenty-eighth attempt at creation, and God was heard to say as He threw this one together, 'Geez, I hope this one works'. I just loved that, but it made me feel very insecure.

I do feel that one has a path to follow, that life's not just a series of random events. I always knew somewhere that it couldn't have been a series of random events, but I resisted so strongly any idea of a guiding principle that was too big for me to understand that I just didn't want to know, and yet it was coming out everywhere in me.

Were you brought up with religion?

I was brought up as a good Catholic girl and, I mean, when a good Catholic girl goes bad, there's nothing worse. A full-on rebellion like mine has to be as good as Lucifer's. So it all had to go. I mean I couldn't say — as a more mature and sensible person might have done — look, that bit's just clearly not on, but that bit's fine. I had to say, all or nothing. And you do miss it enormously. It leaves a terrific hole.

So Catholicism was a strong influence when you were a kid?

Yes, very strong. I loved the choir, and still sing. I'm a member of the Waverley Philharmonic Society. I loved the music. I loved all the good things about it. I loved the early art. I loved the monasticism. I liked the austerity, and the silence. I can't bear noise in the morning. I can't bear to hear talking on the radio. It has to be either silence or something very formal, say Bach — nothing past about 1750, 1780 — until ten. You know, there are laws. There are rules. No chatter. No talk. So I've got that very strongly, that need for silence in the morning. It doesn't give me boils. I've decided that good skin comes from not having that madness of waking up and switching on. I walked into a chap's house yesterday, and the news was on: a man was raped — sodomised and robbed, da-da-da-da. I thought, imagine waking up at seven and switching that on. Now what sort of a day could you possibly have? That violence, that outrage, being blasted out all over the city. Everybody waking up to it. That gives you boils. Spiritual boils. So that's the good of it. It just keeps me calm.

Are you prone to not being calm?

Prone to madness, but getting better, getting much better, yes.

Is that maturity again, do you think?

I hope so. I've also given up the booze, about a year ago. It was knocking me around too much. Couldn't take it any more. And of course booze brings its own madness, after a while. It *is* the madness. After a while it stops being a response to your madness, but it replaces it with a new form.

It is a possession. All addictions are a possession. So since that left my life there's been an enormous improvement in my serenity. And I always lived at a very high level of insanity. I think a lot of writers are terribly at risk there, because of the introspection of the beast, and the fact that I think you probably write from your own obsessions. I'm not too sure about that, but I think that's the case, and I think if you're locked up in your head with your obsessions, and you're drinking, I reckon it's blow-your-brains-out country eventually. I really do. I mean writers' form in this area isn't good. I've never been suicidal. I mean I've sometimes thought, oh geez, it'd be nice if I didn't have to wake up tomorrow, because I don't like what I'm feeling. But I've never ever thought seriously of putting the lights out, ever. It's been a very flirtatious and silly, indulgent thing to think, you know, it might be nice to stop for a bit. But like Woody Allen, the thing that worries me about death is the hours. So, no, I'm very pleased to be alive, and I enjoy my days, very much, now.

Sydney, June 1985

Select bibliography

Fortress, Aurora Press, 1980; Pan Books, 1981.
Tooth and Claw, The Bodley Head, 1982.

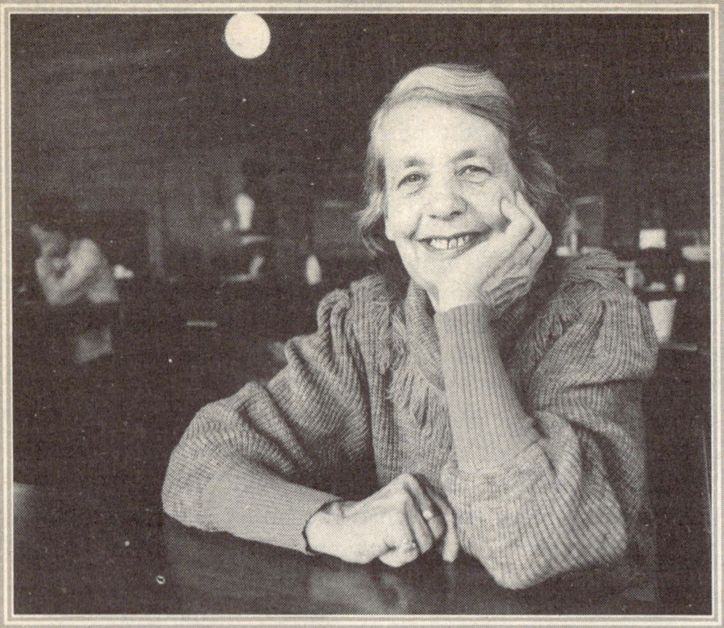

OLGA MASTERS

'All my writing is about human behaviour. There's not much drama, no great happenings in it. No violence. It's about the violence that's inside the human heart, I think, more than anything else.'

Can you tell me when your first short story was published?

In about 1979, in the *Sydney Morning Herald*. I submitted two short stories to the *Sydney Morning Herald*, and they were the first two I'd written. I was aged about fifty-eight, and having written these two short stories I didn't know quite what to do with them. Helen Frizell was editor of the *Sydney Morning Herald* at that time, and she put a piece in the literary pages on the Saturday saying that she would be interested in reading stories no longer than 2000 words in length, and I was so tentative about offering my work that I didn't even send them to her direct. I sent them to Les Murray, the poet and a friend of ours, who was reviewing for the *Herald* fairly consistently at the time, and asked him to read them first, and if he thought they were good enough, to pass them on to Helen. Well, he wrote back to me and said he'd read them both, thought they were quite good, and said he'd pass them on to Helen with his recommendation. Helen bought one, and she said, 'I don't think you'll have any trouble placing the other one'. The other one went on and won a short story award administered by the Fellowship of Australian Writers in Queensland called the Ronald Carson Gold Award. It carried $600 prize money, which was quite good. And that story, called 'The Snake and Bad Tom', went into the book *The Home Girls*. It was the story the judges selected to discuss on the night of the awards, and they compared it to Barbara Banyon's 'Squeaker's Mate', which is a famous story.

You must have been absolutely delighted.

Well, I was delighted but of course a lot happened in between writing those two stories and finally getting the twenty written for *The Home Girls*. I was encouraged to continue on of course, and I wrote more and more. In 1980 I won — shared, with Elizabeth Jolley — the South Pacific Association for the Study of Language and Literature Award and this is administered by various countries in the Pacific. My story was 'The Rages of Mrs Torrens'.

The University of Queensland, which did the judging, rang me and told me that I had shared first prize, and I said to them I wonder would the publishing house associated with the university be interested in looking at all my stories, I had sixteen, and they said they were sure they would. Well, shortly afterwards I got a letter from Craig Munro, who was fiction editor at the time, and he said — to my amazement, because I know how hard it is to get a foot in the publishing door — he would recommend that they be published. And it went from there. I got a contract, and of course by the time the book came out I was well into *Loving Daughters*.

Craig Munro said in his letter 'I would like the collection called *The Home Girls*', and that was it. I used to think I would love to have all my stories in a book and call it *The Home Girls*. Not only because of the story, which I liked and thought was fairly strong as an opening story, but because every story in the book someway involves a home girl, and we are all home girls at heart, I think. There are quite a number of home men, too, and even in stories like 'A Young Man's Fancy', the home was so important to him. The home was so very important to most situations, in the book.

When I finished the last story for *The Home Girls* I didn't want to go off the boil. I thought, well, I've made a good start now, I'll do another story. I might write a longer story, something like a novella. I wouldn't let myself think I was writing a novel. I started *Loving Daughters* as a short story, and it kept going, and I was going to have the child, small Henry, as the main character, and have him reared in an adult situation. He would be a strange little boy, because he probably would not have played with other children of his age, there being no one around him. And I thought what an interesting story. But the minister came on the scene, you know, and the two girls were there, and one can't ignore the love element in the human triangle. And they took the book over. So the book was then not in my hands. I kept on going, and kept on going, and then one day I said to myself, I've got a novel. I always thought other people wrote novels, not me. I didn't think I would ever write a novel, and I had to be well on the way before I had enough confidence and courage to believe that I was actually writing a full-length novel.

It was full of surprises, because I didn't know which girl he was going to get until the actual wedding scene. I didn't know, so I knew the reader wouldn't know. There was nothing to give away, because I didn't know.

Why did you finally decide to give him Una?

Well I think because mostly in life we go the opposite way, to the right way. We all say we wait for Mr Right, but very often we marry Mr Wrong. I thought that was how it would happen, if it were a real life drama, that he would have married Una. And of course she was the stronger one, and she was the more powerful of the two girls, and her power brought him under her spell. But of course it was a story of people reaching out for love. The girls awakened to love through the child, more than anything. Really Una was in love with the child more than with Colin. If ever, indeed, she was in love with him at all. But all sorts of things influenced my thinking in that book, because it was set at a time when I myself first awakened to the world around me. The first date I can remember is 1926. I can remember my mother telling me 'Today is', say, 'the 4th of May, 1926', and I thought, 1926? What does that mean? And that's when I knew that time was being counted.

How long did Loving Daughters *take you to write, roughly?*

Eighteen months, and then there were another three months in revision. It takes me that long. I wrote *A Long Time Dying* in the same amount of time. I'm going to be a bit longer with the current one. I started it at the beginning of the year. It's called *Amy's Children* and I'm a comfortable halfway through, and I've also typed it. I type it as I go, you see. I don't write a complete draft and then go back and type it.

I type each chapter as I finish it. I do all the revision then, and I don't change anything. I won't change anything. If I say something that's relevant to the future I will stick to that no matter what happens. Because I think that that's the way it was. That's the way I saw it, and I don't want to change my own judgement, because if your judgement is not spot on, well, forget it. You start to go haywire. I think other people have their own way of writing. They may write entirely differently, and quite successfully.

Were you writing Loving Daughters *full time?*

The first Literature Board grant enabled me to write full time, and I was one third of the way through *Loving Daughters* when I got the grant. So I really did write it fairly quickly. It would have been quicker than that, only there were some changes in staff up at the University of Queensland Press. I had some revision to do on *Loving Daughters*. Craig Munro was absolutely marvellous. I must give full credit to him, because he pointed out certain weaknesses. I had more letters in it, letters from the minister to his mother in England, and I was critical of myself with regard to those letters. It seemed to me that *I* was writing the letters, not him. And I realised just how hard it was to do. I made my letters very brief after that. Elizabeth Jolley's got a wonderful short story called 'The Well-bred Thief'. It's an exchange of letters between two women, and each of them writes in her own way. I envy her that story. I wish I'd written it.

So you were quite happy to listen to your publisher's suggestions?

Oh, very happy. I'm a journalist, and once a journalist, always a journalist. When you're young and you start off as a journalist, you think those editors and sub-editors are terrible people, to dare to want to change your work. Then after a while you realise that they're a sample of the public and you could be wrong. You feel your work often has a bright edge to it and somebody else doesn't always see that bright edge. But you must listen to criticism. I do believe that strongly.

I think it's a great shame that people won't listen to criticisms.

Do you think journalism has helped or hindered your fiction writing?

Most of the jobs I got as a journalist were human interest stories, and that was a great help, not a hindrance at all, because you would sometimes take quite an ordinary and humble person and write a story about them, and you'd be surprised at the quality that was there in the ordinary human being. I write about ordinary people all the time really. My characters err on the side of being very simple and ordinary, rather than, say, wealthy or exciting, and I think I got that from journalism. I learned a lot about human nature, and human behaviour, as a journalist. I worked on small papers, and you'd go out for a story and it wouldn't be much of a story, but you'd make it into a story. The lesson there was that there is more in life, more in situations, than meets the eye. The deeper you dig, the more you find.

What about the processes of writing? Do you find you have different approaches for journalism and fiction?

Well, my style is simple, as you know. I didn't find I had to change very much when I started to write fiction. I still wrote in a fairly simple, straightforward style, but I had this wonderful bonus of being able to describe, to indulge in a little description, that you couldn't do as a journalist.

You said that you wrote two stories but you hadn't written fiction before that. But did you have an idea in your mind that one day you would write fiction?

Yes. I wanted to write fiction from a very early age, all my life really. And I did make little attempts at it with a pencil and one of the exercise books stolen from my husband's pile (he was a schoolteacher) but I never seemed to make progress. I know now that the characters didn't come to life, they were dead, and I didn't want to write like that. I didn't want to write for the sake of writing. I wanted to write with feeling. I knew there was no feeling there, and it was not until the '70s, really, when I wrote one human interest story that sparked off quite a lot of response. My son was a first grade Sydney football coach, and he brought a team over to play. The editor said, 'Would you go and write a biassed story, you know, you're the mother of the coach.' And I thought, oh, I don't want to do this, I'll just have to go and say to him the day after, look, I couldn't do it. But anyway, I did it, and I surprised myself, and the response to that story was absolutely unbelievable. People rang all next day, and they laughed, and some of them almost cried. One man said to me, 'Oh, I remember the oranges'. And I thought, gee, I've made that man remember, something from long, long ago. That's what writing's all about. It's reaching people through words; and not so much what you say, but what it makes them think of. That story started me. That made me think, well, look, I really will have a go. Surely I'm ready now to do something. Shortly after that I took two years off to try my hand at fiction, because I thought I'd write short stories, and short plays, but I had this awful fear that I might start things and not finish them. But I finished everything. I think the fear that I would perhaps not bring things to a conclusion had the opposite effect.

Was it during those two years that you wrote the stories for The Home Girls?

Most of them, yes. Actually I was back at work when I wrote the story 'The Home Girls', because one of the first jobs I did when I went back to work was to interview a man who had been in charge of a children's home for forty years, and I said to him, have the children changed emotionally over forty years? How do they cope with their plight now, as against forty years ago, when there was a dreadful stigma attached to the split family, and going into a home? I thought today it must be different, because, you know, my children used to sit next to children on either side whose parents were divorced. It was accepted. So I thought the child of today would probably cope much better with that situation than, say, the children of the forties and the late thirties. But he didn't answer me. He went off talking about something else and I tried him again, and I thought, look, I reckon you have never even thought what's gone on inside a child's head. You've brought them in, and clothed them and fed them, and perhaps you've been kind to them and listened to them and talked to them, but you've never thought of their emotional needs, I'm sure of that. He was a very nice man, there was nothing wrong with him, except that he didn't know how to think. And I just went home and wrote 'The Home Girls'.

Almost all of your work is set in the country, and you've lived in the country. Is a lot of it based on your own memories?

My own impressions, rather than memories, although certainly memory comes into it a lot. I'm sure I gathered impressions of behavioural patterns from the people we knew, real life characters, but no one of course is drawn entirely from life. I think very few writers do draw people from life, because you don't really know anyone completely, do you? We think we know people, but we don't really, and that's the same with writing. We get an image of a person, we put a character into their skins. I think we all do it, I mean writers and non-writers, because I don't think any of us ever knows anyone.

When did you move away from the country?

I moved away when I was seventeen, and came to Sydney to work. *A Long Time Dying* is actually set in 1935, a couple of years before I left the country. And they're very impressionable years, when you're in your teens.

Living in a country town must have had a fairly powerful impact on you, then.

It did. And remember, too, that you relied on human beings

for everything. You didn't have television, and you didn't have radio — some people in the town did — so it was all word of mouth, and more or less a study of people, I mean an unconscious study of humans. I was always, like everybody else, fascinated by the aged: you can't imagine how anyone could bother living when they're past the age of twenty-five, and so on. The harsh treatment of the unmarried woman, and the illegitimate child, all those things I noticed. Even young as I was, I noticed it was a terrible thing not to be married. On the one hand you'd have the poor housemother, you know, with a tribe of children, and really a pretty miserable sort of life, and then on the other hand you'd have the spinster, and for some reason or another you believed that the woman with the big family and the dirty little house and no money and no clothes and hardly enough to eat was better off than the well-dressed spinster, who might have been a teacher, or a businesswoman. I remember one woman who opened a shop after working for another man, and it was quite sinful to do such a thing. A, she wasn't married, and B, she didn't seem to want to get married, which was really very very odd: there must have been something wrong with this woman, and she should have stayed and remained a servant to the master. I can remember the criticism of that woman because she opened that shop, and the struggle she had. After a while everybody forgot of course and came and bought her scissors and pins and tape measures and rolls of sprigged muslin and so on.

Were you at that time conscious of being an observer, or perhaps even an outsider?

I think I noticed things and stored them away in some part of my mind, to write them down in later years, because I do notice that I remember more than my sisters do. We do store things subconsciously. In *The Home Girls* there is a story called 'The Greek Way' in which the little girl was teased unmercifully at school. My sister read it, and she said, 'Oh, the Xs, I feel so guilty, the way we used to torment those children at school.' And you see, I must have been storing it away. I didn't think I wrote it from anything at all except my own imagination. It's quite uncanny. All my writing is about human behaviour. As you know, there's not much drama, no great happenings in it. No violence. It's about the violence that's inside the human heart, I think, more than anything else.

Loving Daughters is the kind of book that could have been written twenty years ago. Were you concerned about the fact that it was not contemporary when you were writing it?

Yes, I was. I was very concerned about the limited incidents, the limited scope. I thought, in other hands there might be, oh, a mob of bushrangers coming down out of the hills, and a big shoot-out, or something like that, and that my publishers would be looking for that, but I used to go back and think, no. If you write about life, you write about life, and it was a dull little corner of the world, and there is no changing it. You can't make drama where drama does not belong. And you know, we go through these towns, we call them 'the sleepy little villages'. They are sleepy little villages but still there are human beings in those villages and they're entitled to their story. That was a point. I used to think, when I feared that the pace might be too slow to make it a saleable product, I used to think those people were entitled to their own life, the way it was, and one should not force on them another way that wasn't their way.

I used to think of the main characters in *Loving Daughters*, Una and Enid, and think of my own daughters and nieces, and put them into that situation, and wonder what they would have done. You know, I've got two talented daughters, and I've got many talented nieces: they became teachers and librarians and have good careers, yet they were the same in flesh and blood as those two girls. Una and Enid had the same inborn skills and talents, but they couldn't use them, they wouldn't have any scope to use them. But there was nothing you could do. I mean that was how life was. The only women who had careers were those who said, 'Oh, I'm going to be a teacher' or, 'I'm going to be a nun', and that was it. You know, the others just said, 'Well, you get married, and have children, and that's your life, and up until that time you just look after the men'.

Were you surprised, then, by the positive response to Loving Daughters?

I was more surprised by the response to *The Home Girls*, because I thought the only people who would buy it would be my family. But my husband read *Loving Daughters* and he liked it very much, and he's fairly critical. He's a teacher, he's not a writer, so they're the best people really to judge. I had a lot of hope for *Loving Daughters*. I'd be less than honest if I said I was surprised at the response. I felt confident that it was a good love story. When I was writing it I had my two grandsons in the house and they used to watch 'Perfect Match', and they'd laugh about it and say, 'Oh, isn't he a dag, and oh, God, look at her! Isn't she awful! Ooh-oh!' And they would carry on, but they wanted to know who got who, and what happened. I thought, you little beggars, you laugh and scoff, but you're just as keen, and I thought, everybody is a cupid at heart. We watch romance. We watch the union of man and woman. We observe that, probably more closely than any other human relationship that we have. And that, I thought, would carry the book through.

In Loving Daughters *you do a very startling thing by saying 'They got married', in one sentence, and then you go back. Why did you decide to do it that way? You do that quite a bit, actually.*

Yes, I do, and I'm doing it in this new book too. I don't know why I do it, really. I think I said before that I say something and I'll never change it, you know. For instance, in this book, *Amy's Children,* I said Amy's daughter Kathleen nearly married, but she did not marry this boy she was going out with; in the end she married Joe Miller. Well, now I will stick to that, you see. It may be awkward, it may make it longer and more difficult but I will not change. And I don't know why I do it. It's a puzzle to me. But I think perhaps it makes the reader read on, too. Also that book needed to be lifted in parts. I was consciously using that major step to keep the reader's interest.

I read one review of A Long Time Dying *which said that it's not really a novel. What's your reaction to that?*

I called it a discontinuous narrative, a collection of chapters with a common background, but the first two stories and the last two stories bound it. It was a toss-up whether to call it a novel or a collection of short stories. UQP really called it a novel. They decided what to call it. I was pleased they did, because I thought it was more a novel than a collection of short stories, and this is being a bit commercial, I know, but a novel sells better than a collection of short stories. I think a novel is more readily received than a collection of short stories.

Did you consciously decide to write in that form?

Oh yes, I decided to do that, as soon as I finished *Loving Daughters*. I also thought that I could sell them as I went along, and I did sell four. I didn't really want to sell any more because I thought that was enough.

Did you write them in sequence?

Yes. I wrote them in the order in which they're published. Otherwise I don't think I would have had those first two stories and the last two stories married to each other. People can say whatever they like, but I don't think it's very important whether it's a novel or not. But I wasn't surprised that someone picked it up, because they're looking for that sort of thing.

Do you find reviews helpful?

They haven't made the slightest bit of difference, really, because I'm always so far gone on the next project by the time a review comes out.

Do you think good reviews influence sales?

They don't seem to be a pointer to any sort of result, to awards or to sales. But I noticed the reviews of *A Long Time Dying* came out very quickly. I got very few reviews of *The Home Girls*. They all did it when it came out in paperback, but they didn't do it originally because I was unknown, and it was a collection of short stories. But of course it won the National Book Council Award and then as soon as *Loving Daughters* was out it was reviewed immediately.

Although your work's not particularly feminist in its intent, you seem to be very aware of the divisions between the sexes.

Well, I would say that the division is there, between the sexes. There's no ignoring it, and if you're a truthful writer you'll find it. If you're writing about real-life incidents, and real people, it can't help but surface, and this is what it's all about, isn't it, the present fight for equality? There hasn't *been* equality. You come upon it all the time. I couldn't help finding it, in the early times, when I saw the women tied to the kitchen sink and always just in the supportive role rather than in a leading role. They were entitled to lead, and they had the skills to do so, but it was just not accepted that they should. It seemed that, if you were born a male, you automatically became the person who could make the decisions.

You seem to be careful in your work not to judge that situation.

Yes, yes. Well, it is very difficult to judge, because you just don't know everything. But it's not only in those earlier times, but also in the present day. I can remember when I was reporting there was a function on and one council was represented by a male alderman, and there was also a female alderman there. This alderman got up and, referring to the woman alderman, he said, quite seriously, that when she first joined the council he thought to himself, oh, this'll be good, because there'll be somebody to make the coffee. You would have thought he would have been too ashamed to say such a thing, but, you know, he thought that was right, and that was the way it was. It does make you grit your teeth, doesn't it? But there it is. If you're writing about the real world, real people, these issues will come up because that's the way it is and the way it was.

It's quite apparent that some of your characters, like Enid in Loving Daughters *and Florence in* A Long Time Dying, *are being used by the people around them, but you don't ever comment on that.*

No, no, it comes through. It comes through because they are used, they were used, they allowed themselves to be used because there was no other way out. Florence was the unmarried daughter who looked after the parents, and those were the sort of things that I became aware of when I was very young. I remember going to school, and the teacher had several daughters and a son. One daughter became a nurse, and one became a schoolteacher, and Leila was the girl at home. The schoolteacher's wife took us for sewing, and, you know, ever observant, ever alerted to anything like this that was going on, I still remember her saying, 'Well, Leila was the one we decided would stay at home with the parents.' And that was that. Leila did. I suppose she was discouraged if a prospective boyfriend came to call. That would be it. They would have lived in country towns where there would be very few opportunities of meeting somebody and falling in love, and doing the things that nature intended us to do.

You seem to walk a line of compassion and contempt for country life.

Yes, that's put very well. Can't do much about it, though. The country towns were small, and narrow, and always we're governed by the economy, our lives are structured by the economy. *A Long Time Dying* is set in the Depression. The environment governed people's attitudes, and everybody gossiped because there was nothing else to do — that was their television and their radio, their newspaper.

Do you think you'll always write about the country?

Oh well, I'm not writing about it now. *Amy's Children* starts in the country, but it's in the city. Amy came to the city and worked, and she left her children behind her in the country. It starts in the early thirties and now it's going through the war years. It's going over quite a long period.

Do you find writing fiction personally confronting in a way?

It's very hard. It's a very arduous job. You've got to really get into the minds of the people that you're concerned with, and make sure that they behave in a way that's consistent with their characters. You can't be phony, and you can't push anything, and you can't camouflage, you can't cover up. You've just got to go along at the right pace, and, if you don't know anything about a time that you're writing about you've got to find out.

Yes, do you do much research?

No, I'm not called upon to do research, because I can remember.

The language you use seems so perfect for the periods you have written about.

I think it's very important. That's something that you've got to concentrate on to a great extent, the slang of the times. You know, you couldn't use a term such as 'you've got to be joking'. People didn't talk that way. People said 'whacko', and they said 'OK', of course. 'OK' has been around for a long time.

You also have a lot of descriptions of food in your work, particularly in A Long Time Dying.

Yes, food was very important. Food had more value then because of the scarcity, the tightness of the times, the hungry times I suppose you'd say. And I love writing about food, because I'm a keen cook, really. I think food's a story on its own.

Do you enjoy writing full time?

Yes, yes I do. Well, it's something I wanted to do. Everybody who writes dreams of writing full time, I think. I've been doing it since 1982 when *The Home Girls* came out. You produce a lot more when you're writing full time.

Do you find you write at fixed times every day?

I get up at half past four in the morning. You see, when I went back to work, after taking the two years off, I worked part time then, and I would have gone from Sunday to Thursday without writing, and that's too big a gap. So that's when I started getting up very early. I made sure I carried on whatever project I had going. I still do that. It doesn't matter what I'm doing. Every day, every single day, as they say.

Do you think there have been any advantages or disadvantages in starting your writing career relatively late in life?

Ah, well, the tremendous advantages are that you can enjoy this time of your life. I would have been burnt out if I'd started writing at thirty, or twenty-five. I think I'd have written it all. You don't go on and write and write and write. Most writers have a span of time in which they do their best work, and their early work is a little bit tentative. Then they get into a period where they write their best, and then they possibly go off a bit. Well, you know, I missed that, because I'm not thinking beyond the Bicentenary collection. That will give me five books — *Amy's Children, A Long Time Dying, Loving Daughters, The Home Girls,* and the Bicentennial one. And

I love writing columns, because you write about life, and it's satisfying. I'm looking forward to a bit of a break, because I've been going constantly since 1982, and I was going along steadily before then. You get very involved when you're working on a project, and you get nervous about leaving it, for fear you'll lose the threads. It's a very committed occupation, and it's a very lonely one, too, because you can't say to anyone, what will I say now? What do you think I should say here? Because you'd be a pretty terrible writer if you did that, wouldn't you?

I read that Shiva Naipaul said, 'Writing demands an immense amount of physical stamina', and I think it does too. For one thing, apart from all the family around you (and I've got a large family), you've also got your fictional family, and, you know, a woman of my age normally would be engrossed in her grandchildren, if she didn't have a career, and so you go against nature a little bit. Last Sunday we had a party here for a niece who's getting married, and I was amused. There were about six children coming, and I never gave a thought to the kids. We were having chicken and lasagna, and I made quiches, and I was making cream puffs, and of course my sister-in-law said, 'Now for the children we'll have ...' And she knew exactly what her grandchildren like. I don't know what my grandchildren like! On the other hand, the grandchildren become very interested. Little Clare is very interested in my writing. She wants to be a writer like Granny, so you have that compensation. Whereas on the one hand you don't know what they eat, you don't know their sizes when you go to buy them something for a birthday present, on the other hand you at least know they like you for what you can do.

Austinmer, September 1985

Select bibliography

The Home Girls, University of Queensland Press, 1982.
Loving Daughters, University of Queensland Press, 1984.
A Long Time Dying, University of Queensland Press, 1985.

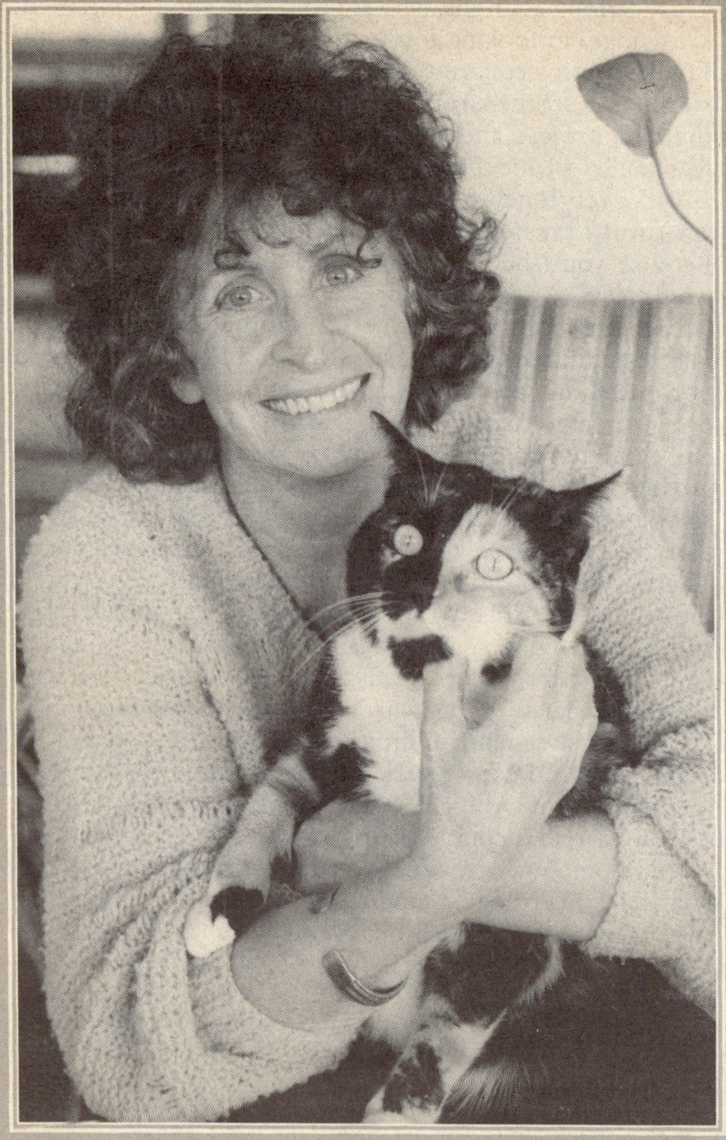

GEORGIA SAVAGE

'Writing is not a matter of how long you sit at it. It's a sort of waking-hours job. You're doing it all the time. I don't cut off from it. It's always there.'

Was there a specific point in your life when you decided to be a writer?

Yes. When I was about thirteen a relative lived with us, and she was my fairy godmother. She let me borrow her nylons, her make-up, her perfumes, and her books and her typewriter. I used to write really dopey things and pretend that I was a reporter on the paper. In those days of course girl reporters only worked on the women's pages, so I used to do a lot of wedding reports and things like that. Nobody knows this, that's all terribly, terribly buried in my dim past, but it is true. And I used to imagine myself going on and becoming the first woman war correspondent, because I've always been keen on war. Not the idea of war, but what happens to people in wars, has always fascinated me.

When I was about sixteen, I started writing short stories. I wrote a bit of poetry which I didn't show to anybody, but everybody does that. I did most of my writing in school, at the back of the classroom. I even wrote novels at the back of the classroom when I was a bit older. But I started off with short stories, which I hid in the bottom of my wardrobe in my room. My mother found them and read them out to her women friends at an afternoon tea party. And I was so mortified when they goohed and gaahed that I didn't write again for twenty years.

But you still nursed the desire to be a writer?

Yes, I always wanted to be a writer. Then I got very heavily into living and there was no possibility of writing for a long time.

What do you mean by 'heavily into living'?

There's a dreadful old song title that typifies the first twenty years of my adult life: 'Too Many Parties and Too Many Pals'. To put it another way, I was always mad about men — still am. I've wasted a lot of my life on them.

Do you have regrets about that?

No, I'd go back and do it all again.

When was your wish to become a writer realised?

I guess I would have been pushing middle thirties, and I thought, if I don't do something about writing now, I never will. And I had, I think, four years off work. I always worked. I had to because of the circumstances of my life.

I left the job where I was because it was not a happy place to be working, and I had a lot of responsibility and strain. It was one of those situations where the young woman in the place had to carry a burden that simply wasn't fair. I left because my health was in danger of breaking down over it.

What sort of writing did you produce during that period?

Oh, it's better not to talk about it. I was heavily into my William Faulkner period. I think we'd better leave it at that.

Did you try to get published at that time?

Yes, I did. I think I did my very first draft of *Slate & Me* then, and another novel, which I later burned. And one more novel, which was lost in the mail. I've had lots of laughs thinking about the Australia Post people out on the country road lighting the billy with pages of that novel, you know, which was the fate it deserved, by God. But I was learning to write. I didn't know much about good writing. Sitting at the back of the class writing all the time, I didn't pass any exams and had no education.

Did you continue writing when you went back to work?

Yes, I wrote the first draft of *The Tournament* in my spare time at work, and I taught myself to be able to put it away and then pick it up again, which was very good training for a writer, because I taught myself to concentrate with a certain single-mindedness.

How long did that go on?

A couple of years, maybe even three years, and that would have been some time in the seventies. I did another draft of *Slate & Me* at work too. A lot of people write at work. I think especially women writers write at work. I guess it means that you probably don't do your job very well. You see, I lived in Mooroopna and worked in Shepparton, so I could use my lunch hours and my morning and afternoon tea breaks. I was working in income tax and after the end of the income tax season there might be three months when you didn't have much to do.

And what was involved in getting The Tournament *published?*

Before that was published I'd sent away *Slate & Me* a couple of times and had it back. I'd sent *The Tournament* away, and had it back, and editors kept saying the same thing to me. I thought naturally that they just didn't recognise a bit of shit-hot talent, you know, but they kept saying the same thing. They'd say I had writing talent and that I should learn to use it. I started to think, if they're all saying the same thing there has to be something in it. So I set myself to learn what was wrong with my writing, which I did by studying what I considered good writing, studying it absolutely in depth, analysing the first page of something, a classic like something of Salinger's, and analysing the first page of my own writing.

A certain series of events happened in my life at the one time. My mother became ill in Queensland. At the same time I had a story accepted for the *Bulletin* literary supplement, and I thought, I have to do something really serious about writing. I should leave my job, and go to Queensland so that I can be near my mother and share the visiting with my brother. And at exactly the same time I got into an Open School of the Film and Television School, to do a little course there, and it was sort of all buoying me up to have the courage to say, well, I'll dice my job. And while I was down in Melbourne, at the Film and Television School, John McLaren had met Caroline Lurie, the agent, at lunch and asked her if she'd be interested in my work. And so she asked if she could see some of it, and she saw it, and said she would be interested in my work.

So I went back up to Mooroopna and put my house on the market, and gave notice at work, and I suppose it took three weeks or a month only to sell my house, and by that time my mother most unfortunately died, which was really grim, because I'd planned to have some time with her. I went to Queensland in 1980 and I had four years there.

I hadn't been up there very long when I had a letter from Caroline to say that she'd sold *The Tournament* to Hale & Iremonger. That was rather interesting because they were certain that it was a hoax, that Caroline Lurie and whoever was purporting to be Georgia Savage were doing an Ern Malley, and that it was really written by a young man. And I more or less had to go to Sydney and flash my raincoat, you know, and say well, it *was* me, I was Georgia Savage.

Did you find that surprising? That they were so convinced you were a male?

In a way I was flattered because I had written as a male, and it meant that I had brought it off. Apart from that I thought it was a bit silly because I felt there was no reason why a woman couldn't do that.

How did you become confident about writing as a man?

It didn't ever enter my head not to. When I was a kid at school, and used to write film scripts and things, I had a friend and she and I used to act out the things we wrote in class, and we would have to take the role of Heathcliffe, or whatever, and it just didn't occur to me not to. There's no reason why people can't swap sex.

You said that you studied and analysed what you considered to be good writing. After that, did you rewrite The Tournament?

I only ever worked over *The Tournament* once. I'm well aware that it could do with heavy reworking, but it would lose the spontaneity of somebody talking, and especially somebody like the character Finney, who tried desperately hard to be hip. The first time I sent it away I was advised that it bogged down about two thirds of the way through, and I did the old Scott Fitzgerald trick of taking the boggy bit and putting it at the front, where it didn't matter if it was going slowly, and that was about the only change I ever made in that.

It's a very unusual story. Was it based on a real incident?

No, not at all, because I am an imaginative writer, and I make things up for my own pleasure. I write for my own pleasure. I don't write really for any other reason, except entertainment for myself. Although that, I think, is a phase I'm growing out of. I feel that I have some things to say and I should be saying them instead of just writing for kicks.

What about your second novel, Slate & Me? *What was involved in the process of writing that?*

Well, I had put that away saying that one day I was going to sit down and rewrite it. When I arrived in Queensland, in my mother's house, I got it out to rewrite it, and it was so dreadful that I got rid of it so that I couldn't copy it. I rewrote the same story and then sent it down to Caroline.

How long did it take you to rewrite the whole story?

Off and on, eighteen months. But I go very slowly, because I have very bad osteoarthritis in my hands. I can't type any more, and some days I can't write, so that I do as much as I can on a good day, and that's it. In Queensland where the air's damp I had a lot of trouble with my hands, and so it was really difficult for me.

When you went up to Queensland, having made the decision to write, was the transition a difficult one?

No, no, because I didn't ever want to go out to work. I can't understand why anybody would ever ever ever want to go out to work. I think you would have to be mad. After all, the main privilege of the very rich is not going out to work, and why people even consider that going out to work gives them an identity, when you can sit down and do nothing and watch the grass grow, I don't understand. So no. It was just wonderful. It was like, you know, the school holidays coming, and so on. I thought it was marvellous that I was free finally to be myself, because I am a dedicated bum. I put a lot into being a bum and I think I do it well.

When you had that time to yourself, did you find that any working methods emerged?

Yes, I always write all the morning, and I think all the afternoon and always think for a couple of hours in the middle of the night. I had probably been doing that for a time before I left work — not working on my writing all the morning, of course, because I wasn't free to do that, but thinking about it all the time. I think most writers do. It's not just a matter of how long you sit at it. It's a sort of waking-hours job. You're doing it all the time. Well, I am, anyway. I don't cut off from it. It's always there.

Why did you decide to come to Melbourne?

Because I always wanted to. My husband was a Melbourne bloke, and we planned that one day we would come to Melbourne, and we started looking for houses in Melbourne not terribly long before he died. He died in 1974, from heart trouble, and we were looking for a house in Melbourne then. Our social life, and especially my social life, had been in Melbourne for a long time. Although I lived in Mooroopna, we came down here for our social life, and then my son came down to Monash. He's here, and there are only the two of us left in the family, so there was every reason to come here. But, paradoxically, while I was in Queensland I missed Victoria desperately, and if I saw something about Melbourne

I literally cried. But now that I'm down here I miss Queensland. My mother was up there for many years, and I used to visit her in my holidays. In a way I think where your mother is, that's home, because nobody ever looks after you like your mother does. Even when my mother was very old, and I stayed with her, I was not allowed to do the vegetables, or do the dishes, or do anything. She looked after me. So that's really where the heart is, I think, where mother is, and I will always be split between these two home things. I think the only way to solve it is to try to spend my time in both places. Maybe in the winters I could have a caravan or something and put it on a friend's place up there.

Queensland politics of course are something that I couldn't cope with. But after I'd been up there for practically the whole time and was ready to leave, I met people who felt the way I do. They *are* there; it's just that you don't come across them, especially not on the Gold Coast. You'd find more of them in Brisbane.

Did you have a more specific reason for returning to Victoria?

I came here primarily to work on the film script of *Slate & Me*.

Did you enjoy doing that?

No. I found it traumatic and degrading. Let's put it this way: John Le Carré said that seeing your novel made into a film is like seeing a living beast turned into an Oxo cube. It's a perfect analogy because, as a medium, film is so limiting. In a novel you can do anything; on film you can't. It's as simple as that. You're limited all the time by the budget and, worse, by the limitation of other people's creative abilities. I used to believe that film making was a team business — it's more a factory business. Most film makers aim for the lowest common denominator, that is, bums on seats. This attitude gives the distributors total power over them. The same situation, if applied to the writing of novels, would mean that we'd all be writing with a view to selling in Big Ws.

Then why did you get into it in the first place?

I was starry-eyed about making a good film. Professor Manning Clark wrote to me saying that with *Slate & Me* he believed I'd written a novel which would make a film comparable to Graham Greene's *The Third Man*. I hoped that was true. I certainly tried to make it true. I worked on three drafts of the script and believed that we had a good one. Then I was sacked. It happens all the time, partly because in the film industry there is a tradition of hatred for the writer. It's especially strong in the case of a novel being adapted for the screen.

Why do you think this hatred exists?

It's a fascist sort of industry. And writers can think, so film people fear them, just as the Catholic Church and the Communist party fear anyone who thinks.

Would you allow any future novel of yours to be made into a film?

Yes, definitely, because although I'm desperately sorry that a disembowelled version of my novel is to be made into a film (a gumleaf western, I call it), I learned a great deal. For one thing, I learned that several producers wanted the rights to the book in question, and next time, instead of being in such a hell-fire of a hurry, I'd wait a couple of years until all the bets had been called.

Can you locate the inspiration for Slate & Me and Blanche McBride? *Was it based on a particular incident?*

No, it wasn't based on any incident, but when I was a child and we all used to go out with my grandpa in his very old Dodge car (which my grandmother wouldn't let him drive over forty), we used to drive down the Tamar, in Tasmania, and I'd have little fantasies about being kidnapped, and getting away. That was always there apparently, because it finally came out. The two boys I based very loosely on one boy that

I know well and am very fond of. But there's absolutely no true story in it, not at all, it is just imaginative.

Most of the action deals with the psychological tussles that go on between the characters. Did you do any research for that?

No, I didn't need to. I've had a lot of experience of people. I'm interested in psychology. I'm also interested in psychiatry, and I have always read those things, but I read that sort of thing just because it interests me, not as research.

You don't confine yourself to reading fiction?

No, I'm a manic reader. I'm one of those people, and I think there are many of us, who read the label on the jam tin if there's nothing else to read. I couldn't live without reading. I prefer reading to watching television, for instance.

Have you always been like that?

Yes. And that's partly because I suppose we lived a fairly lonely existence. After we were married, Ron and I went to live at Longford in Tasmania, and because we were so poor we didn't really have any friends, and — truly, don't laugh, that's what life's like if you're really poor — and, although of course we did have very good friends, what I mean is we didn't have friends with whom we could have discussed things like psychology, and so on. I was forced to read because of that, and then we went to live up at Redcliffs, eleven miles from Mildura. We lived at the pumping station, which was about four miles outside of Redcliffs. It was right on top of the red cliffs themselves, on the Murray, and there was a tiny little community there called Cliffside, and there was nothing to do but read. So one read. And reading becomes a disease, as you probably know.

Getting back to Slate & Me and Blanche McBride, *why did you decide to structure it in such a way that you change perspective all the time?*

I worked that out when I got it back one day from wherever I'd sent it. I spent a long time thinking about it and decided it was a very thin little story and needed a really dramatic form. I'm very interested in form. I think we should all be thinking about it, because I think too many people are writing the same thing. There is nowhere much to go unless you start looking at form.

I was talking at a school not very long ago about that particular book, and a year twelve student said he'd liked it very much because it was about something, and most of the books that are written in Australia at the moment are just about middle-class couples in their mid-thirties breaking up. And I was inclined to agree with him. People write about that because it's all they know, which is fair enough. That is what you have to give, so you give it.

I should say, of course, that I got the idea of doing those different voices from one of William Faulkner's books (I think it's *As I Lay Dying*) which impressed me tremendously. It's a book that I have always loved, and so I stole that from there.

You've mentioned Faulkner a few times. Are there other writers that you are particularly fond of?

Yes, I'm a great Nabokov fan, and for almost as long as I can remember I've been very keen on Russian writing. I've read a lot of Russian writing. I go back and read the same things over. I've read *War and Peace* several times, and Dostoyevsky I keep going back and reading. Some of this I do because I've never had the money to buy books. I've been re-reading some of Solzhenitsyn. I love his writing. In *Cancer Ward*, when the chap goes out to look for his apricot tree, that seems to me to be the high point of literature in this century, because there was a man who'd come out of the cancer ward and he was going to look for a tree in flower, and it just seemed to me the most wonderful thing that he found it.

I read Salinger's stuff over and over, because I just love him. I love his mind. I suppose the author I love most of all is Colette. She's the person who made me into a gardener

— that's my great joy in life. And I also admire Jean Rhys and her talent enormously, especially *Wide Sargasso Sea*.

Do you think, then, that Australian literature has a fairly narrow focus?

Well, it's broadening all the time. Australians have been writing about Asia and things like that. I think that's marvellous, and there are people like David Malouf, who certainly couldn't be called narrow in any way. And I don't think Elizabeth Jolley could be called narrow. I admire her, and I admire her work very much. But I think there are quite a lot of writers who are going along a fairly narrow track, yes.

Do you think that has to do with the fact that Australia is a relatively young country?

No, I don't think so, because some of those writers have travelled extensively. I think it probably has more to do with the fact that they've grown up and lived the first fifteen years of their adult lives in an affluent society. That's all. And so they write about relationships breaking up because they don't, as I said to that young man, have anything else to write about. And later on, when things happen to them, if things happen to them, they write about other things.

So, it seems that you don't enjoy that type of content either?

Well, no, because there is nothing in it for me. But I think some of it is very popular, and obviously has a place, because there is something in it for a lot of people in the same boat. So many middle-class people have relationships breaking up, and they like to read that sort of thing, because I suppose it comforts them and they're looking all the time for help in what has gone wrong between men and women.

What are you working on at the moment?

I have finished another novel which is to be published by

the University of Queensland Press. It is totally different, absolutely different, from the others. Every time I write something I want it to be different. That's something that I set myself, that I would do something different every time. As I've developed — and I think writing has developed me (it's certainly a two-way process) — I've decided that I have things to say, and I'm going to seize the opportunity to say them. I'm a dedicated feminist, but I'm old enough to be a realist too. I'm fascinated by male-female relationships, and that's one of the things I've been writing about.

I set myself to write about a woman in her mid-thirties and to show, as she went through life on what I suppose I would have to call a spiritual journey to some kind of self-realisation, to show her encountering what I believe are problems that are universal to women: the loss of a man that you love (because everybody goes through that whether you lose him to another woman, or just to a career, or because of death, or war, or something) and things like abortion, and difficulties with a daughter. I've noticed that in nearly every anthology of women's writing most of the stories are about 'What my mother did to me'. So I decided to turn it round and write of 'What I did to my daughter'.

And so, I set off to write about these problems and had some difficulty getting it into what I felt was the right form. But I believe I have achieved what I set out to do; I'm very pleased with what I've done. Part One of it is a series of short stories, or almost short stories, told by the main character, Vinnie Beaumont, and Part Two is, I suppose, a novella which ties the stories together and concludes them. I feel I've brought it off and I think it's good to be using this form because people are so conditioned to seeing things in blocks. I found with *Slate & Me* that people, especially young people, liked that sort of block form, and so I thought I would explore it a bit more.

I've just started another novel about a little girl who runs away from home, and a very middle-class family, after being sexually assaulted by her father. She takes her eight-year-old brother with her. I've done the first chapter of that, and I'm just about ready to start on the second chapter. I'm going to do some more of this exploration of our sexual attitudes, and what I believe has gone wrong between men and women in that.

When did you begin to see yourself as a committed feminist?

Always. All my life. My mother obviously got it over to me that my brother would be allowed to lead one kind of life and have things like sexual freedom, and that I would have to lead another because I was a girl. I rebelled against that. I tried to just take equality, which I believe you have to do. Nobody gives freedom. Slaves are never given freedom. You only get freedom when whoever is the master sees that you will die rather than give in. It's no good saying you *want* your freedom, you have to *take* it.

Did you become in any way directly engaged in political action?

I was certainly politically involved during the Vietnam War, but then everybody was, so there was nothing very wonderful about that. You didn't have any choice, really. And I'm madly anti-nuclear now. When I was over at the Perth Festival as one of the speakers, I started my little talk with an anti-nuclear message, which I repeated at the end of the talk because I don't think that anybody should be speaking in public today without mentioning the nuclear threat.

Would you address such an overtly political issue as nuclear war in a book, do you think?

I think probably you have to, if you can find a way not to be boring about it, because it's no good hitting people over the head with something. If people have bought your book because they think it's going to entertain them on a wet Sunday afternoon, you can't bore the breeches off them.

I read on one of your blurbs that you were a 'well-known reviewer'. Are you still writing book reviews?

I did reviewing for the *Australian Book Review*, and that's a dodgy subject with me, because I don't think that I was ever a really honest reviewer. I've been offered reviewing work since I've been back in Melbourne, and I'm refusing to do it at the moment because I know how hard it is to write books, and how you sweat over them and how they matter to you, and I couldn't ever say anything rude about anybody's work.

Did writing book reviews help your own writing?

Yes, absolutely. I was a very conscientious reviewer and I used to read everything twice. Learning to criticise like that, to do it to the very best of my abilities, certainly helped me tremendously, yes. It was invaluable. The best lessons I could ever have had. And by learning to do that, I applied it to other books that I was reading and worked out how people were doing things, and why they were doing things, and often thinking that they shouldn't have done things. Which leads me to say, as I've sometimes said when I've been speaking in public, that I think you can teach yourself to write by analysing books. Not necessarily good books, bad books too. Work out what's wrong with them and see if you can improve them.

How do you go about analysing a book?

I suppose primarily by looking at the structure of the entire novel, and breaking it down into sections, and looking at the structure of different parts of it. With writing that impresses me as being very beautiful writing and very easy writing I try to work out why it flows, and what structural devices are used in the sentences to make the writing flow, and so on. I can't really be more explicit, because, you know, all writing is different.

Are you happy being a writer?

Yes, it's the most wonderful existence, because I don't get up in the morning. I stay in bed and write. And you own every day. When you wake up in the morning, the day belongs to you. So it's wonderful. You have to put up with being poor. But everything else about it's wonderful.

What about the financial aspect of it?

Oh it's too terrible to think about. I'm old enough to be able to get the Widows Pension, so that I can live on Social Security. This year I'm on a Writers Fellowship and after that I'll just have to go back to Social Security. I know it's supposed to be terribly demeaning, but I don't mind. I feel that I work very hard, probably harder than most people, for my little bit, which I'm incidentally very grateful for. I'm lucky in that I want nothing out of life, just to be left alone to write. I don't want trips, or jewellery, or parties. I like parties, but I can do with fairly modest ones. There's nothing that I want that I can't have without money, so that makes life fairly simple for me.

Is the solitariness of writing a problem for you?

No, no. I think it's probably true of nearly all writers that we have two absolutely separate sides to our personality; there's one side that craves solitude, and another side that has to dash out and do a bit of raging. I think you do your living in short bursts, because if you rush out and rage it's very debilitating, and you need to go home and regroup. Also I think writers are fairly sensitive people, and I think they sometimes find it difficult to cope with seeing a lot of the human race all at one time. I think they're often so shocked by the things people do and say that they like to sneak away home again. Perhaps I'm being very hard on people, but I think that's true.

Do you still work in the mornings?

Mostly, but that's partly because of my hands, you see. I can't type any more. Which is annoying, because I was a very fast typist. It's annoying, and it's also expensive to have to get work typed. It's a hard thing to be a writer and not be able to write, sort of, but I don't think about it, because I think it's better not to dwell on it. I've thought of using a tape, but I'm very much a writer who writes by sight as well as sound. I like to see the sentences, and be able to look at their construction. That's very important to me. So I have to devise things for myself to do in the afternoon that are to do with my writing. I plot and plan and work out characters, and things like that.

Do you spend a lot of time redrafting and reworking?

Yes, sure. I always hope that it will become less. I've always had to do, say, five or six drafts, but I was very pleased to find, in the last three chapters of my new novel, that three were enough. But that was because I went more slowly, instead of gushing everything out, which I'd always done in the past. I thought before I wrote. And perhaps I'll be able to cut that down. But I wouldn't ever be able to get down under three. Nobody could.

When you're working on a novel, do you have anyone that you talk over your problems with?

No, I think I've always been unlucky in this regard, that I've lived in places where there was nobody. I think it must be wonderful to have somebody to discuss things with. I think it must be just the best thing that could ever happen to you, if you could use somebody as a sounding board. I haven't ever had anybody, in that way, and it's something that I feel I've missed in life. I think I would have found some short cuts in my work, if I'd had that.

Do you feel that you're part of a literary milieu?

Oh, yes and no. I suppose I am, yes, because that's where my friendships lie, it's where my interests lie. The people I'm closest to are all connected in some way with writing. Except for my old cronies in the country, whom I love —

you know, the old stalwarts who will always be my friends and couldn't give a stuff about writing.

Do you think you've had a good run to date in your career as a writer?

I would say a very good run. I've been very happy, yes. But then I haven't asked for much, so perhaps there are two sides to that. Yes, I think I've had a very good run.

What about your writing more generally, in terms of what you want to say, and your ambitions?

I'm quite happy with the way I'm going. Perhaps nobody else would be, but I'm happy with what I'm doing. It's fulfilling me, and I think if that is all my writing does, then I have been extraordinarily lucky in my life. That's what I ask out of life, just to be a fulfilled person.

What are your thoughts about the future of Australian writing?

I'm wildly optimistic about it. In Adelaide at the 1984 Writers Week there was an absolute wave of young writers present. They're bright, educated and very aware of what's going on in the world. A lot of them know what it's like to be without a job and they've turned to writing partly because of that. I'm sure they'll have a lot to say and I'm looking forward to reading it.

Melbourne, August 1985

Select bibliography

The Tournament, Hale & Iremonger, 1983.
Slate & Me and Blanche McBride, McPhee Gribble/Penguin, 1983.